Couples had begun to slip away into the woods. Pierre took Mireille by the hand, and they made their way by a forest path to a hidden place where fallen leaves had made a natural bower. The drums were softer now, distant and seductive, and it was very peaceful as they sank into the bower, the stars bright in the sky.

Mireille breathed deeply of the quiet night, Pierre's arm about her. She could not share the silence. Her heart was beating to the compelling thunder of the drums, the thunder of her own blood. She was a woman tonight, a woman who wanted what every woman wanted and needed, a man to hold her and make demands upon her compliant body.

Pierre understood the mood of the night, the graceful curve of her arms raised to him, the invitation of her lips. The banked leaves were as enveloping as any feather-bed, the air warm and balmy. They made pagan love on that pagan shore beneath the pale moon.

Barbara Cooper was born in Montreal, Canada, the second of five children. She was educated there and earned an Arts Degree from the University of Montreal. She met her first husband working at the Canadian Atomic Energy Project at Chalk River. They made their home in Oxfordshire and later in Lancashire. When he died she turned her hand to part time work to have time to bring up her three children. Now married again, she writes romantic fiction.

Barbara Cooper's two other Masquerade Historicals are *The Choosing* and *Fortune's Kiss*. She has also written a longer novel, set in Canada in 1922, called *Beyond Paradise*.

PALE MOON RISING

BY

BARBARA COOPER

MILLS & BOON LIMITED
15-16 BROOK'S MEWS
LONDON W1A 1DR

First published in Great Britain 1987
by Mills & Boon Limited

This edition 1987

ISBN 0 263 75719 6

Set in Monotype Times 10 on 10 pt.
04-0487-81000

Typeset in Great Britain by
Associated Publishing Services
Printed and bound in Great Britain by
Cox & Wyman

CHAPTER ONE

MIREILLE'S ANGER BOILED over. She had appealed to this man, this Albert Morel who called himself Monsieur le Secrétaire as if to emphasise his own importance. What was he, after all? Not the Governor of the colony of New France, not the new *intendant*, who were in Québec. This Albert Morel was only in charge of the civil affairs of the town of Trois-Rivières.

'I asked for your help, Monsieur.' She knew she had to keep her temper in check. A long strand of curly fair hair freed itself from her kerchief and fell over her left eyebrow as she shook her head. She tried to push it back with a trembling hand. 'I wish to see my cousin, Capitaine Charles de la Croix. He is stationed here, is he not?'

'*Oui, vraiment*. He was posted here in April and has been here ever since,' Monsieur le Secrétaire permitted himself a frosty smile in her direction. 'It is regrettable that he isn't here today. He is in Québec.'

'But he will be back?'

'One supposes he will return in a few days,' Monsieur le Secrétaire agreed in his small, pale, colourless voice, which even in the confined space of the church sacristy scarcely carried to where Mireille stood only a few feet from him. 'Mademoiselle will see him then.'

Mireille reflected that the voice suited the man. He was small, pale and colourless too, and sat perched on a stool with a ledger spread open before him on the shelf which served as a desk. Now he gave his attention to that ledger, dismissing the girl by his action. She looked at him and bit her lip. How could she make him understand? She must see Charles.

'Please, Monsieur, you don't understand!' She cleared her throat, ready to begin again.

His pale grey eyes fastened on hers. '*Au contraire,* Mademoiselle, I understand very well! You asked to speak to someone in authority. They brought you to me. I am authority here. You tell me you are Mireille de la Croix. For your sake, I chose not to hear that. Mademoiselle, you would do well to take yourself back into the hall and choose yourself a husband. Does it not occur to you that by wasting your time with me you are missing your best chances? Go quietly, Mademoiselle. I am doing you a kindness.'

Mireille gulped. She could not face going back to the church hall.

'It's barbaric,' she declared. 'How can one choose a husband in such a way?'

'The other girls have made no complaint,' she was told. You knew the terms of coming here. The King of France has provided you with a dowry and only wishes you to marry one of his settlers in return. It's a fair exchange, isn't it?'

'But I don't know any of those men,' Mireille protested. Nor did she want to, she added to herself. One swift glance around the hall on first entering had been enough to convince her of that. She supposed they were worthy enough men, honest men, hard-working, but she had not come to marry one of them. She had come to Charles—and Charles wasn't here.

'Nor are you likely to make their acquaintance if you don't take your courage in your hands and go out and talk to them.' Monsieur le Secrétaire was being as patient with her as if she had been a child. 'Come, they're not such bad fellows. One of them will want to marry you.'

'But I don't want to marry them,' Mireille threw caution to the winds. 'I want my cousin.'

'You want to marry him?' Albert Morel's expression was stern. 'You cannot. He is a soldier, not a settler. I warn you, Mademoiselle, if you have come here under false pretences, the consequences may be dire.'

'The consequences will be dire also, if I am forced to choose among that rabble.' Mireille's eyes flashed with disdain.

'Ah-ha, we come to the heart of it.' Monsieur le Secrétaire put down his pen. 'Mademoiselle fancies herself as above them, somehow!'

'I am well born,' Mireille whispered, sensing that her words had further antagonised the only man who could help her. 'I am Mireille de la Croix, not Marie Decarie.'

Monsieur le Secrétaire sighed, 'So you persist in that story. You force me to arrest you—to take action against you.' He looked down at the papers spread before him. 'Yes, there is a Marie Decarie among these names. You have taken her place in order to come to this cousin of yours. This is a serious matter, a deception against the King.'

Mireille's heart sank. Now she was in real trouble. Why, oh why, had she appealed to this man? 'Please,' she whispered. 'I meant no deception.'

Monsieur le Secrétaire gave her an icy stare. He seemed lost in thought, tapping his pen idly against his cheek.

'I wonder,' he murmured as if to himself. 'Yes, I wonder.' He got down from his perch and went to the door. From there he summoned someone in the hall and held a low-voiced conversation.

When he had shut the door, he came back to the high stool. 'You won't have long to wait.' He surveyed her. 'Perhaps I may be able to help, after all. Your voice tells me you are an educated girl, at least. That haughty look of yours says perhaps you speak the truth. And you are comely enough to attract a young man's eye. Maybe you will do.'

Will do for what? Mireille longed to ask, flushing to the roots of her hair. She was not used to being regarded as this man was doing. She was not a horse or cow up for sale. Wasn't she? she asked herself silently, enduring his appraisal. Were not all those little brides in the hall up for sale—a sale arranged by King Louis XIV in this year of 1666 for the convenience of his settlers? He had given each girl a dowry, and Monsieur le Secrétaire had arranged that the men should be gathered in the hall. Each girl had only to strike a bargain with a man, and marriage followed immediately. What sort of marriage would come from such a transaction?

Under a pale moon last night on board *L'Hirondelle,* she had asked that question aloud, and her friend Émilie had answered, 'As good a marriage as any; perhaps happy, perhaps not, as God wills. It is woman's lot to endure.'

Mireille had longed to shake her. How could she accept it so quietly, so willingly? She had not accepted the marriage arranged for her. She had run from it. Nor had she told Émilie who she was, even then. Time enough to speak out when the ship reached Trois-Rivières. She had thanked her stars, and the good Sainte Anne who had guarded her so far on her perilous journey, when they had reached Québec and her name had not been called to disembark there. She had been among those chosen to go on to Trois-Rivières. To think she had been pleased about that, rejoicing that everything was going in her favour because she knew Charles was stationed here.

Mireille had stood for a long time under that pale moon last night, deciding what she must do, how she must speak, to whom she must appeal to summon Charles to her side. She had been calm then, sure of herself. After all, she was Mireille de la Croix. She had only to tell them so and she would not have to face the ordeal of the would-be husbands.

Standing now in the tiny sacristy, she asked herself how she could have been so naïve? Albert Morel only a few minutes ago had stated she had a haughty look. She doubted if she wore it still. She leaned against the wall, anxious and frightened, and marvelled that this morning she had put on her best dress, a blue brocade which brought out her fair colouring, and had tied a blue kerchief round her head, singing.

How sure of herself she had been as the girls had left the ship, marching two by two along the quay, belongings in bundles over their shoulders. She remembered she had clapped her hands and laughed as she stepped out with Émilie. Émilie had had to wear the dress she had worn all the way across the Atlantic. It was her only one.

Émilie had been dour. Down the gangplank, her feet had been slow, dragging, not beating to the music of the army band drawn up there. Even with the sun shining in August splendour and the dear earth firm against the soles of her sabots, Émilie's stride had been unwilling. She looked only at the ground.

The ground was muddy from yesterday's rain, Mireille had observed, and Émilie had agreed, and kept on staring at it. She frowned and paid scant attention to Mireille's description of the sturdy little houses with their pointed roofs and their gaily coloured doors.

'A housewife is hanging out her washing.' Mireille had tempted her friend to view the spectacle of shirts and sheets fluttering in the breeze by nudging Émilie and pointing to the line strung high over the road from one upper balcony to the other opposite.

Emilie had risked a quick glance. '*Enfin,* pray for a fine man,' she had counselled. 'One who will praise you for the whiteness of your wash—and will not beat you too much.'

That had shocked Mireille. Of course it was different for Émilie, she told herself comfortably. She had no cousin Charles to turn to. She would just have to make the best choice possible among the men sure to be assembled in the church hall to which they were going. In an hour or two, Émilie and the rest of the girls would be wives—happy wives or unhappy wives, but wives indeed—that was what they had come for.

'Just look,' Mireille had pleaded with her friend. 'Don't you want to see the town you've come to?'

Émilie would have none of it. 'Call this a town? It's

a huddle of houses behind piles of logs thrown together for protection. I saw it all from the ship. No, no, better to look down, to look meek, to pray for guidance.'

'That's just so that no one will see you're cross-eyed,' sneered the girl behind. 'Skelly-eyed Émilie,' she chanted. 'Come for a husband, she'll be lucky if she finds one! But if she does, will she see one man or two?'

Émilie ignored the sally, but Mireille stuck out her tongue and her foot at the tormentor without succeeding in tripping her. 'Fatty, fatty!' she jeered. 'Will your fine man take you or the cow from the dowry to his bed?'

A real squabble would have started then, but for the eye of the chaperon falling upon them and Émilie seizing hold of Mireille and dragging her forward a few places. 'I've told you and told you not to tangle with that one! Why do you never learn?'

'Because she insults you,' was Mireille's quick reply. 'I know what you've done for me. If it hadn't been for you, I would have had trouble all the way across the ocean. You always stood up for me against the others.'

'It was nothing.' Émilie forgot to look at the ground. 'I am big and strong, and they were afraid of me because I might put the evil eye on them. Why should eyes be evil because they are not quite straight? Well, no matter,' she had shrugged. 'It served us well enough.'

Mireille had clasped Émilie's hand. 'I hope and pray you find a fine husband,' she whispered.

'Et tu, m'amie,' was Emilie's quick return. 'Straighten your collar, pull your kerchief back a little to show the colour of your hair—that ripe wheat shade is sure to attract a handsome fellow.'

Mireille had done as she was told. Émilie was still determined to take care of her and to push away her gratitude, but Mireille knew well how much she owed her friend. The other girls, as if sensing there was something different about her, would have teased and bullied her. True, she had had no problems about giving a passable imitation of Marie Decarie's accent and way of putting things. After all, she had talked to the farm girls, played with them as a child on her father's seigneury. It was the subjects the others talked about incessantly which defeated her. They spoke of boys and men, and what they got up to in barns, and nudged each other. They gloated over the fact of King Louis providing them with a dowry to marry one of his New France settlers. They enumerated its components over and over like a kind of litany—an ox and a cow, two pigs, a pair of chickens, two barrels of salted meat and eleven crowns in money.

Mireille acknowledged it would give them a start in life which none of them could have hoped for or aspired to as orphans or farm hands. But it was fixed, settled. She wanted to hear more of the wonders of this new world she was approaching.

She sometimes hovered near the sailors describing the Indians, the Hurons, Algonquins and Iroquois, and their fearsome ways. There was one of the ship's company who had lived among them for a time and Mireille would dearly have loved to talk with him, but the chaperon was horrified at the suggestion and pulled her out of earshot.

Mireille had wanted to hear more of this exciting new land, about the enormous inland lakes that the old sailor called the Finger Lakes because of their resemblance to a hand. But it was no use. She was not allowed to ask questions. She was forbidden even to look in the direction of the crew.

It was just the same now, Mireille reflected as she leaned wearily against the wall. Monsieur le Secrétaire was working busily on his documents, and she was made to wait, silent and submissive. She felt mutinous, and opened her mouth to enquire what was happening. Before she had a chance to utter the words, the door was opened from the other side and a man was thrust into the room.

The man paid no attention at all to her, but strode up to Monsieur le Secrétaire. 'I might have know it!' he exclaimed. 'It was you who had me brought here. What are you up to, Albert? Am I free to go?'

From a man who had presumably been held prisoner somewhere and brought here under orders—and none too gently, judging by the way he had been shoved in—Mireille thought it was a strange sort of greeting. He appeared to have no fear at all of Monsieur Morel.

'You are not free to go.' Albert favoured the newcomer with a smile—a genuine smile this time. 'At least, not yet. I have something here that may interest you.' He waved in Mireille's direction.

The girl was suddenly subjected to the most intense glance from this stranger. His eyes were very blue. That was her first impression of him—that, and the alertness of his whole bearing. Here was a man who waited for no one, who looked as though he might leap towards her and seize her. She shrank back a little.

He bowed to her. 'Pierre Charbonneau, at your service, Mademoiselle. There is no need to be frightened. I won't bite you!'

Mireille was relieved when he turned to Monsieur le Secrétaire. 'Let's have the whole story, Albert. Who is she? What are you plotting?'

'All in good time,' said Albert. 'Do you find her agreeable to look at?'

Once again, those blue eyes raked Mireille. 'She's very pretty,' was his verdict. 'A little on the small side perhaps, but well enough formed.' For the first time, he gave her a warm, merry smile which changed his whole face, and robbed his words of any sting. 'Come, Albert, is she one of your little brides?'

'Indeed she is. Just landed this morning, and she tells a strange story—one which I thought you might find of interest.'

Pierre Charbonneau swung round to face Albert Morel. 'Let's hear it, then.'

'She shall tell you herself, but I'll give you the bare bones first. She claims to be Mademoiselle Mireille de la Croix, cousin to Charles, but she travelled to us under the name of Marie Decarie. Perhaps you would care to hear her explanation, Pierre.' Albert waved one hand at Pierre and the other at the girl.

'Certainement,' Pierre nodded. 'Who is this other girl—this Marie? Where is she—are her papers in order?'

'As to the papers,' Albert replied, 'they seem good enough. I suppose there is such a girl and she applied for the King's dowry—then changed her mind, and Mademoiselle stepped into her place. *Est-ce que c'est vrai?*'

'Oui, c'est vrai.' Mireille nodded her head and the kerchief fell away to her shoulders exposing a riot of yellow gold curls. 'Marie was one of the farm girls. She was left an orphan and penniless. She had no dowry. She wanted to marry a young man from a nearby town. When he suddenly came into some money, they eloped.'

'And this money—this windfall—you had a hand in this, did you?' It was Pierre Charbonneau who asked.

Mireille did not answer. Some of her mother's jewellery had provided the cash, but she saw no need to enlighten him or Monsieur le Secrétaire about that.

'So, then, Marie's papers fell into your hands conveniently?' It was Pierre who kept questioning. 'Why? Why were you so determined to remove yourself from the scene?'

'Because my father's lands had been left to me, with my uncle as guardian, and he was determined he was going to marry me to his son to keep the property in his hands.'

'The son was not to your liking?'

'No, he was not—nor ever would be. A horrid, spoiled half-grown boy of sixteen who pulled the wings off butterflies and boasted about tumbling all the kitchen-maids in the district. I hated him!'

'Dear me, Mademoiselle.' Pierre's expression gave nothing away of his feelings. 'You seem singularly unfortunate in your cousins—an offensive youth on one side of the ocean, and Charles on the other!'

'There's nothing wrong with Charles!' Mireille sprang to his defence.

'Except that he's not here,' Pierre suggested. 'I suppose he's the son of a younger brother and has no fortune, but still, you turned to him.'

'I had no one else to turn to.'

'Quite so . . . The plan then that you concocted—how did it go? Was Charles to be your husband instead of the other butterfly?' Pierre waited for no comment. 'A good enough plan, given an ambitious man and a pretty girl. When he left the army he would seize back your land. You wrote to him, I suppose?'

'There wasn't time, and I was afraid my letter might be found anyway.'

'You showed considerable iniative,' Pierre's praise sounded more derisive than laudatory. 'It's unfortunate your plans miscarried here.'

'Will you help me, Monsieur Charbonneau?' Mireille appealed directly to him.

He came a step nearer to her and the girl couldn't help but notice that Albert rubbed his hands and winked at Pierre.

'As to that,' Pierre's voice was soft, his eyes kind, 'my help might not be to your liking.'

'Why not?' Mireille studied him, puzzled and uneasy. Now that he was closer to her, he seemed bigger, menacing. His face was dark—as dark as a farmer's. It was not a gentleman's face, was the thought that flashed into her mind. Yet he stood confidently, sure of his strength and of himself. She sensed that. His voice was cultured, but higher and more melodious than she would have expected from such a tall man. His shoulders were broad, his waist neat, his hips lean, and he was dressed in clothes such as she had never seen before. His leggings were long and fringed and made of softest leather. She wanted to put out her hand to touch it, but didn't. His jerkin, too, was leather of a lighter shade than the breeches, but adorned with beads, and was fringed as well. Round his throat he wore a silk scarf in a mixture of browns and oranges. His hair was shoulder length, thick and shining black. But it was the eyes which held hers. They were so blue and observant.

'Why not?' she repeated, her voice husky, her colour rising. 'If you could send to Québec for my cousin . . . '

Both men laughed at that and shook their heads.

'I wonder,' said Pierre, 'if your cousin were here, how he would deal with you. He's a great one for correctness in everything. He loves the majesty of the law.'

'Ambition rides high with him,' Albert observed. 'If he dealt as I should deal with you, you would be whipped through the streets of Trois-Rivières and put on the first boat back to France. It is what you deserve!'

Mireille clasped her hands together to stop their trembling. 'But—but—I meant no harm,' she stammered.

'Sham bride, counterfeit bride!' Monsieur le Secrétaire hissed at her. 'You stole someone else's identity and would even steal the King's dowry for your own. You must know that's serious. Have you ever been beaten, Mademoiselle? They use a whip here, and aren't gentle about it. It would be a pity to see such soft flesh bleeding.'

Mireille licked dry lips, her heart thudding painfully in her chest. 'I haven't taken the King's dowry,' she whispered. 'And I've told you who I am.'

'That is in your favour.' Albert nodded and looked to Pierre Charbonneau. 'Would you say there were extenuating circumstances? Do you think something might be done for her?'

Pierre was silent for a moment, his face unreadable. 'I begin to see why you sent for me,' he told Albert. 'If Mademoiselle were safely married and disinclined to speak of her reasons for coming . . . '

Mireille did not understand him, but she saw he was the one to appeal to. 'Please, Monsieur,' she begged. 'Help me?'

'Ah-ha, you don't know me! Friend Albert will tell you what a rascal I am, what an unworthy character, fined and thrown into prison for his misdeeds.'

'What misdeeds?' Mireille's voice trembled.

'For daring to flout His Majesty's directives to his loyal settlers, for trading among the Indians without one of those coveted licences for doing so.'

'What licences?'

'Why, in his wisdom, the King has decreed that settlers must settle, that only a very few of them shall be allowed to trade, and among that number my name is not written, even though I have served King and country.' His face was stern.

'Why not? What have you done?'

His face creased into that winning smile again. 'It's not what I've done. It's what I haven't done.'

Mireille was not sure if he was teasing her. 'What —what haven't you done?'

'A simple thing,' he shrugged. 'I've never married —never found myself a wife.'

'Never married?' She was sure now he was playing some kind of game with her.

'Only married men may claim a licence for trading with the Indians,' Albert supplied. 'A wife brings a man back to the settlement.'

'Otherwise, he might stay always with the savages, choosing some dusky beauty instead for his comfort.'

Mireille drew back from Pierre. Did he have such a one for his comfort?

He was laughing at her, knew exactly what she was thinking. 'Comfort is a fine thing,' he told her.

Albert broke in, 'Every time a bride-ship puts into port, bachelors are encouraged to come forward to claim brides—otherwise they're fined. So far, Monsieur Charbonneau has managed to avoid most of the bride-ships by being in the forest, but this time a patrol led by Capitaine de la Croix has seen fit to bring him in and hold him by force in the prison so that he may make a sensible choice and regularise his position. Mind, there's no guarantee a licence will be forthcoming, but he has friends who may intercede for him. In short, he needs a wife.'

Mireille drew in her breath sharply.

'I see you understand.' Pierre's voice was still soft. 'It would seem only fitting to claim the King's dowry—an amusing idea, don't you think?'

'Particularly since Charles was the one who brought you in to face justice,' said Mireille.

'Touché,' Pierre agreed. 'Does Mademoiselle not find it droll?'

Mademoiselle did not. She had no wish to be a pawn in whatever game they were playing with Charles. She wanted to see her cousin. At least she would know where she stood with him. This Pierre was not the sort of husband she wanted. He was a lawbreaker. He had admitted that himself.

'There are fifty girls outside, out there in the hall.' Mireille pointed in the direction of the closed door. 'There is nothing to stop you choosing one of them.'

'Nothing except the fact that I am languishing in prison! Everyone knows that. What's the matter, Mademoiselle de la Croix, am I not to your liking either?' His eyes pierced her with a cold stare. 'I am as well born as you, little bride, whatever you may think to the contrary.'

Mireille bit her lip. It would seem he had an uncanny ability to read her mind. 'I never said anything about your birth or position.' She pulled at the curl over her ear, a habit she had never lost from childhood in times of nervousness.

'You are entitled to know of my position. I have land and a house. You will have a roof over your head —quite a comfortable one.'

'I didn't doubt that, but—but this wife of yours will not see much of you. When you have your licence, you mean to leave her and go among the Indians again, do you not?'

'All the more reason to choose such a one as you, a girl of some determination and stubbornness. I don't want a clinging wife.'

Mireille did not know whether to be flattered or insulted by this statement. He was cold. He was wily.

He was determined on his own way. No, the whole thing was preposterous!

She opened her mouth to tell him so, but he forestalled her.

'We are neither of us prize packages. How do you suppose you would fare if Albert set you among the settlers out there?' His hand pointed to the door now. 'Can you keep house, Mademoiselle? Have you the strength to wash and sweep and fetch wood and water? You look none too robust to me.' His blue eyes rested on her trim figure. 'More important, can you cook?'

Mireille felt her face flush under his gaze. 'I am strong,' she protested. 'Why, when most of the others were seasick, I was walking the deck with the wind at my back.'

'A wonder you weren't blow overboard,' was his soft comment.

'I can bake bread,' Mireille went on as if he had not spoken.

'That's a beginning,' he conceded. 'But what about meat and fish and gruel? There are no servants here.'

'I could learn. I'm not stupid.'

'Excellent! By the time I return, you might be a passable cook. I shall just have to be patient.'

'I didn't say I was going to marry you. You take too much for granted! Besides, how long will you be away?'

Pierre shrugged. 'A year—eighteen months, perhaps.'

'A year?' Mireille could not believe what she was hearing. But worse was to come.

'Time enough for the first little one to arrive. *Tiens,* Albert,' he addressed the clerk now. 'A son or daughter would ensure my return, would it not? How right, how wise, our good Sun King is. He knows the pull of children.'

'Absolument. Un vrai roi,' Albert agreed.

Mireille felt as if the breath had been knocked from her body. This was no easy way out that Monsieur Pierre Charbonneau was offering her. He meant to claim her as wife. She rebelled at the thought, and yet—and yet—he was an attractive man. There was a quality of strength and good humour about him. He was more truly masculine than cousin Charles had ever been. She could do worse. He was no rough settler such as those she had seen in the hall. She would not dismiss him out of hand.

'I might never return,' Pierre went on in a conversational tone. 'The trade of coureur-de-bois is a hazardous one. I might lose my life in the rapids or at the hands of some angry brave. Then everything would be yours. You would be free to turn to cousin Charles—or anyone else you fancied.' He smiled at her. 'Do you find that tempting?'

'I wouldn't rejoice in anyone's death—violent death,' Mireille replied piously.

'Well said,' Pierre's eyes danced. 'But only consider what freedom would be yours!'

'I am considering it,' Mireille admitted.

'Honestly spoken, if not very flattering.'

Mireille turned to Monsieur le Secrétaire. 'I suppose I may refuse his offer?'

'Mademoiselle would be unwise to refuse,' Albert replied smoothly. 'The alternative is not pleasant.'

'You wouldn't be willing to wait for Charles to return?' She knew the answer to that before Albert spoke the word No. But she persisted. 'It would only be a few days.'

'In all likelihood it would, but it would solve nothing,' Albert assured her. 'The girls who come on the bride-ships are not permitted to marry soliders. They are destined for settlers. That is the King's order. I cannot change that.'

'Then either I marry Monsieur Charbonneau or I am sent back to France?'

'And punished in the process.' Albert clasped his hands together. 'It is regrettable, but it is so.'

Mireille felt panic rising in her. She tried to make her voice calm. 'I have no choice, then. I must—I must accept Monsieur Charbonneau.' She turned to him. '*Eh bien, je suis heureuse . . .* ' Her voice shook and then broke. She was not happy; she could not be happy to accept such an offer, but the best she could do was to accept it with good grace. If she had to spend her life as this man's wife, it seemed sensible not to antagonise him at the start by declaring how hateful she found the idea.

'I am happy too.' Pierre Charbonneau took Mireille's hand in his. If he noticed that it was trembling, he made no comment, but raised it to his lips and kissed it gently. 'We shall suit each other well enough.' He turned enquiringly to Albert. 'What now? Do we find a priest?'

Mireille envied his casual acceptance of the inevitable. She wished she could be as cool and collected as Pierre appeared to be. She wanted to snatch her hand from his, to scream and howl. None of this had gone as she had planned. She had thought it was going to be simple: that Charles would have married her; that he would have returned to France with her and reclaimed her birthright. Instead, she must exchange vows with this stranger, about whom she knew next to nothing except that he needed a wife so that he might go his own way, leaving her a prisoner in this wild new land. It was not fair! She hated him for forcing her to such a life. In a few minutes she would be tied to him irrevocably.

'Allons!' Albert slid from the high stool. 'I myself shall escort you to one of the good fathers and shall be your witness.'

Mireille wondered sourly why he should look so pleased with himself. Why was he so determined that Pierre Charbonneau should marry? Did his neat clerk's mind see everyone in orderly ranks of two? Was he married himself? She shivered. She would not like Monsieur le Secrétaire as husband. No, Pierre Charbonneau was preferable to that bloodless specimen. At least Pierre was a man. Her mind refused to follow that train of thought. Pierre Charbonneau had declared he meant to make her his wife in every respect.

As one in a dream, Mireille followed Albert out of

the sacristy into the big hall, where the others were gathered. The girls, the other brides, were standing in the centre in a loose sort of circle as if huddled together for comfort. Before them stood the men. They, too, were in small groups, nudging each other, staring at the girls. It was like a country dance before the men had found their partners. But these partners were for life, Mireille reminded herself.

She felt Pierre Charbonneau's hand against her elbow as he guided her forward to where Albert beckoned them.

He stood beside a priest who had an open book in his hands—a small, white-haired man, who reminded the girl of the curé in her own village. Ah, if Père Richard were here and she were standing before him with Charles, how differently she would feel!

Mireille blinked a tear away. Charles was not here. Pierre Charbonneau was, and they were waiting for her to begin. The priest gabbled the opening words of the ceremony, eager to get them out of the way before other couples stood in line for his services.

Pierre made his responses, and Mireille made hers, still not quite believing that this was happening to her. When the priest pronounced them man and wife, he blessed them and gestured to them to move away. Immediately Albert waved them to another man, tall and gaunt, who told them he was the appointed notary and would inscribe their names and details. Nothing appeared to be expected of Mireille. Between them, Albert and Pierre answered all his questions.

The girl looked about her. She was pleased to see that her friend Émilie had two suitors, and that she was looking from one to the other, deciding which to have. One was short, shorter than Émilie, but handsome in a florid, fair way. The other towered above her, and seemed not to have quite so much to say about himself. Still, he smiled, and his teeth looked white and strong. He was not as smartly dressed as the fair man, who wore a cool jacket which flared out from his waist, and green breeches to the knee, with high boots of leather.

Mireille was not close enough to hear any part of their conversation, but she knew Émilie well enough to guess at how her mind would work. What was it she had said on the way to the hall? Pray for one who will not beat you too much. The big man would have a great deal of strength, but the small one might be mean. He looked as though he spent his money on himself. The other might have no money.

Mireille had not had to make a choice. It had been decided for her. Was that better or worse?

She was given no time to consider further, for Albert seized her arm.'Put your X here,' he instructed.

Mireille hesitated. 'I can write,' she whispered.

'There's no need,' he whispered back. 'A cross will suffice. It's all that's expected of you.' He put the pen into her hand.

For an instant the girl debated whether it was worth defying him, but a single glance at his face deterred her. She inscribed an X, and then another on a second paper.

'Très bien,' said the notary. 'Your marriage lines, Madame.' He gave a paper to her, and another to Pierre. 'Entitlement to the dowry,' she heard him say. 'Collect it tomorrow at the market.'

That was all. It was over.

Dazed, without time for a backward glance to see how Émilie had fared, Mireille was hustled from the hall and on Pierre's arm through the door out into the summer sunshine.

She blinked, the heat hitting her in a sudden wave. She was married—married to this stranger—his for life.

'Ah!' exclaimed Pierre, taking in a great gulp of air. 'How good it feels to be kissed by the sun, to be free. I could dance and sing. *Allons,* Madame Charbonneau, we shall go home.'

'Home,' Mireille echoed, and the realisation was like a blow to her heart. France was no longer her home. Her home from now on was here, with him. She shivered. She had no desire to dance or sing.

'Come on!' Pierre sounded impatient. He took the bundle of her belongings from her and hoisted it on his shoulder. 'It's some distance to walk, and you will not know the way.'

She thanked him and walked beside him while the path was wide. In a few minutes they came to the end of the row of houses, and he led the way along a much narrower lane of sorts, tree-bordered and dusty.

Mireille followed him in silence.

CHAPTER TWO

MIREILLE HAD IMAGINED no picture of the house Pierre Charbonneau owned and to which he brought her. It seemed to her that they walked for quite a long time. Though the day was hot, the path was shaded, and occasionally she could see the river glinting in the distance. Birds sang, and once she saw a squirrel running along the branch of a tree, and called to it. But it only stared at her and came no nearer.

Pierre had a long, easy stride, which appeared effortless but which forced her almost to run. Twice he waited for her to catch up, and she envied him the leather mocassins he wore on his feet. If she had shoes like that, she knew she would travel more swiftly. Besides, he had no skirts to hamper him, skirts which caught in the underbush and had to be pulled clear.

'Indian maidens wear short skirts,' he commented, as he saw her struggle. 'They have no false modesty about dress, nor do they suppose the sight of a girl's leg will so overcome a man that he will pounce on her like a bitch on heat.'

He only laughed when Mireille drew back from him at this plain speaking. 'We're rougher here . . . say what we think and feel. You'll get used to our ways.'

Not another word was spoken until they reached a sort of boundary line of logs. He scrambled over it and then helped her to surmount it. 'This is my land now,' he announced, gesturing largely with one hand.

Mireile was not sure how much land was encompassed by that negligent gesture, but she was surprised to see that trees gave way to cleared land, and that a crop was planted there. 'Beans and corn,' she hazarded a guess, and was rewarded with a nod. 'Did you plant them?'

'No, I was trading at planting-time, but I have an arrangement with a neighbour—a good fellow who keeps me in vegetables in return for furs, and he stables my cow and horses.'

The house was long and low and built of logs. It had a log door, and windows facing the cleared field. The number and size of the windows surprised Mireille. She counted four, and that was just in the front. The fur trade must supply a few luxuries, then.

Pierre opened the door and allowed her to enter. It was light and spacious inside. The floor was wood and so were the walls, some light wood which shone in the sunshine. There was an enormous hearth, and a wide chimney-piece that held carved figures and a clock. A large table ran along one wall with benches on either side, and two wooden chairs stood before the fireplace.

'Not the usual type of house'—he acknowledged her stare—'but we are far enough from the centre of the town to be free of some of the petty regulations that abound there. It is more in the Indian style than the French. You're surprised by that? I suppose you think the Indians are mere savages with no ideas of their own?' He did not wait for the answer. 'It's time you revised your ideas! The tribes and nations of the Iroquois and Algonquins have lived in this fertile land for centuries. They could teach the French many things—had they ears to listen, and eyes to see.'

Mireille was fascinated. Here was a man who knew about this new land and its peoples. She wanted to sit down and listen to him, but he was walking her towards one of the doors that led off the main room.

'The bedroom.' He pointed unnecessarily towards the wide unmade bed which stood in the middle of the floor, with blankets on it, and furs.

Mireille drew nearer to see the furs, and touched one. It was soft and sleek.

'Seal,' said Pierre. He picked up another. 'This is

beaver. There's fox there, too, and sable.'

Mireille gasped at their quality. 'They're worth a fortune!'

'On a cold night, they're worth more than that! You'll be glad of their warmth.'

She could imagine that!

'Come, you'll want to see your domain.'

Reluctantly, she followed him to a second door. It opened on to a kitchen, a bare sort of room with a big cooking-fire at one end and a window at the other.

Mireille knew it was a cooking-fire because of the large pot which was chained above it from the ceiling. The fire was out, but there was a great quantity of ashes in the grate.

Mireille's glance slid away from it to the window. She walked towards it. From there, because some of the trees were cleared, she could see straight down to the river. It looked cool and inviting. She wouldn't mind a walk down there, and what pleasure it would be to sit in the sun by its banks.

'What a lovely vista!' she exclaimed over her shoulder to Pierre. 'Who cut down the trees?'

'I did. I wanted a clear view of the river—not for the sake of its beauty, but for its practicality. It's best to see who's coming and who's going. Attacking Indians mainly come by canoe, and though they're clever about concealing themselves, a man who is used to the ways of the woods and their inhabitants is sometimes forewarned.'

Mireille didn't ask how—she didn't have time. Pierre's hands were on her shoulders, turning her round to face the kitchen.

'First the pump, I think.' He pointed to the object, where it rested with its spout directly above a small sink. 'You must learn to work it.'

Mireille's unwilling feet took her across the room. She knew nothing of pumps and how they produced water. Servants attended to that. She was about to tell Pierre so, and to add that there was one thing she wanted above all others—to have enough water to wash herself all over and change into her other dress. He was directly behind her as she opened her mouth to speak.

'Put your hand to it,' he directed.

Mireille was too astonished to do anything except obey him. Her hand went out to the handle. It was very heavy. Her other hand went to help.

'It's not moving, is it?' Pierre made no move to help, but watched her struggles.

'Please,' Mireille panted, 'help me.'

'You're going about it the wrong way,' he answered but he picked up a jug of water from the floor under the sink. 'You must prime it first.' He poured the water on to the pump.

Again Mireille tugged at the handle. This time, a trickle of water flowed from the spout.

'Harder, harder,' he directed.

She obeyed with mutiny in her heart. This time the water gushed out.

'Don't waste it! Fill the jug. Remember, if there is no water for priming, it's a long walk down to the river. You're lucky to have a pump. Some families have to make do with frequent trips with buckets to fetch water.'

'Lucky!' Mireille echoed, 'I don't call it lucky to have to struggle with such a beast.'

'Fetch the cooking-pot,' was his next directive.

'Fetch it yourself,' said Mireille, her anger rising. She glared at him.

'Temper, temper!' he chided her. 'The kitchen is your province. There are no servants here to obey your slightest command. I warned you about that.'

Mireille bit her lip and walked towards the pot, her head high. It was a large iron pot, within her reach, but very heavy. 'I won't be able to carry it when it's full of water,' she protested.

'I hope you won't be so foolish as to try,' was his daunting comment.

She brought the pot to the sink, and made a face

when she saw its contents. Her nose wrinkled in distaste. 'What is it?' she asked in alarm.

'I'm afraid it's rather cooked in.' This was not an apology. 'Your cousin Charles was in too much of a hurry to incarcerate me in the local gaol to bother about such niceties as removing the dinner from the fire! It boiled and bubbled until the fire burned out. It needs cleaning.'

Mireille was well aware of what the pot needed. She could see for herself, and she could see too that Pierre expected her to attend to it. But first she begged to change her dress. Her blue brocade was too fine for the task, and she changed to the cotton one she had worn on the voyage. It was a pity that she had no large apron to cover it.

'I—I don't know where to start,' she admitted on coming back to the kitchen.

'There's no need to cry about it, poor little bride!' His tone was bracing.

Mireille felt like hitting him. He had no need to rub it in that she was his bride, his wife, to order about, to treat as a servant. Emilie's words flashed into her mind: 'pray for one who will not beat you too much.' She bit back the angry words she longed to shout at him.

'If I hack at it with a knife,' he surprised her by saying, 'and you scrape at it, between us we may succeed.' He suited his actions to his words, and between them they began to move the congealed mess.

It took some time, and Mireille was hot and perspiring by the time they had finished. She pushed her hair back from a shiny forehead with the back of her hand.

'I think the only thing to do is to bury the remains outside,' was his verdict. 'There is a cesspit past the shed.'

He led her to it and she threw the rubbish in, shuddering a little and looking away.

Pierre replaced the cover. 'You must bear in mind that it's there. You wouldn't want to fall in!'

Mireille fled back to the kitchen, and he followed at a more leisurely pace.

'Fill the pot with water now and leave it to soak. We'll fetch sand later, and scour it out. There are other jobs to do.'

Mireille was glad to leave the pot, but dismayed to hear there was more in store.

He turned his attention to the hearth, and handed her a small shovel-shaped tool and a scuttle. 'Kneel down and clear it. A new fire will not burn there until it's done, and the careful housewife keeps the fire burning always.'

'Why?' Mireille demanded. 'It's warm enough here, surely.'

He sighed and patted her on the head. 'I see it's going to be longer than I thought to train you in self-sufficiency! But I'll explain,' he added, as Mireille jerked her head away from his hand and squatted on her haunches before the ashes.

'You get hungry like the rest of us?' he enquired softly. 'You expect hot meals, have a hot drink before you go to bed or first thing in the morning? Yes, I see you do. You're probably hungry now.'

'Yes! Yes, I am.' As though to emphasise the point, Mireille's stomach rumbled. She blushed in mortification, but Pierre laughed.

'A hot meal is out of the question now.' He looked undecided for a moment. 'But start to work, and I shall see what I can find. There might be some cheese and fruit.' He strode towards another door in the far wall. 'I'll look in the larder.'

Mireille could hear him rummaging about as she shovelled ashes into the scuttle, and began to cough as the dust caught in her throat. It was very quiet in the house. She could almost have sworn she was alone as she got to her feet and looked for somewhere to get rid of the collected ashes.

Pierre startled her by appearing at the back door, with something in his hand. He put it down on a small table and waved her out. 'On the rose-bushes,' he instructed, 'It helps them to grow.'

Incredulous, Mireille looked for rose-bushes, and found them a little way away. They were blooming, a riot of red and pink blossoms, and she bent to inhale their fragrance. What a strange man he was; but perhaps he hadn't planted them.

'The pride of my garden!' He smiled at her as she upended the scuttle over the roots, 'But no lovelier than the face bending above them.'

Mireille straightened up, her back catching her. Compliments were out of place when she looked as she knew she must look, and yet his eyes were serious.

'We shall eat outside,' he declared. 'Sit on that tree-stump, and I'll bring the food.'

It was a very large stump, and it was good to sit down. Pierre joined her there, bringing bread and cheese, a jug and a cup. The bread was buttered, and it was fresh. She didn't question, but bit into it , ravenous. He watched her eating, and then poured from the jug to the cup and handed it to her.

She looked at it and tasted. 'Fresh milk!' she exclaimed, taking a long draught. 'Where did it come from?'

'Why, from the cow, of course,' he told her blandly.

'I know that,' said Mireille. She might have said it more sharply, except that the food had mellowed her a little. 'You said your cow was stabled with a neighbour. How does he know you're back?'

'We keep watch of who comes and goes. One of his children will have noted our arrival.'

'Are the neighbours close?' Mireille had a sudden longing for another girl her own age to talk to, another wife.

Her hopes were dashed with his answer. 'Close enough to be neighbourly—far enough away not to be a daily nuisance.'

Mireille had no idea how far that might be, but pursued the subject no further. It was pleasant after all to sit in the sun, to eat and drink her fill. If the truth were told, she had a bigger share of the lunch than Pierre did, but he made no comment. He even allowed her to sit for a few minutes after they had finished, and Mireille's eyes, in spite of her efforts to keep awake, began to close. She would dearly have loved to stretch out on the ground and drift into sleep.

However Pierre declared there would be time enough for sleeping when the sun went down. For the present, more work awaited her attention.

She slowly rose to her feet.

'You will want to know where the woodpile is,' he said. 'And the privy too.'

Mireille felt the colour rising in her cheeks. His casual reference to such a thing embarrassed her more than a little.

Pierre seemed quite unmoved. 'You are as the rest of us, are you not?'

Mireille could only mumble that she was, and he left her to enjoy a little privacy. When she rejoined him by the house, he piled logs of wood in her arms and then loaded himself in the same way.

Together they built the logs into the makings of a fire, and Mireille had her introduction to the art of starting a flame by rubbing two sticks together as the Indians did. She protested that a flint would be easier, but he brushed aside that suggestion.

'You'll be grateful to me for the rest of your life for this lesson,' he told her.

So Mireille persevered, and eventually was rewarded by a tiny burst of flame which he helped her to nurse into fuller life with shavings of birch-bark. Only when the logs had caught, and the fire was fully established, was she allowed to rise from her knees. By now, her hands were filthy, her hair in considerable disarray, and she was hotter than ever, and more tired, too.

The pump did not present such insurmountable difficulties this time, and Mireille laved her face and hands gratefully in the cool water. When she would have tidied her hair, Pierre simply took the remaining pins from if and gave her a leather thong to tie the whole long mane of it in a bunch that tumbled down her back like yellow gold.

'Pretty,' he said, his hands lingering on it. 'We must keep it safely attached to your head. Some wild brave might fancy it at his belt!'

Mireille shivered—not at the touch of his hand, she told herself, but at the sombre tone of his voice.'What—what do you mean?' She stammered, not quite understanding his words.

'Why, our English and Dutch enemies to the south have learned to distrust the boasts of the Iroquois. They demand proof of Frenchmen who are killed by tomahawk or arrow, so the Indians bring scalps to them.'

A chill of startled fear shook Mireille, but not for one moment did she doubt what Pierre had said. Automatically, her hand flew to her hair. Yes, it was still in place. Pray God she kept it there!

Pierre went to the wall of the big room, from which he took down a musket.

That did nothing to allay the alarm that she now felt. 'What's that for?' she whispered.

'To defend ourselves. In all likelihood, we won't need it now, but we're going down to the river, and I never stir far from the house without a weapon and ammunition.' He patted the pouch, which hung now from his belt.

'What are we going to the river for?' she asked.

'Questions, questions!' Pierre grumbled. 'Still, I suppose that's the only way you'll learn. It shows a certain intelligence on your part—as well as a complete lack of knowledge of the way of life you have pitchforked your way into.'

Mireille was unsure whether to be flattered or insulted by this remark, but she had no time to decide which pose to adopt.

Pierre continued,'We are going to fish. A healthy young appetite like yours will need food. We must provide against that.' He handed her an object resembling a spear, but which was quite unlike any spear that Mireille had ever seen, being much shorter and lighter. He also gave her a net attached to a stick, and a bucket.

'Am I your slave, then?' Mireille demanded, indignant to be bearer for him. She half expected him to be angry, and did not care if he was. She was unaccustomed to being treated in this way. At home, the only things which had been expected of her were to sew a fine seam and be waited on—not to do the waiting on for such a man as Pierre!

Pierre did not lose his temper. He answered her, as he might have a child, 'Don't you understand anything of what I've been telling you? I need my hands free in case I need to use my musket.' He stroked the weapon lovingly. '*Allons, ma petite.* I don't mean to alarm you, only warn you of the dangers. If your eyes get any bigger, they will jump out of your head.' He patted her on the shoulder.

It was a kind sort of pat, Mireille told herself, but she resented it all the same, and jerked her shoulder away.

Without a word he led the way out of the house and past the cleared land, down through the trees. Mireille followed, her eyes darting from tree to tree, half expecting some naked warrior to appear from behind their shelter, but they arrived quite safely at the water's edge. Mireille was then allowed to hold the musket, with strict injuctions to be silent and motionless.

Pierre took the spear from her and slid into the water, leaving his moccasins beside her on the shore. He did it quietly, so quietly that the water barely rippled at his approach.

In a moment, Mireille was astonished to see him raise the spear; a second later, a fish was impaled on it and thrown to her feet. He picked up a stone and hit the creature sharply on the head.

'Watch carefully,' he instructed. 'The next one you must deal with.'

'It's cruel! It's barbarous!' Mireille panted, sure that she could never kill a fish—no, not if her life depended on it!

'Nonsense!' said Pierre. 'That carp is a fine fellow and meant for my supper. Now I shall find one for you.'

Mireille wanted to stop him, to prevent him somehow, but she eyed the fish and knew Pierre was right about it being a fine fellow. It took him a little longer to find a second to join the first, and he held it for Mireille to deal the *coup de grâce,* instructing her as to the exact spot the rock should strike. 'Open your eyes,' he commanded. 'Squeamishness is out of place. This good creature deserves a quick clean death, not a lingering one.'

Mireille took a deep breath, and struck as Pierre directed. 'Two is enough?' she pleaded as he approached the water again.

'Yes,' he agreed, finger to his lips. 'But I saw a big eel that can be pickled for the future.'

So Mireille waited. The eel was not only larger; it was wily, and took a bit of catching. Eventually it was she who, venturing to the water's edge, kicked off her sabots and netted it.

Pierre was pleased. 'Well done, but where's the musket?'

She pointed to the sand, where it lay beside the fish. She didn't need him to remind her of what might have happened, and she ran back to it.

It was none the less a cheerful twosome who returned to the house, Mireille carrying the fish and a bucket of sand, Pierre the fishing equipment as well as his gun.

Work was not yet finished. There were fish to be gutted, the cooking-pot to be scoured clean with the sand, and corn to be picked. Then Pierre showed her where to gather wild onions and mushrooms. By the time everything had been done, Mireille was more than ready for her meal, and impatiently she waited for it to cook.

Pierre had to instruct her in that as well. The fish must be baked, he decreed, with the onions and some herbs, and then the mushrooms. The corn was boiled in the big pot. There was milk to drink, and berries followed with it.

'You see we're self-sufficient,' Pierre said as they ate. 'There is fish and game in abundance. Tomorrow I shall show you how to shoot, for you will need fresh meat sometimes during the winter when I am away.'

When Mireille heard these words, she knew a moment of despair. Granted he was a hard taskmaster, what would she do without him in the hard months of snow and ice? Why did he keep harping on about being absent?' It sent shivers down her spine.

She rubbed her eyes, resting her elbows on the table. It was all very well for him to smile and say how she would manage. She knew she couldn't. She wanted to put down her head and howl, even plead with him not to go. Only pride held her back, and the fear of the wedding night looming ahead of her. Perhaps, by morning, she would be glad he was going.

'Tired?' asked Pierre, without waiting for an answer. 'Never mind, there are only the pots to do now, and the kitchen fire to build up for the night.'

Mireille rose wearily to her feet. By now, she knew well enough who would be attending to those duties. The light was beginning to fade by the time she finished her chores, but Pierre had dealt with the eel.

'We'll sit outside for a little,' he suggested, 'now that it's cooler.' He took her arm and led her out to a rustic bench by the door.

Mireille was glad enough to sit down and to put off the moment when they would get into the now tidied bed. She did not want to meet Pierre's gaze. She wondered what he expected of her—a simpering smile, a look of eagerness. She wasn't smiling. She wasn't eager. An owl hooted mournfully nearby, and she jumped. She heard a wild animal call in the distance.

'What is it?' she asked.

'A fox—it's nothing to be afraid of. There are still many wild things in the bushes.' He gestured vaguely towards the line of trees. 'But nothing like it used to be. When I first came here, I met a bear just where we're sitting.'

'A big one?'

'Big enough! I was lucky. He left me alone, and I had no desire to harm him. We just looked at each other and called quits.' Pierre laughed.

When she looked at him, she wondered for a moment if he expected her to be impressed by his bravery, but he was too matter of fact about it.

'You never married before?' She was curious, in spite of herself: he was a puzzle to her in every way. He went among the Indians, he met bears head on, and yet he knew all about looking after himself and keeping house. 'You never wanted a bride from those who came on the ships?'

'No, I never wanted one of them.'

'Why not?'

Mireille was uncertain whether he would tell her or not, and found she was holding her breath. There was no reason why he should. He meant nothing to her. She might have been married to Charles if the day had gone right. That would have been a different kind of wedding night! Charles would have smiled at her, told her she was beautiful, desirable. She sighed.

'A wife ties a man down—if he lets her. I want to make a good life here, a better life than I would have had in France. I'm a second son. A second son has to fend for himself. I joined the army and took my discharge here. I own the land. One day there'll be a fine house here, and children who can carve a future for themselves.'

Mireille shivered. He was talking of children again. He meant what he said; she knew that by now. The night loomed darkly before her.

'Besides,' Pierre continued, 'I think marriage should

be a happier event—an affair of the heart—not by command of the King.'

'So do I,' she whispered. 'Oh, so do I!'

He reached out and took her hand in his, giving her the ghost of a smile. 'Poor little girl, it's all been too much for you, hasn't it? I wonder what you make of me. Do I frighten you?'

Mirielle was experiencing the strangest of sensations. Her hand seemed to slip into his so trustingly and her whole arm was tingling where it touched his. What was the matter with her? A little kindness, and she was ready to fall into his arms. She reminded herself of the tasks he had imposed on her. He had not chosen to marry her, but had been forced into it. At least, if he had been in the hall and picked her out from the others, she would have felt he had selected her, liked the look of her. But he had married her because Charles had arrested him. It was a form of revenge. So she snatched her hand away.

'Yes,' she declared. ' You do frighten me! You don't even like me. I don't like you, either.'

She felt him draw away from her. Why had she let her tongue run away with her? Just when he had softened towards her.

'You don't have to like me,' he informed her coldly. 'I understand there are many marriages like that. You have only to obey me, and take care of my property when I am absent.'

'When you are absent! What kind of marriage is that?' Mireille felt goaded beyond endurance. 'You can't get away fast enough.'

'There would seem little to stay for,' was his short and bitter rejoinder. 'You've already told me you don't like me. You have none of the womanly accomplishments. You don't know how to cook or wash or manage a home, but by heaven you will by the time I leave you! And you'll stay faithful to me while I'm away—I shall see to that.' He put his hands on her shoulders and shook her.

It didn't hurt her, not physically. As shakings go, it was gentle, but in some deep corner of her being it wounded her to have him speak to her, to think so little of her. She knew she had brought it on herself. She'd snapped at him, pushed him away. That knowledge made it no easier.

'Leave me alone!' she gulped. 'I've had enough of you—enough of marriage to you—slavery is what I'd call it! You talk of being free, but what freedom do you give me?' Her eyes swam with tears, but she brushed them angrily away. 'I want to go to bed. If there is one more task before me tonight, please tell me quickly. I'm so tired.' Head up as proudly as she could manage it, she swept past him and into the house. She threw her clothes off and put on her shift. If he was coming, let him come. She wouldn't fight him, wouldn't whimper. It was, after all, part of the bargain. She belonged to him. She fell on the bed, dry-eyed.

Pierre, too, had risen to his feet. Now he paced up and down the narrow strip in front of the house.

You talk of being free, but what freedom do you give me? She had flung that taunt at him, and it hurt. He knew he wasn't a cruel man—he had taken pity on her, hadn't wanted to see her flogged through the town. It had seemed a solution for both of them. He was tired of trying to avoid fines and imprisonment. Marriage with Mireille had appeared the answer—neat, tidy and with a hint of amusement about it. What a joke it would be to see Captain Charles's reaction.

Where had it changed? She had stood up to him, worked hard and well. It had been pleasant to have a companion, a girl who did not chatter all the time, was willing to learn from him. He had enjoyed his day. Why didn't she like him? He liked her well enough except when she gave him a fight . . . Even then, there had been something admirable about her, something brave. She must have known he could have beaten her or forced her to be welcoming. But he could not do that to her. She was defenceless.

He smiled to himself. Well, he must win her round. An enemy on one's own hearth was an enemy indeed.
He went in and bolted the door against the night. His wedding night.

CHAPTER THREE

PIERRE ENTERED THE bedroom. In the light of the moon which shone through the window, he could see Mireille lying under a thin blanket. One arm was thrown back against the pillow and her eyes were closed. She looked so like an exhausted child that he stood for a minute and watched her breathing.

He opened the window and stretched a piece of netting against it to keep mosquitoes and flies away. Then he undressed and stood naked by the bed. Still Mireille did not stir.

She had told him to be quick, but he had no intention of following that instruction. He slid into bed beside her. She trembled, but did not move as his arms closed about her.

'There's nothing to be frightened of,' he whispered. 'I have no desire to force you. Tonight I shall only hold you. Even horses have to be gentled before they are broken to the saddle.' He almost laughed aloud at his own words. Whatever was he about, comparing her to a horse?

Yet he had had a mare once whose eyes had been the same shade of melting brown as this girl's, and she had been nervous of him, too. He had talked to her and patted her, and finally she had taken an apple from his hand and then given him her trust—and her devotion. Honoré he had called her, and he had mourned when she had been shot from under him. He found himself telling Mireille about the mare. 'The best horse I ever had,' he confided. 'So quick, so dainty on her feet. You have a look of her.' He rubbed Mireille's back with one hand casually.

'I am not a horse!' she grumbled, but he felt the stiffness gradually receding from her spine.

'No, of course not,' he agreed, his mouth close to her ear. 'But you have the same thoroughbred air, and the same appetite.'

It was hardly romantic language, he chided himself, but the girl seemed to find it comforting in spite of that. She had lovely skin, and her hair where the moon caught it was like spun gold. Ah, on such a night to hold a girl like this . . . No, no, he pushed the thought away, but it was a long time since he had held a woman of his own race. He sighed. Soldiers were not monks, nor had ever been. Patience was the only way with this one.

'I—I have never been with a man,' Mireille whispered.

'I should hope not!'

'Do they all sleep naked?'

'Not all,' Pierre felt a stir of interest in his own body. If she kept asking him questions like that, he wouldn't answer for the consequences!

'Does—does my cousin Charles have some girl he pays court to?'

Pierre resented cousin Charles being brought into the conversation. 'There are not many girls in New France of marriageable age.'

'Then he doesn't.'

Was he wrong, or was there satisfaction in her voice? 'Not to my knowledge, but it can't matter to you.'

'He is the only relative I have here.'

'You don't need relatives. You have a husband,' was his sharp rejoinder. He had no time to waste on relatives! 'Turn round and face me.'

He felt the fear rise in her again. 'You said you weren't . . . '

'I know what I said. Turn round.'

'But you're naked!' Her protest was only a thread of sound in the quiet night.

'I have a fancy to hold you as a husband holds a wife.'

She turned in his arms, tender breasts against his chest through the thin material of her shift.

He liked the way she fitted there, but she was shaking, and as he searched her face to find her mouth to kiss her fear away, he tasted the salt tears on her cheek.

'What are you crying for?' he demanded roughly. 'Don't you like being in my arms?'

'I know you are my husband—and I must submit . . . ' she whispered. 'But . . . '

'I don't want a wife who submits.' He pushed her from him. 'I want a wife who wants me. What's wrong with you? It's a perfectly natural thing I want—a joyful thing—yet you draw back. Has some man assaulted you?'

'No, I swear it isn't so!'

'Then what is it?'

'I had a serving-maid, and Alphonse caught her in the barn.'

'Who's Alphonse?'

'The other cousin—the one I left France so I wouldn't have to marry . . . '

'The one who tore the wings off butterflies?' Pierre caught her hand. 'You saw him with this maid?'

'Yes,' her sigh was heavy. 'It was horrible, and afterwards she wept, and she was bleeding.'

'Pig, *cochon,* that you should witness such a thing! I promise it won't be like that—nor will it be tonight. Turn round and let me hold you as we were before.'

Mireille turned very quickly.

Again Pierre rubbed her back. This time, she allowed herself to rest against him. She yawned and rubbed her eyes.

'Go to sleep,' he instructed. 'It's late, and you are tired.' He began to sing softly to her, a gentle song he had learned when he was a boy and sometimes paddled to when he was alone in his canoe.

Yes, one night, if he but waited—held back—she would turn to him. There was fire and warmth beneath her fear. His voice drifted to a stop with the last words of his song, and he thought Mireille slept.

She whispered something, and he strained to hear her words. What was it she said?

'I like you better than Alphonse—and you're better formed.'

He smiled. Yes, she would turn to him. It was only a matter of time, but it was a long while before sleep overtook him. A strange wedding night, he mused as he waited, watching the moon grow big.

In the morning, Mireille awoke to find herself alone in the big bed. She stretched; disappointed, somehow. He wasn't there. The sun was shining in at the window, and it was a lovely day. She greeted it with more enthusiasm then she had felt at a day's beginning for many a week. The hard voyage was over. The uncertainty was over. What if there was a different sort of uncertainty hovering over her? There was Pierre. Ah yes, there was Pierre, and he had been kind to her last night, had seemed to understand. Today, she'd try to please him. She might tell him she'd like to have a bath, to wash her hair. Heigh-ho, it was time she was stirring!

She got out of bed.

The day did not go quite as she had planned. After breakfast—a plate of porridge which Pierre had ready in the big pot—he announced that they were going into town to collect the dowry and some flour and yeast. She would have a chance to prove she could make bread.

The market was a busy affair. Not, of course, like the large markets she had seen in France, but still there was a great deal of activity, a great many beasts to be claimed, a great many stalls selling all sorts of things from leather to cloth, to wine, cakes and cheeses.

Some of the other girls from the boat were there, including Émilie with the large man. She hugged Mireille and introduced Georges. Pierre already knew him. They left the two girls talking while they chose the best ox and cow they could find.

Émilie confided that her man was a carpenter, and he had a fine house. He had not beaten her at all, but was good to her. He did not mind about her eyes not matching, and he had promised to buy her some cotton to make a dress. She wanted to know how Mireille liked married life.

Mireille in her turn felt she must boast about Pierre. She was telling Émilie about going fishing, when Monsieur le Secrétaire strolled up to them and passed the time of day.

He was all smiles this morning, and full of affability and compliments for the ladies. As he raised his hat to leave them, he said to Mireille, 'Tell your husband, Madame, that Capitaine de la Croix returns tomorrow—or so I hear. He will be interested to know.'

Mireille wondered why Pierre would be so interested to know. Surely it was rather something to hug to herself, someone from home. She acknowledged to herself that she was curious to know how Charles would greet her. Would he have heard? No, how could he? It was only Pierre, herself and Monsieur le Secrétaire who could tell him, and she saw no reason why that gentleman would. She was not even sure if Charles would recognise her. In the three years since she had last seen her cousin, she had grown up a lot. She'd tell him, if he didn't know her. But would it be wise? Was that exactly what Pierre would expect her to do? There was something strange about the whole situation. She puzzled about it so much that she was silent nearly all the way home.

Pierre made no comment. He was busy leading the ox, which was loaded down with flour, the two squawking chickens and the barrel of salted meat. Georges had promised to bring the two pigs by cart.

Pierre had pocketed the eleven crowns, and Mireille noted that he had made no offer of dress material for her. And she was left to lead the cow! Fortunately she was a docile animal and was content to come quietly, only stopping now and then to fill her large mouth with some succulent plant. The ox, on the other hand, took all his attention.

Once home, the animals were led into the barn. Mireille expected that she would be taught to milk the cow, but when she mentioned the subject, Pierre told her she was a bit premature. The cow must have her calf first, and that would take time. She blushed to have to be taught the facts of life, as he informed her that one of his neighbours had a fine bull.

They shared between them a large meat pie, which Pierre had bought in town, and a flagon of beer from the new brewery in Québec. That restored her spirits considerably, and she went so far as to volunteer to bake bread with the precious yeast she had obtained. That pleased Pierre, as he declared he must construct some sort of pen for the chickens.

Mireille liked making bread. She always had, though her mother had said it wasn't lady's work. Still, she had never put a stop to her visits to the kitchen at home to help in the baking. At least the dough kept her hands soft, was her mother's verdict.

Now she looked at them. They were soft no longer—not after yesterday's cleaning of the grates. She sighed for those years of being a lady. What would her mother make of this life her daughter was forced to live? Mireille pounded at the dough, taking out some of her anger. What was she so angry about? Pierre had been kind to her last night, was mostly patient with her. Yes, but for how long? She struck the dough again.

She had built up the fire before she started and put on the big pot to heat water, for she meant to wash her hair while the bread was proved. When she had pushed and pummelled the unresisting dough to her heart's content, she covered it with a cloth and put it in a warm spot near the hearth. Quickly she cleared the table and ladled the hot water into a large bowl.

A glance out of the door assured her that Pierre was still at work, and she whipped off her dress and one of her petticoats, and bent her head into the water. At home, she had never had to wash her own hair, but she knew quite well how to go about it. Soon the water was filthy, and she was struggling with dripping hair and dumping the bowl into the sink.

That was when he chose to come in. He laughed to see her antics, but he helped her with the heavy bowl. Once it was emptied, he stood back and looked at her a gleam in his eyes.

'What a sight to greet a man,' he exclaimed, and Mireille's hands flew to her exposed breasts. 'No, no, don't cover them up! I am your husband, after all.' He took down her hands very gently, and surveyed her.

She did not know where to look—certainly not at him, for there was such a hungry look to him. She bit her lip, and murmured, 'I must rinse my hair, and fill the bowl again with clean water.' She raised her hand to the small towel, which barely caught the drips.

'Allow me?' Pierre took the towel from her, and wiped her neck and shoulders and down into the cleft of her bosom.

He was so close that she could feel his breath on her neck, so close that she could see the paler downy hair that stretched from his ear to the top of his jaw. It softened the jutting angles of his face. That face now bent closer to her, and he kissed one rosy nipple.

Mireille felt such a thrill of sensation, of anticipation, that she thought her legs might give way beneath her. They trembled so much that she leaned back against the sink. Now she was completely hemmed in by him, the bowl resting drunkenly under the pump.

Pierre moved his head and kissed the other thrusting nipple.

The girl was so startled and overcome that she offered no resistance when he rained gentle kisses on her tender flesh. His hands stroked her upper arms and then her shoulders, leaving streaks of dirt where they encountered droplets of the water from her hair.

'Zut!' He clicked his tongue against the roof of his mouth. 'Only see what I have done—spread the good

dirt on your white skin. Let's fill the bowl again and I shall wash my hands and then you, and together we'll rinse the soap from your hair. You will want to dry it.'

Mireille turned quickly to the sink and clutched the big ladle. She could not describe, even to herself, how she felt. Her breath was short, her heart thudding against the thin cage of her ribs. Why had he stopped? Of course she didn't mean that, couldn't mean it. He had taken her by surprise. She didn't want him near her. And yet, as she rinsed her hair and he rinsed the black smudges from her arms and shoulders, she had to acknowledge that it was pleasant to have him drying her shoulders, to see the admiration in his eyes.

She was all the more startled and affronted when, her hair now wrapped in a bigger towel, he held out his hand to prevent her moving the bowl from the table.

'Aren't you going to wash your dress and petticoat?' he demanded. 'They look as though they need it.'

'Yes—yes, they do,' Mireille admitted. She was unwilling to add that she had never washed a dress, and did not know how to go about it. Besides, who was he to comment on her clothes? At home, she had had several dresses. Here, she had only this one, which she had worn for most of the voyage, and her best, which had seen an outing yesterday for the landing. It was the blue brocade.

She was undecided for only a moment. She picked up the brown cotton frock and dumped it in the water. She supposed it would prove no more difficult than her hair. But there she was wrong. It was so soiled that she had to soap it again and again, and rub the spots to try to remove them.

Pierre had lost interest and gone outside. For that she was grateful, she told herself. Now she had nothing to cover herself with, and the bread was ready for more kneading. She ran to the bedroom and found a shirt of Pierre's, and came back. Afterwards, when she had the bread baking and the clothes and herself washed, she would dress properly. But first she must dry the table off, and attend to the dough.

The plan might have worked if she had been given time to complete the whole, but up to her elbows in flour, she heard the sound of a cart. It was Émilie's husband with the pigs. What could she do? Finish the bread at least, and hope against hope that he would not come into the kitchen.

But there her hopes were dashed. He wanted water for the horse, and Pierre insisted he must have a glass of beer. Mireille was cut off from retreat. She had only time to remove the wet towel from her head and wrap it willy-nilly round her waist, knowing full well that an expanse of leg from above the knee to the ankle was exposed, for the waist-petticoat she had retained was very short.

She greeted Georges with as much dignity as she could muster. Under the circumstances, that was not very much. She endured Pierre's disapproving stare, flushing, and raising flour-streaked hands to push back her damp hair. She could have cried with mortification.

Georges said he could see she was busy, and left as soon as he had finished his drink. Pierre accompanied him back to the cart. Then, with a sinking heart, Mireille saw him head back for the kitchen door.

Before he reached it, he called out to her. 'Come here, now—at once. Hurry!'

'I'm not dressed,' Mireille wailed, but she did as he asked.

'One of the pigs has got loose,' he shouted at her. 'You stand there, and I'll beat it towards you.'

Mireille stood. The difficulty was that when the pig eventually headed in her direction, it was coming at such a speed and with such a look of ferocity on its face that she was frightened and stepped aside. The pig swerved, and both of them were on the ground in a patch of mud. Her towel flew from her waist, but the pig was caught by Pierre.

'Well done!' said Pierre, rushing the recalcitrant beast

to the barn and a secure tethering.

Mireille picked herself and the towel from the ground. She tried to brush off the mud.

'You'll never get rid of it that way!' said a voice above her.

She looked up, startled, to see a soldier in full uniform on a large black horse. Too shocked to move, she stared up at him. What a contrast he presented to her dishevelled state! In his blue coat piped with white, his plumed hat, his musket carried in a sling over his shoulder, he looked the thorough officer he was. Even his long leather boots turned back half-way to his calves gleamed in the sunlight. His mount shone, too, and reared back a little from the girl. The officer gentled it with one strong hand.

'Well, well!' he exclaimed. 'Do I have the honour of addressing Madame Charbonneau?'

Mon Dieu, thought Mireille. That voice! It is the voice of cousin Charles. She was so astonished, so embarrassed by the bizarreness of her situation, that she was dumb. She could only bite her lip and stare.

'Come, I won't bite you,' the vision on the horse continued. 'You have a tongue—just say Yes or No.'

This was quite beyond her. In any case, she was saved from answering by Pierre's return. He put his arm about her shoulders. At first, she found that oddly comforting—until he spoke.

What brings you here?' he asked the horseman. 'As you can see, I've bowed to the King's wisdom and found myself a wife. You catch her unprepared to greet you.'

'So I see!' A frosty smile crossed Charles's face. Quite obviously he did not recognise the girl. His lip curled as he took in her awkward state. 'It appears you treat her well.'

'How I treat her is no concern of yours,' Pierre replied. 'She is my wife. If she's a little slow to learn the domestic round, you have no need to trouble yourself about it. I suppose you came to see for yourself what prize I'd landed!'

Mireille felt the shock of those words in her very heart. It was not her fault that she wasn't a prize. None of it had been her fault. If she had been allowed to get on with her own affairs, to bake the bread, all would have been well . . . Oh, the bread! It would be burned. She ran for the house, and the smell met her at the door.

The bread was burned. It had risen beautifully, but it was black on top. She pulled it from the heat, and scorched her fingers in the process. The pain made her cry out, and tears came to her eyes.

Pierre had followed her in. He took in the scene at once, and led her to the sink and cold water for her hand.

'Poor little one,' he murmured. 'Nothing's gone right for you, but I wonder you didn't claim kinship with your cousin.'

'How could I?' the girl demanded furiously. 'Look at me! I couldn't bear to have him see me so.'

'Why not?' The blue eyes were sharp. 'Because he isn't your cousin—or because he wouldn't want to recognise such a girl as you?'

Mireille stamped her foot in rage. 'He *is* my cousin.'

'Strange he didn't claim you, then.'

'He wouldn't expect to find me half naked, muddy, chasing a pig.' She sprang to Charles's defence.

'Had he been other than the grand Capitaine de la Croix, he would have looked beneath the dirt and seen a lady.'

Mireille winced at that. She turned away from him.

But he did not let her escape, and turned her firmly round to face him. 'I would have recognised you for the one you are. I would have opened my arms to you and laughed and called out, cousin.' He suited his action to his words and opened his arms.

Mireille made no move to enter them. She was angrier than ever. 'Would you? You called me a prize.'

'Well, so you are—the wife I've drawn.'

'I hate you,' she snarled at him. 'You don't think me a prize at all. I'm not a prize. I can't do anything. Any of those girls on the boat would have suited you better.'

'How do you know what suits me? Have I complained?'

She shook her head, willing herself not to cry, to let him see it mattered what he thought of her. It doesn't matter, she told herself.

'I heard it in your voice, what you thought of me when you called me a prize,' she muttered unwillingly. 'Why don't you end this marriage—tell them I came under false colours—have me sent back to France? At least there I knew who I was—what was expected of me.'

She felt wretched and alone. It was the biggest mistake of her life to have left France. She had begun to think so on the boat, when she had been with the other girls and started to realise the comforts of the life from which she had cut herself. Now it came over her in a rush. She was not suited to being a settler's wife. Too much was expected of her—and all of it dirty, demeaning work. Since Pierre had said nothing and was standing watching her, she continued,

'You could have it annulled . . . It hasn't—we haven't . . . ' she faltered under those cold blue eyes. 'Well—we didn't . . . '

She was not allowed to go any further, for he put his hands on her waist. 'We can soon remedy that!' Before she even guessed what he was about, he had lifted her from the floor and was carrying her to the bedroom.

Mireille kicked and struggled. 'What are you doing? Let me go.'

He threw her on the bed and in one easy movement was on top of her, imprisoning her with his body, his lips on hers.

She hit at him with her fists, but he laughed and kissed her again, and drew the shirt she had filched from him over her head. Then his kisses were directed to her trembling body—down her neck, over her shoulders, to the soft curve of her breast.

'No,' she whispered. 'No, no,' as he slid out of his deerskin trousers, one hand still on her threshing legs.

She was never sure quite how he accomplished it, but she found her petticoat torn from her waist and thrown to the floor. Surely she hadn't helped him! No, she could distinctly remember the tearing sound as it was ripped away. But she had done nothing to prevent him from taking off his tunic. Ah yes, she had almost rolled off the bed then, striving to be free of him.

They were together, both naked, as she was pulled back to his arms. She fought him, and somewhere in that struggle of arms and legs and warm, aroused bodies, she felt her strength leaving her. His lips were so demanding, his masculinity so overpowering, his will so much stronger than hers. He did not have to force her legs open. They opened of their own accord, and he took her.

She gave a gasp of pain, then found her body moving in accord with his, stretching and arching and accepting him. When it was over, she lay in his arms, spent. He slept, but he still held her.

So this was what it was—this fierce coupling between man and woman. Not quite so frightening as she had expected, but wild and—she searched for a word to describe it to herself—free, was the one which sprang into her mind. There was a kind of release in being free of clothes, of all restraints, of letting the body follow its own inclinations. No one had ever told her it would be like this. Was this how Alphonse felt? She dismissed that thought very quickly.

Of course this wasn't love. Love was gentler, more considerate. Love was sung about, had poems written to extol it. No, this was passion. How was it she had never known passion before?

Mireille slept. When she woke, she found Pierre holding her no longer, but looking at her body. She stirred and would have covered herself, but the covers had all slipped from the bed.

'Well, wife!' he greeted her. 'There'll be no more talk of annulments, of going back to France. Here you are, and here you stay.'

Mireille resented the firmness of his voice. In fact, she told herself rebelliously, she resented the whole high-handed way he had used her. She was not just a possession of his, whatever he might think. She turned her back on him, forgetting she was naked, and he slapped her bottom lightly.

'I know you heard it! Just keep it in mind.' His hand lingered, moving from her buttocks down her thigh. 'I'm almost inclined to repeat the performance.'

Mireille rolled to the far side of the bed, evading his hand.

'Perhaps not now, he conceded. 'There is the bread to salvage yet—and your dress to hang out if you are to have anything to wear tomorrow!'

That persuaded Mireille into action. She rose from the bed and looked for some clothes.

'Émilie's husband bought her some material to make a new dress at the market today,' she pointed out. She picked up the torn petticoat and held it up for his inspection.

Pierre tossed her the shirt which she had been wearing before. 'I'll have to think about it. You have only the two dresses, have you? The one you're washing and the one you wore yesterday.'

'That's all,' Mireille agreed, slipping the shirt over her head. 'I haven't even a big apron. That would do well enough in the kitchen.'

'If that's all you want,' Pierre slid into his trousers, 'there's one in that chest over there. Sometimes one of the town women comes to straighten up the place.' He fished an apron from the trunk and handed it to her.

Though it was much too large for her, Mireille was pleased to have it. She wound it round herself, and it served as skirt and apron.

Pierre bent over the trunk again and pulled out a pair of moccasins. 'These look as though they might fit you.'

Mireille tried them on, fingering the elaborate bead-work on them. 'Whose are they?'

'Yours now,' was the only answer he gave her. 'I think it's time we introduced you to the neighbours. We'll have a party.'

'A party?' Mireille echoed. 'What sort of a party?' She was delighted with the idea.

'An open air sort of party. I shall go hunting for a deer tomorrow—we can roast it over an open fire—perhaps a turkey or two. Depends how lucky I am. I might take Georges with me.'

'Yes, but when will the party be?' Mireille asked impatiently. 'You'll have to invite people . . . '

'That's easy enough. They don't need much notice. What else would they be doing? Of course they'll come, tomorrow or the day after—it depends how the hunting goes. A messenger can be quickly sent round. I think we'll invite your cousin Charles. You can wear your good blue dress—it's a bit better than most of the women will be wearing, but Captain Charles will recognise you in it, won't he?'

'Yes, I suppose he will,' Mireille was puzzled why it should be important that Charles acknowledge her, but she didn't question Pierre. It was enough that he meant to have a party—a party in her honour. He had not said exactly that, but surely that was what he meant.

She turned to him with a smile. 'If you go hunting tomorrow with Georges, do you think I might spend some of the day with Émilie?'

Pierre considered it for a moment. He shrugged. 'If the housework is done first, I don't see why not. It's only a step into town, after all.'

Mireille would have called it more than a step, but she wasn't going to argue about it. He had given his permission, and that was enough. She led the way to the kitchen.

CHAPTER FOUR

IT WAS AFTERNOON before Mireille set out for Émilie's. She wore her old brown cotton, which had washed and ironed better than she might have expected. Her hair was fastened in a neat, thick braid that hung down her back. Pierre had helped her with the braiding in the morning before he set off. He had said an odd thing—that he had not seen such long, thick, fair hair since Marianne's.

When she had asked who Marianne was, he had looked as though the words had just slipped out and he was not going to add anything to them. But she had asked again, and he'd said gruffly, 'Marianne was a Dutch girl—very young, thirteen, fourteen. I freed her from the Turks.'

'The Turks?'

'*Oui, vraiment!* I fought against the Turks. I won my first promotion there. Marianne was the spoils of war, in a way. I was able to return her to her parents.'

'And were they grateful?'

'They'd given her up for lost. They couldn't believe she was their daughter come back from the dead.'

'But she was?'

'She was—and she wasn't.'

'What do you mean?'

'She had been a prisoner of the Turks.'

'What does that mean? Had she been . . . cruelly used?'

'Not cruelly, but she had been in the harem of an elderly Turk.'

'One of his wives, you mean?'

'A concubine.'

'What's the difference between a concubine and a wife?'

'Nothing in actual fact—but a wife has status, the protection of a husband's name.'

'Did she want to go back to her parents—this Marianne?' Mireille had felt there was a parallel between herself and this Dutch girl, and wanted to know more about her.

'She wanted to go back to her own people. What else was there for her except to become a camp-follower? There were some who would willingly have turned her into that.' He had turned away again, as if tired of the subject.

But Mireille could not leave it alone. 'What happened when you returned her? Did her parents know?'

'I think perhaps they guessed, but they took her back just the same.'

'And—what then?'

'I don't know. I had to rejoin my regiment.'

'*Tiens!* You must have some idea. You can't just stop there!'

He gave her a lazy smile. 'You're very curious about her! She was, of course, a very pretty girl, and her family were rich.'

'Is that supposed to answer my question?'

'*Certainement*. She would not have made the marriage that might have been expected of her originally, but a young man without money or an older man who valued her gifts acquired in the harem might well have oblige-d—and been pleased to do so.'

Mireille's mouth opened to ask what these gifts might be, but she decided against further questioning. She could puzzle it out for herself.

At any rate, Georges had arrived then and insisted on leaving his dog with Mireille to accompany her on her walk into town.

'What can Pierre be thinking of to let you walk

alone? No, Diablo shall accompany you.' He whistled, and a large black dog came to him. 'Don't be afraid! In spite of the name, he's very gentle—except to enemies.'

Diablo looked reproachfully at Mireille as though he knew he was going to miss a day's hunting, but he settled quite happily at her feet. Now he accompanied her to town, walking majestically before her and sniffing the air with great care. When he came to a sudden stop where the path met the more open outskirts of the town, he stopped, and growled deep in his throat.

Mireille was drawn from her reverie of a Turk's harem to the present day. '*Qu'est-ce que c'est,* Diablo?' she asked sharply, but the dog only barked and prevented her from moving forward.

'This is ridiculous!' Mireille's heart was beating fast when yesterday's horseman appeared at a trot out of another path at right-angles to the one she travelled.

The rider pulled to a halt, and Mireille looked up into her cousin's eyes. This time he recognised her. 'By all that's holy,' he exclaimed, 'it's Mireille! Coz, how you've grown! It is Mireille, isn't it? Yesterday, I wasn't sure. Something about you—the way you stood, perhaps—kept reminding me of you, pushing at my brain . . . ' He leaped from the saddle and held out his arms to her.

Mireille ran into them. 'Charles, Charles, how good it is to see you—if only you had been in Trois-Rivières two days ago!'

They were both speaking at once, Mireille half laughing, half crying, Charles wholly astonished at the explanations pouring from her lips.

Diablo was pacing around them. 'Call off that animal,' Charles begged, 'and start at the beginning. Why should Alphonse want to marry you? The last time I saw him he was a lumpish, grubby boy. What was your father thinking of to countenance such a match?'

Mireille signalled to Diablo as Charles led her to a fallen tree-trunk, and the dog whined softly.

'Has he been trained to allow no dallying on the

way?' asked Charles. 'How like Pierre Charbonneau to keep him—and you—so close to heel!'

'He is not Pierre's dog!' Mireille did not like the way her cousin spoke. 'Diablo belongs to Georges.'

'No matter,' Charles shrugged and brushed leaves away from the trunk before he handed Mireille to a seat. 'There, that will be comfortable enough—it's in the shade.' He stood above her. Diablo lay at her feet, watchful.

His very watchfulness made her feel guilty—but what was there to feel guilty about? Charles was her cousin. They had played together as children—well, perhaps not exactly played together—Charles was nearly ten years older than she—but they were cousins. There could be no harm in passing the time of day with him. In any case, tucked away as they were behind the trees, no one could see them.

The whole story came out—the flight from Alphonse, the voyage across the Atlantic and all its dangers and tedium, the hasty marriage to Pierre. 'Just think,' Mireille finished it off. 'If you had been here, I might have been married to you at this very moment! That is—if you would have had me.'

Charles raised Mireille's hand to his lips and kissed it, then held it in his own. 'How can you doubt it? I would have jumped at the chance!' His brown eyes, so like her own in colour, seemed to darken with emotion.

For a moment, Mireille thought that emotion might be anger, even hatred. Why should he hate her? Of course, it was Pierre he hated. Pierre had laughed when he had proposed marriage, and asked her if she didn't find it droll. There was something between the two of them—something she did not understand.

'Pierre Charbonneau knew who you were?' Charles made her go over the whole thing again.

Mireille could not see the point of that: what was done, was done. Besides, looking up at Charles, she compared him to Pierre—and not as favourably as she would have expected. The flesh round his eyes was puffy. His hand where he had removed his glove was white, the fingers stubby. His complexion was not bronzed as Pierre's was, but ruddy, and she could see the first faint lines of veins threading his cheeks. Diablo stirred at her feet, and she removed her hand from Charles's. For a moment she thought he might kick Diablo, but the dog bared his teeth in a ferocious grin. It was clear to her that Diablo didn't like him.

'He told you he wasn't married?' Charles paced up and down before her.

'*Oui*. He said that.'

'And you believed him?'

'Why should I not? A priest married us, and Monsieur le Secrétaire was witness.'

'That doesn't mean anything. How would they know?'

'Know what?' she demanded.

'Mind, I have no proof. I always thought the reason Pierre Charbonneau wouldn't obey the King's edict was because he couldn't.'

'Couldn't?' Mireille's mouth was dry. 'You mean . . . ' She found she couldn't get the words out.

Charles supplied them for her. 'That he had a wife already.'

'Who?'

The question hung between them.

Charles had stopped his pacing and come to a halt before her. 'No, I may be wrong.'

'Who?' Mireille repeated.

'Just a girl,' Charles shrugged. 'Tell me . . . I suppose your marriage . . . You and he . . . ' Charles coughed delicately, one hand to his mouth, his eyes moist, sympathetic. 'It has been consummated?'

Mireille drew back, yesterday afternoon suddenly a sickening memory. She nodded.

'I'll say no more.' Charles sat down beside her. 'It's better so, after all.'

'Better for whom?'

'For you, of course! It's a long way from the Low Countries. Who's to know the exact truth?'

'The Low Countries?' She repeated the meaningless words. *Bon Dieu,* he meant the Dutch girl. Had Pierre married her?

'Marianne?' she whispered. 'You speak of Marianne?'

Charles was evidently surprised. 'You know of her? He told you?'

'He said he returned her to her parents.'

Charles smiled. 'I have no doubt he did. But in what condition?'

'What condition?'

Charles reached out and patted her knee, and Diablo raised himself and put his muzzle there.

'I have no wish to hurt you. You care for him.'

Mireille denied it, and Diablo gave her a reproachful look. She commanded him to sit.

'You know what she was, of course—this Marianne—a girl of the harem. Well, soldiers are not the nicest of creatures, and after a battle the spoils fall to the victors. The French were the victors.' Charles raised his shoulders in a very Gallic gesture. 'Who can blame him? She was an exceedingly beautiful girl—and young. And he was not the first.'

Mireille bit her lip. Pierre had said Marianne was pretty—and rich. Had he tired of her and brought her back to her family? What else was it he had said? She strove to remember the exact words—he had been unwilling to tell her what had happened after Marianne had been brought back. Her parents might have bought her a husband. No, she wouldn't believe it of Pierre. He would have told her. Would he? Why should he, if he wanted to hide it from her? She had known him only two days, been married to him for two days. But it all hung together. If Marianne's family had wanted to give her respectability and yet keep her with them—no, it wasn't true! Charles was just trying to stir trouble. She remembered her mother had once said that of Charles-—that he brought discord with him. She had never believed it, always thought Charles a sort of hero, but now, was she so sure? In this new life, she wasn't sure of anything.

'Best to forget it all.' Charles rose to his feet and helped her up. 'We don't know, do we? Besides, he might be free by now. She might have died. We'll say no more about it.' Charles walked to where he had tethered his horse, and in one quick movement had mounted it. He saluted Mireille. 'Till we meet again, Coz, at this party of yours. Shall we pretend we've never spoken today? Let your husband introduce us for the first time, and feign surprise?'

'Yes,' Mireille agreed. 'If you like.' She patted Diablo as if to reassure herself that he, at least, was real. He whined softly and led her from the spot.

All very well for Charles to tell her to forget Marianne. If it were true and Pierre was married to her, this was a bigamous marriage. The enormity of that conclusion was frightening! Lord, what had she landed herself in? Yet--it might not be true. She might be worrying herself needlessly.

She could ask Pierre. No! No, she couldn't. She shrank away from that. But she didn't love him. The marriage could be annulled—it was only of two days' duration. Two days might be enough to have landed her with a child! Whichever way she looked, she was trapped. She wished she knew. No, she didn't. Pierre was her husband. He had not treated her badly. No? He had forced her to work with her hands, taken her by force. Not exactly by force, she admitted honestly-—when it came to it, she'd been willing enough. She could realise now that he had not behaved like some rough, selfish oaf. Pierre must have had some experience of women—of Marianne? Her mind tried to block that thought out. There was no reason to be jealous of a girl like that—like what? Marianne had had no more choice in what had happened to her than Mireille herself had. She could understand her better than Pierre, or Charles.

Charles was right. It was better to say nothing, to blot the ugly suspicions out. None of it was fact, nor was there any way of finding the truth. She had no knowledge of Marianne's full name, even.

It was a very subdued Mireille who reached Émilie's house. In truth, they were the exact opposites of how they had been on landing day. Émilie was bubbling over with her good luck and her fine home, whereas Mireille was upset and abstracted.

'What's wrong?' Émilie kept asking her. 'Does he beat you, this fine new husband?'

'No.'

'He hasn't bought you any clothes or ribbons or gloves?'

'No, but it doesn't matter, anyway.' She had other things to think about than ribbons.

'He's going back into the forests and the Indians might kill him. Is that it?'

Mireille shivered. That might be the answer, after all! If Pierre disappeared, none of it would matter—it would never come to light. Somehow, that didn't seem very satisfactory, either. She couldn't explain it. Nor could she tell her friend what was troubling her.

'He says he'll be gone for eighteen months—maybe two years!' Mireille allowed a tear to cloud one eye.

Émilie hugged her. 'Ah, men . . . Fools! To find a wife, and then to leave her! It makes no sense at all.'

It might make no sense to Émilie but it was beginning to make a great deal of sense to Mireille. Did Pierre mean never to come back?

'Perhaps he'll change his mind?' Émilie offered. 'At any rate, Georges and I will see no harm comes to you. When he—when Monsieur Charbonneau—goes, perhaps Diablo could stay with you. He seems to have taken a great liking to you.' She pointed to the dog, which had not left Mireille's side since she had arrived. 'A dog is great company.'

'Yes,' agreed Mireille. 'A dog is great company. I would feel safer with a dog.'

Charles allowed the big black horse to stroll through the forest, following the path.

Merde! It was the devil's own luck that he had not been at the quay when Mireille had landed. Everything would have fallen into his hands then—the girl who had turned into quite a beauty, and her fortune. It would have been a pleasure for him to have wrested it from Alphonse's grasp. What a clever move that had been of Mireille's Uncle Alain. Well, he had tried to seize a splendid inheritance for his son—and failed. Alphonse had no real title to it. He was only a cousin on Mireille's mother's side of the family.

Now, Pierre Charbonneau could claim it all. Always Pierre Charbonneau managed to be one step ahead of him, to snatch the prizes from him. He had as much talent as Pierre, had shown as much bravery in the field, yet Pierre had won the medals and the first promotion. He had also won Marianne! Ah, she had been every man's dream of voluptuous, welcoming woman. He had freed her and was taking her into his own care when Pierre Charbonneau had appeared on the scene. He had declared the girl should go free—that French officers could do no less for her—and Pierre had fought him for her.

Unfortunately, the Colonel had agreed with Pierre, and ordered him to return her to her family, with leave of absence to do so. No doubt, on that journey home, there had been many opportunities for Marianne to show her gratitude. As for the rest of it, it could have happened in that way—who was to know? It would not do Mireille any harm to harbour suspicions of her fine new husband!

Charles mused on, an idea knocking at the back of his mind. Mireille's father was a canny man. He must have appointed Uncle Alain as guardian to his daughter, and Mireille had refused his choice of husband. He had not given his permission to Pierre, nor ever would. The property must pass to the next in the male line of de la Croix. That was himself.

But, of course, that was only if Mireille wasn't there to make a fuss, to petition the courts, to come to some arrangement with Uncle Alain. If Mireille weren't there . . . If Mireille . . . he put it into words for the first time . . . if Mireille were dead. That was unthinkable, of course. She was young and healthy, and as yet had no children. A son might well inherit. The marriage had been consummated—she had said so. Pierre Charbonneau would not waste any time in that direction.

Still, there was time—time, perhaps, to prove a bigamous marriage or for Mireille to disappear. The life of a settler was precarious. So was that of a coureur-de-bois!

He would watch and wait, and bide his time. He meant to have the de la Croix land. He was the male heir—not Alphonse. When he left the army—as he would if he could afford to, he would not take land in this new country—this wilderness. Its roughness and its solitude turned his stomach. He wanted to return to softer climes, to ease, to luxury. Mireille's land would see to that. At least he had the time to think about plans and strategies; time before Mireille spawned a son. For, unless he mistook his man, Mireille's father would have provided for that eventuality.

Charles smiled grimly to himself and set his horse at the gallop. An ambitious man must be ready to be governed by the wind of opportunity.

It was late when Pierre and Georges returned from the hunt. Diablo heard them first, and begged Mireille to open the door to run to them.

The girl knew that was what he wanted. It was surprising how soon she and the black dog had come to understand each other. She let him go, and he came back with the men. They had found a young deer, and the two turkeys Pierre had promised.

The three of them feasted on pickled eel and the

remains of the burned bread. Then Georges called to Diablo, and they left.

Pierre yawned hugely. 'It is time for bed.' He pulled Mireille from the kitchen. 'These few dishes can wait till morning. We'll be up early to get all in readiness. It was a grand hunt today. I've walked my feet off. How was your day, Mireille? Did you have a good gossip with your friend?' He held her by the hand, and led her to the bedroom.

'Bien sûr,' Mireille replied, wishing she had the courage to ask him about Marianne. 'Émilie has a nice house—bigger than this. But they've haven't the sort of furs you have.'

Pierre smiled. 'We have, you mean. Not many have the furs *we* have. We'll have some of them made into a coat for you, come winter. Would you like that?'

'Very much!' She was delighted at his suggestion. She had had a fur cape—a short fur cape, left behind in France. 'Which fur would be best?'

'Beaver is nice, or fox—you shall decide in the morning.' He yawned again and shrugged off his clothes, sliding into his side of the bed.

Mireille followed suit more slowly. Let it wait till the morning, along with the dishes and the decision about the coat. What difference could one more night make? If she was married, she was married. If she wasn't . . . She shivered as she got in.

'Cold?' asked Pierre, and drew her close.

So tender was his voice, so gentle his embrace, that Mireille nearly cried out to him. She longed for the reassurance of knowing she was properly married. Pierre might not be the man she would have chosen, the man her father would have chosen for her, but up till now she had thought he was her husband. Oh, why had she ever had the misfortune to meet Charles today? She could not get his innuendoes out of her mind—and that was all they were, she acknowledged to herself. He had said he had no proof.

When she opened her mouth to speak, to demand an

explanation, Pierre's mouth fastened on hers before she could begin. She abandoned herself to the comfort of his presence. He was claiming her as wife by his actions. He had married her before a priest. That was enough. She returned his kiss, hoping to lose herself in the pleasure her body could take and give.

In the morning, there was no time for talking. Pierre had to find a messenger to take round his invitations; he had to prepare the deer and the turkeys. Mireille was glad to see that three men and a boy appeared as if from nowhere to assist him.

The boy ran round to friends telling them of the party that evening, and the men built a pit for the fire to roast the deer. They also made a spit to turn it on, and helped Pierre with its skinning.

It fell to Mireille to make a soup of the turkey livers, necks and wings, which simmered in the big pot over the kitchen fire, and to which she added onions, beans and carrots as one of the men brought them in.

She baked, too, another batch of bread, and this time the loaves were golden and crusty—perfect. Pierre said they were, as he sniffed them hungrily.

After Georges had delivered a barrel of beer and some home-made wine, he had a bowl of the soup and a hunk of bread. He had brought a message from Émilie, asking if she should wear her new dress. Mireille said Yes to that.

She was beginning to enter into the spirit of the party. It would be good to meet her neighbours, Pierre's friends. She laughed at her fears of yesterday. Of course she was married. Was he not saying publicly that it was so?

The weather was fine. The sun shone all day, and by evening there was the promise of a moon as the light began to fade. People started to arrive—men, women and children. As Pierre had said, none of the women was as finely arrayed as Mireille was in her blue brocade. He was obviously proud of her, and introduced her to one and all, his arm round her waist.

The beer and wine flowed, the soup was praised, and the smell of deer and turkey roasting was tantalising in the cooler air of evening. A big orange moon—a true harvest moon—bathed the whole scene in a warm golden glow.

It was when the deer and the turkeys were being cut and distributed that Captain Charles de la Croix arrived on his black horse. He was in army uniform, and pulled off his plumed hat as he dismounted before Mireille.

His arrival caused stir enough, as several of the guests had to move quickly to avoid his horse's dancing hooves. But when Charles exclaimed, '*Mon Dieu,* it can't be—yes it is! Why, cousin Mireille, what are you doing here?' and stepped forward to hug and kiss her in delighted and noisy appreciation, the guests drew closer to enjoy the reunion.

Pierre, too, drew closer, and though he did not remove the girl from her cousin's embrace, he began to speak, which caused them to part.

'My wife,' he proclaimed. 'Strange that you didn't recognise her the other day.'

'Not so strange!' said Charles. 'I didn't expect to find her in the fields. It's not her proper place.'

It was not Pierre who answered this sally, but Monsieur le Secrétaire, who stood beside him. 'As to that, good Captain, we are all workers here.'

Mireille had not been aware that Monsieur was one of those invited. Now she turned to greet him, and to offer him and his wife refreshments. She was surprised by the sight of Madame Morel. Where her husband was small and thin, Madame was tall and plump, and very much younger than Albert. She had a pretty little girl by the hand, whom she introduced as Albertine. 'Named for her father, of course,' she explained, and Albertine curtsied to Mireille.

Mireille took the child by the hand to fetch her some turkey, and Madame Morel followed them. Charles came right behind, leaving Pierre with Albert.

If Charles had hoped for some private conversation with Mireille, he was frustrated, for Madame kept close beside her.

Mireille found she was glad of that, for she wanted no more tête-à-têtes with Charles. Eventually he gave up and attached himself to a very pretty young girl, who could have been no more than thirteen or fourteen.

'About the only unattached girl in Trois-Rivières,' Madame Morel offered in an undertone. 'And I doubt her father will allow the Captain's attentions!'

Mireille had thought Madame rather bovine and dull, but she perceived a look of acute intelligence in her large grey eyes and decided that first impressions could be deceiving. It made her pause. Here was someone else who did not have too high an opinion of her cousin!

'You are fortunate in your husband,' Madame Morel went on pleasantly. 'He is brave, well born and generous. I'm sure you'll be very happy with him.'

Pierre had said he was as well born as herself, but she had not quite believed him until then. There was an air of complete honesty about this woman. But it was a mystery to Mireille that he had no airs and graces: he talked to everyone as if they were the same. Not as her cousin Charles did, she acknowledged to herself. He gave the impression he was above other people. Why should that be? And why should she be noticing it only now? The change was in herself. She was not the same girl who had left France. The voyage had forced her to look at herself, to make a few changes in her ideas and attitudes. Émilie and the other girls had seen to that.

When everyone had eaten, they gathered in small groups at first, chattering and laughing. Then they came into a big circle around the burning fire, and someone began to sing as they sat on blankets and furs on the ground. They sang the songs of home—the soft love-songs of France, the wilder vagabond songs of the coureurs-de-bois. An old man among them told the story of the *loup-garou,* the hound of the skies.

While they were all experiencing a thrill of alarm at

this macabre tale, they heard the sudden sound of horses' hooves and the jingle of harnesses, and they all rose to their feet, alarmed. For they had most of them experienced surprise attacks, fury by night.

A party of six soldiers rode in. 'Is Captain de la Croix here?'

'What is it?' asked Charles, striding forward.

'An attack. Come at once!' was the quick reply. 'A child captured, a cabin burning. We're to set off in pursuit.'

There were horrified cries, demands for explanations, for the name of the settler, but there was no time for that. Charles mounted his horse, and they were gone, leaving the party no longer a happy occasion.

People stood guessing whom this calamity had happened to, then they began to gather sleepy children, holding them tight, and started to leave.

Mireille watched them go, calling farewells, huddled together. Émilie gave her a quick hug, and so did Madame Morel, shrugging plump shoulders. 'Now you know the fear that lives among us. Pray God it comes no closer!'

She began to tremble uncontrollably. Pierre came and stood beside her, his arm about her. It was strange what comfort his presence gave. She turned to him, and he held her as the last guests went down the path.

CHAPTER FIVE

IT WAS NOT until the next day that Pierre began to question Mireille. He took her by surprise as they were eating breakfast.

'Tell me,' he began quietly. 'What did you talk about when you met your cousin Charles on your way to Émilie's the other day?'

Mireille choked on a crumb of bread as she put the slice down on her plate. 'What—what do you mean?'

'You didn't tell me about it'—Pierre's eyes were hard—'but I understand you had quite a chat with him. Come, what did you talk about? Did you get him to agree to claim you as cousin—or have you some other plot between you?'

'There is no plot between us,' Mireille protested. 'And he is my cousin, whatever you may think. I'm sorry I didn't tell you about it. I wasn't sure . . .'

'Not sure about what?' he interrupted. 'Not sure that I'd be interested? Certainly not sure that I'd find out.'

Her temper began to rise. 'I don't know how you found out. Did Diablo tell you?'

'Dogs don't speak!' For the first time, there was a glint that was almost laughter in the grim gaze.

'I suppose someone saw us. It doesn't matter. Do you have to know everyone I speak to?'

'Not everyone, but I won't have secrets between us where Captain de la Croix is concerned. What did you speak about?' He reached across the table and took hold of her wrist.

The pressure he exerted was considerable—and painful. Mireille bit her lip and snarled at him, 'Let me go! I'll tell you, since you're so determined to know. We talked about you.'

'What about me?' His grip did not loosen.

'He said . . . ' Mireille faltered. 'He said the reason you hadn't married according to the King's orders was because you were already married.'

'Did he now, and who was the lucky lady—or did he not mention names?'

Mireille could not read Pierre's feelings from his face, but it seemed to her that he had paled.

'Marianne,' she whispered. 'Are you married to Marianne?'

'I am not married to Marianne—and never was!' Pierre released her hand abruptly—so abruptly that it fell to the table with a thud, and she began rubbing it to ease the pain. 'But if I had been—what would that matter to you?'

'It would matter if you still were!' Mireille retorted. 'For no man can have two wives—not at the same time.' For some strange reason, her spirits began to lift. He had never been married to Marianne. He had said so, and she believed him.

'No man can have two wives,' Pierre echoed. 'Well, I'll tell you something, little golden hair, so that your cousin won't have to. I had another wife—before . . . '

'Before . . . ' Mireille repeated, the ground suddenly swept from under her feet, her bread uneaten on her plate. 'Before what?'

'Before you came.'

'Who was she—is she?'

'She's dead. She died having our son.'

'And the son?'

'With his mother's people. They would not give him to me.'

'Why not?'

'That is the Indian way.'

Mireille's hand flew to her mouth. 'The Indian way . . . She was an Indian?'

'A Mohawk maiden, as dark as you are fair, but with

such a light of love in her eyes. Eyes that a man might lose himself in—trusting eyes.'

Mireille felt as though he had struck her. Perhaps this other girl had had reason to trust him. 'What was her name?'

'Little Beaver.'

'And the boy?'

'Silver Badger.'

'Do you ever see him?' Why was it such torture to question him—to hear his answers? Why did she keep on? she asked herself.

'And you were truly married? Before a priest, as we were?'

'Not before a priest—but truly married according to the customs of her people.'

'How can you call that truly married?' Everything in Mireille refused to accept it. He was a Frenchman, and his religion bound him as it bound her. It was a sin to marry without a priest. She told him so.

He seized both her hands. 'How comfortable you make it sound! Do you call this a marriage that we have? You running to your cousin . . . not wanting me? My marriage with Little Beaver was the real one . . . There was no drawing back with her.'

Mireille snatched her hands from his. She wouldn't listen to him, couldn't listen to him. She rose, and would have run from the room.

He stood in front of her, preventing her. 'Sit down. I haven't finished.'

'As far as I'm concerned, you have!' She was trembling. 'I suppose this Little Beaver had a choice. I had none.'

'Yes, she had a choice. You have one now. You can sit down and listen—or you can run away. That's what you did from France, but has it solved your problems?'

'No,' she screamed at him. 'Just presented me with new ones!' She was breathing heavily. She hesitated. Then she sat down.

Pierre pulled another wooden bench close in front of

her and sat down. 'I suppose you can't help the way you are—brought up in a comfortable home, living an orderly, safe life. What do you know of the way life is? The struggle and the fighting—the treachery—and sometimes the goodness. Mireille, when love is offered freely, it is a gift to accept—to treasure. What does it matter where one finds it? Love and trust go hand in hand.' His blue eyes held hers. 'Trust me, Mireille. I have not lied to you. I will not.'

She was moved, but not ready to give in. 'You don't trust me,' she objected.

'Don't I? I want to. The biggest act of trust I ever made was in offering to marry you.'

'How was that?'

'Knowing the family you came from—I looked at you, and found myself wanting to believe you were not like cousin Charles.'

Mireille drew back, insulted. 'What's wrong with him? I can understand why you and he are enemies, but what I can't understand is why Monsieur le Secrétaire, Albert, is so against him. Is that because of you?'

He sighed. 'I see I'll have to tell you the whole story. Albert had a brother. He was in the Turkish campaign—not as an officer, but as a soldier. Richard was only a young lad. He was in your cousin's company, and unfortunately in the pillaging which took place after the victory, it was Richard who appealed to me to save Marianne.'

'Unfortunately?'

'Fortunately for Marianne, unfortunately for Richard, for Charles did not forgive him. As soon as I had departed for the Low Countries, Charles denounced Richard to the authorities on a charge of looting. Richard was found guilty and put to death. Your cousin was at his execution.'

Bon Dieu, could this be true? Mireille shuddered at such treachery—and yet, even as a boy, revenge had always been his code. Alphonse had told her that; but Alphonse had never been his friend.

She did not want to believe it, and denied it to herself, turning on Pierre angrily. 'So Charles had his revenge! Are you any different from him? You revenged yourself—Albert revenged himself—by marrying me. I see why he arranged it. I see why you fell in with it. I suppose you mean eventually to return to France and snatch my inheritance back from Uncle Alain—as Charles would have done.'

'If that's what you think of me, I can't stop you!' There was dislike in Pierre's expression. 'I don't want your lands. I am well able to provide for myself and my wife.'

'Not want them?' Mireille was affronted, 'No sensible man turns his back on such bounty.'

'I don't want them. Let your cousins fight over them.' He leaned forward. 'But you would be wise to take care.'

'Take care of what?'

'Your life, your health. Captain de la Croix is a dangerous man.'

'I think you are a dangerous man, too.'

Far from making him angry, this statement seemed to please him. 'Pray heaven your cousin thinks so as well! We shall prepare for him. It's time you learned to handle a musket.'

'To use against Charles?' There was fear growing beside the anger in Mireille. Pierre couldn't be right—but if he were . . .

'Possibly.' Pierre shrugged. 'I think that more to be feared from him is the knife in the back. First, you must promise not to meet your cousin on your own—never to be alone with him.'

'How can I promise that?' Mireille objected. 'I didn't meet him by arrangement on the path the other day. He rode up to me.'

'Didn't it strike you as odd that he should be along there, waiting?'

'No, why should it? We met by chance.'

'Did you? I fancy the chance was on your side, not his. Promise me.'

'Will you believe in my promise—knowing the family I come from?'

He considered her for a moment, studying her face.

Mireille found she was holding her breath. Would he trust her word?

He nodded. 'Yes, I think I shall. Promise. Trust must begin somewhere.'

'Very well, I promise.'

'*Bien.* Finish your breakfast; then I'll give you a lesson in shooting.'

Mireille had little appetite for her bread and milk, but Pierre cut himself another slice and poured more milk. The confrontation had done him good. It was the girl who brooded on his words. He had been married to an Indian girl and had a son. And, moreover, he compared her unfavourably to Little Beaver. He had turned all her values upside down, called her cousin a villain, made her question her ideas of marriage and religion, and now proposed to train her to defend herself. Did he not think she might turn the musket on him? No, he was a man. Men had an overwhelming confidence in themselves. Mireille bit into her bread savagely, feeling the hurt of his assessment of their union. One day she would pay him back for those words.

The shooting lesson was not an unqualified success, and Pierre soon realised that. Mireille was slow at mixing powder and shot, was nervous of holding the weapon, closed her eyes to aim, and never came within distance of taking the whole thing seriously. There was only one time, when she turned the musket on him, that he had the faintest hope she might one day be a possible markswoman—and in that moment he knew a sharp, tingling fear, but she pointed the muzzle at the ground at his command.

Impatient with her, he asked, 'Don't you know we're

fighting a war with the Iroquois? You must learn to handle this weapon.'

She loaded it again. 'Are we—are we fighting a war—now?'

'*Oui, vraiment*. Oh, not this very day, this very moment, but why do you suppose there are more than a thousand men from the Carignan-Salière regiment in the colony now, and more expected? It is war.'

She held the musket in her arms, not as a weapon, but as one might cradle a baby. 'With so many soldiers here, it will be a short war.'

He took the gun from her, chiding her for her careless handling of it. 'What makes you think it will be a short war? For your information, the French army marched against the men of the Five Nations last January and were hopelessly defeated.'

He had the satisfaction of seeing Mireille's eyes widen at that. 'A thousand men, and they were defeated—you must be mistaken! How could it be?'

'Quite easily. An army which marches in bitter cold and snow into hostile bands of men who have fought in these forests all their lives is destined for defeat. They would not listen to the settlers' advice.'

'Were you with them?'

'No, I didn't even know they were going. I had been trading beyond the Finger Lakes. It was a long journey-—eighteen months. I returned in time to see the remnants of the army creep back.'

'Will they go out again?'

'It's rumoured so, but this time it's to be hoped they'll show more sense and go about it in a different way. They have taken on Indian scouts, and enlisted some of the settlers.'

'Have they enlisted you?'

'Not yet.'

'Do you mean to go with them?'

'I don't know. *Peut-être*.'

'But you were in the army, so aren't you obliged to go?'

'I took an honourable discharge after the Turkish war. I came to settle here, not to be a soldier once again. I had enough of that.'

'But . . . '

He could see there were more questions on her lips. He didn't want to hear them, didn't want to answer them. He gave her back the musket. 'We aren't out here to talk. Shoot.'

That silenced her, and he was glad to see she was beginning to put some urgency into it. She actually kept her eyes open to sight the target.

'Better,' he conceded. He made her try again. And again. And again.

Until she was so tired that she snapped at him, 'Does it all have to be done today?'

He looked at her and then some slight movement—a shadow, perhaps, near the barn—made him exclaim, 'Load it again and come with me.'

Mireille was too tired to protest. She did as he told her, and followed very quietly as he put his finger to his lips.

They halted by the barn door. Was she mistaken, or had it been tightly closed before? Now it was open the barest crack.

'Cover me,' Pierre instructed. 'I'm going to open it and go in.'

Mireille raised the musket to her shoulder, her heart pounding, the hair at the base of her neck rising. She couldn't explain it, but she knew there was someone in the barn.

Before Pierre had a chance to do more than open the door and flatten himself against the wall, a little boy stood in the entrance.

It was a moment of total surprise. Mireille slackened her hold on the musket, and would have reached out for the boy except for Pierre's hand on hers.

'He has freed me,' said the boy.

'Who are you? Who has freed you?' was Pierre's

response. He did not move from his position against the side of the barn.

The boy answered the second question. 'White Fox has freed me. He took me from the other.'

'White Fox!' Pierre cried out. 'Let me hear your voice! Are you alone?'

Mireille could hardly believe her ears. Who was this White Fox?

Whoever he was, he replied, 'I am alone, O brother Fox. I come in peace.' His French was passable, but he said more in another tongue.

'I welcome you in peace,' Pierre answered, and took a step towards the door. 'Come to me.'

'No, brother, you must come to me, for there are eyes everywhere.' Again he added something that Mireille could not understand.

It appeared to convince Pierre. He moved into the barn, and the boy ran to Mireille. She had no idea who he was or what was happening, but she held the musket at the ready while the lad clung to her skirts.

What should she do? She could hear a low-voiced conversation on the other side of the wall. In fact, the whole encounter had been conducted in soft tones, which had made it more frightening rather than less. She slid towards the door and peered in. Pierre and an almost naked Indian were embracing each other. Astonished, she took a further step towards them, the boy with her.

'Put down the musket,' said Pierre. 'White Fox is a friend.'

Mireille lowered the musket, but she held it still.

White Fox inclined his head to her as might a king, but made no other acknowledgment of her presence.

'White Fox has returned Daniel Lamont, the boy who was captured by another Indian—a Seneca,' Pierre explained. 'It is a proof of his good intent.'

'Then he is to be thanked.' Mireille turned to the boy. 'Is it true—were you taken by another?'

The boy nodded. 'Yes, that other burned down the

house. Where is my mother? This one won't tell me.'

Mireille felt sickened. She did not know where Daniel's mother was, but she could guess. She looked at Pierre.

He shrugged and asked White Fox something in his own tongue. Whatever he replied made Pierre's face grim. 'Take the boy to the kitchen and give him some milk.'

Mireille would have obeyed, but White Fox barred her way out in one swift movement. 'No,' he exclaimed. 'Let them stay. There is danger here for me!'

Pierre snapped his fingers, and Mireille sat down on some hay, the musket beside her, the boy Daniel in her lap. He leaned against her, one thumb in his mouth, his eyes half closed. She guessed he was not more than four or five. Poor mite, just a little dark-haired lad who'd lost his mother—and his father and his home, in all likelihood. She held him to her.

White Fox began a long speech in his own language and Mireille had the opportunity to study him. She found him fearsome with his head partly shaved, his thick black hair drawn into a single quiff that ran along the centre and was braided down his back. There was a streak of green dye painted across his forehead, and another of purple, which ran from one lean cheek across a hooked nose to the other cheek. His eyes were small, dark and rounded. His chest was bare and bronzed, and there was a thick purple line across that, too. He wore fringed leggings with a bead pattern, and moccasins. When he turned suddenly, his head tilted as if he heard some noise beyond ordinary hearing, she was discomfited to discover that his leggings covered only the front of his body—the back was bare, lean buttocks totally exposed. That made him seem even more formidable. Yet Pierre had called him 'friend'.

Pierre answered in the same tongue, then both of them dropped to their haunches, and White Fox began again.

'Speak in French,' Pierre directed. 'I wish the woman to hear.'

'I ask my brother to return with me.' White Fox did not appear at all put out as he switched his language. 'His people and his village need him. Silver Badger would welcome his father. He asks about him. Three summers have gone by and he has never seen him.'

Mireille saw a muscle twitch in Pierre's cheek, but he made no comment.

White Fox continued, 'We are blood brothers, are we not? When one is hurt, the other suffers. The enemies of one are the enemies of the other. My people's enemies press upon us. My brother's help is needed.'

'White Fox speaks in riddles.' Mireille noted that Pierre had adopted a different way of speaking, following the same style as the Indian. 'Of what enemies does he speak? Does he mean the Frenchmen among whom I live? Does he forget than I am a Frenchman?'

'White Fox does not forget,' was the quick rejoinder. 'He does not ask his brother to take arms against the French. He only asks his brother to come and build such a defence about Silver Badger's village that all within will be safe against any enemy—English, Dutch or French.'

Pierre considered that in silence.

White Fox waited for an answer with an impassive face.

Mireille waited, too. Pierre could not accept. Little Daniel, with a tired sigh, relaxed completely against the girl, and slept. She saw Pierre glance at him. His own little boy would be about this size, she supposed.

'Does my brother tell me that the English and the Dutch make war against his people? It is my understanding that it is the French who mean to march against them. Their great King has sent his soldiers—soldiers who sent fear into the men of the Five Nations, even though the icy hands of winter forced them to withdraw. Next time it will be different. Already the men of the Onondagas, the Cayugas and the Senecas have sent peace parties to Québec. Why do not the Mohawks do the same?'

'Though the soldiers of your King be as the sands of the sea and they march together as one man and the sound of their musketry is louder than thunder, the Mohawks believe their cause is right, their strength is as the strength of ten. They do not sue for peace with one hand and practise treachery with the other, as do the Senecas. It was a Seneca who burned the boy's house.' White Fox gestured towards the sleeping lad. 'A Seneca who would have taken the boy to his village, and kept him.'

'White Fox deserves great credit for his timely rescue. The people of Trois-Rivières will wish to express their gratitude to him. But I think my brother makes a small mistake. Agariata was a Mohawk, was he not? And he was put to death not long since for boasting of the death of a Frenchman to the commander of the French army. Is this not the reason why the Mohawks know peace is not within their reach?'

'Agariata was a fool. He paid for his folly.' White Fox acknowledged it. 'Many of my brothers want only peace.' The Indian's expression was brooding. 'Why do the white men settle on our shores? They want land. They hedge it off with fences, and call it theirs. Land belongs to no man. It is for all to use. The white man is not willing to share it with us.'

Mireille was listening attentively to this high-flown dialogue. It amused her to hear the Mohawk talk. She had thought of all the Indians as savages, as people who spoke in grunts or simple words, yet this man had mastered French as well as his own language, and seemed to glory in long sentences and elaborate ways of expressing himself. And his ideas were so different from any she had ever heard. He said that land belonged to no man. How could that be? He talked of his brothers wanting peace. Wasn't that strange, too, for a fighting nation? Everyone knew the Indians were ferocious enemies, who tortured their prisoners and scalped their enemies.

She puzzled over it, moving the boy so that his head

lay against her lap, and he did not even stir in his sleep.

'If the land belongs to no man,' said Pierre, 'how is it that my brother's people live in a village and want to raise a fence around it?'

'Red Fox goes to the very heart of things. My people now ape the white man's ways. They want to protect their women and children and the old customs. They huddle together for security. Will my brother help?' There was no pleading, no begging, in White Fox's voice.

Mireille had to admire the dignity of that simple request. She looked at Pierre. She could see he was more moved by that than by all the rhetoric which had gone before.

It was perhaps because White Fox, too, was looking towards him, that none of them realised that Charles de la Croix stood in the open doorway until they heard his voice. 'Stop where you are! I have you covered.' His musket was raised.

'Put your weapon down,' said Pierre. 'This man has come in peace.'

'You may believe that. I do not!' Charles's musket was at his shoulder. 'I intend to make him my prisoner. He shall face French justice.'

'Don't be ridiculous!' snapped Pierre. 'White Fox is my friend. He has returned the boy.' He pointed to the sleeping Daniel.

'And what of his mother and father? Can he give back their lives?' demanded Charles.

'Of course not,' said Pierre. 'But he didn't take them.'

'Is that what he says?'

'Yes.'

'He can tell it to the court! But I know that I have followed him here.'

'Followed him?' There was disgust and incredulity in Pierre's voice. 'You aren't capable of following an Indian's trail! Somehow you stumbled upon him and skulked around my barn till you heard us talking, then chose your moment.'

That taunt went home. Mireille could see the white lines around Charles's mouth, the angry tilt of his head. 'We shall see whose word is believed on that.' He addressed the Indian who had been standing impassively during this exchange. 'Move, you red bastard!'

Pierre stood in front of White Fox, his body shielding him. 'This man is innocent. How will it look to the Mohawks when they hear how he has been treated?'

'It will look as though we realise they are enemies, and will be treated as such. Get out of the way.' Charles's musket was fixed on Pierre. 'I shall not hesitate to shoot you!'

There was such a look of determination, of triumph, in Charles's eyes that Mireille's hand stole to the loaded musket, ready primed by her hand and hidden in the hay because of the way Daniel was lying.

For a moment the two men stood motionless as statues. Mireille saw that Charles's finger tightened on the trigger. She knew suddenly that he meant to kill Pierre. She half thought that Charles would not live long after that, because she sensed the Indian was ready to leap.

It was perhaps an instinctive reaction on her part to the curl of hatred on Charles's lips. She never knew afterwards how she had managed it so smoothly. As Charles's finger whitened against the stock, she raised the musket and fired at him.

The shot took him in the arm and deflected his aim. But—not soon enough. She saw the stain of blood that spread from Pierre's shoulder, down his leather tunic.

She cried out in horror, 'Pierre, Pierre! He's killed you.' She pushed the boy aside, and got to her feet.

Before she could reach him, White Fox was upon Charles and had felled him with a blow from the head of the short axe he wore at his waist. He bent down and hit him again. Then his eye found Mireille as he raised the axe.

Stunned by the swiftness of the action and by the awful consequences, she screamed, 'Two dead men!

They were alive a minute ago. What have we done?' She ran to him, her fists against the Mohawk's chest, not frightened for herself, too overcome, too hysterical to consider what he might do. Her words came out in a howl, a high keening cry in a voice she didn't recognise, didn't even connect with herself, until White Fox stuffed something into her mouth to stop her shrieks. For one frantic moment she stared at him, brought back to her senses.

Without a word or any suggestion of his intentions, he caught her firmly round the knees and lifted her on to his shoulder, struggling, kicking.

He ran from the barn, carrying her imprisoned by one steely arm against him. Across the open space he streaked in a burst of speed, to the shelter of the trees. At the same mad pace, he made his way to the river and a canoe.

She did not know where it had been hidden, or how he managed to deposit her in it and paddle swiftly from the shore. She did not know, because she had fainted away.

CHAPTER SIX

MIREILLE LONGED TO wipe the moisture from her face. Nearly crying with weariness, her whole body ached. Her feet in sabots and thick stockings were numb now. In the heat of the sun, her dress clung to her body, itchy and hot. Her head ached, her eyes smarted from the glare of sun on water.

She had come back to consciousness, tied hand and foot in the bottom of the canoe, her gaze on the sky. At first she had not known where she was, and had struggled to get up. A sharp word from White Fox had quietened her—that and the paddle raised above her head in menace.

'Be still, no harm will come you.'

As a gag effectively silenced her, she had no choice but to do as he said. In any case, she had begun to realise she was in one of of those frail boats called canoes, and the sound of the water through the thin bark wall so close to her ear frightened her. If the canoe should overturn, she would have no chance at all of saving herself. She longed to ask where White Fox was taking her, why he was taking her, but she could not even do that. What did it matter, anyway? Pierre was dead. She had seen him fall with her own eyes, had seen his life's blood stain his tunic as it sped swiftly away.

Mireille had no idea how long White Fox had been paddling. She was cramped and stiff, and sunk in grief. She could not quite understand her grief. She wasn't sorry that she had fired at Charles, that she had wounded him. He had deserved it—he should have listened. She knew in her heart he wouldn't come after her. Pierre would have—had he lived. She didn't know why she was so sure of that, but she was; she couldn't get it out of her head. Pierre would have matched this Indian in skill and cunning. Charles would not—he could not. She must just resign herself to being this Mohawk's prisoner. She would have to learn to live among his people if that was to be her fate. She rebelled at the idea, shuddered at it, wanted to scream and beat her heels against the bottom of the boat. Perhaps it would be best to tear the frail birch and sink into the cold, chuckling water. A glance at White Fox ended that speculation. He would hit her with the paddle before she could accomplish anything.

The fears went round and round in her head. Always the water whispered to her, the blue sky stretched above, and she was carried further and further away. She had not eaten since breakfast, and the sun from being high in the sky came nearer the horizon. She had forgotten about hunger, but thirst was a raging torment.

She judged the afternoon was far advanced when she felt the canoe change direction. Would it be four o' clock, or five? she asked herself as it ground on to a beach of some sort. She was lifted out of the canoe and deposited with no ceremony on the shale.

'It is no use trying to escape,' White Fox informed her. 'I shall untie you.' He suited his actions to his words, and Mireille found her feet and then her arms freed. She pulled the gag from her mouth. As pins and needles of discomfort shot through her limbs, she writhed and rolled from side to side to ease them.

It was some time before she asked him the questions: 'Why have you taken me away? Where are you taking me?'

'To my village,' was the terse reply. 'Up, up, on your feet, we haven't time for chatter. We must make haste.' He was darting careful glances over the river. 'Pick up one end of the canoe and we shall carry it.'

'Why?' she asked as she got to her feet.

'To get to the next body of water—to put pursuers

off the track. Move, and let your tongue be stilled.' He fingered the axe at his belt.

Mireille did as he directed. Between them, they lifted the canoe on their shoulders, she in front, he behind. She had no hope of escape, no idea where they were going, but she saw there was a narrow sort of path between the trees, and she followed it.

Her pace was not fast enough for him, and he pushed her on until she was nearly running, sabots slipping, perspiration dripping down her face. Hot, exhausted, panting for breath, arm raised to support the canoe, she was forced on and on until the hem of her dress caught fast in some underbrush. She sobbed, and struggled to free herself.

White Fox lowered the canoe and came towards her, a knife in his hand. She was too tired to move, and waited for the blow to fall, for that knife to end it all. Dully, she hoped only that it would be quick.

To her surprise, she realised White Fox had bent down before her and seized the bottom of her dress. With two hacking motions he shortened it to the knee. She made no protest.

'Rest,' he told her.

She dropped to the earth and lay there without a word.

White Fox rummaged in a pouch tied at his waist, and offered her water from a leather container. She drank it greedily. A strip of dried meat followed. She regarded it suspiciously, and then ate it as she saw he was wolfing down its twin.

'How much further?'

'We make only a short portage, but you must move faster. You are too slow.'

Mireille closed her eyes. If this was a short portage, what was a long one like? She felt she could not move another step.

'I go as fast as I can.'

'An Indian maiden would not be so slow.'

'I am not an Indian maiden.' She sat up, her back

propped against a tree-trunk. 'Let me go back. You're safe now.'

'What nonsense the white girl talks! How would you find your way back? No, we go on together. Now.'

'I can't!' Mireille's hair had come loose during the progress through the forest, and she tried to pull it together so that it did not fall down her shoulders.

White Fox gave her the thong which had bound her hands, and she used it to tie her golden tresses back in one big bunch. He watched her.

'We have wasted enough time. We go on.'

Between them, they raised the canoe, Mireille swaying on her feet.

' We must make haste. If we should fall into the hands of enemy Indians, you will not enjoy their attentions.' He clutched the long hank of her hair to emphasise his point, and pulled on it.

She shuddered and began to step forward. He had succeeded in frightening her thoroughly, although he had no need to raise his voice or to strike her. Branches swished against her face and against her bare legs, for her stockings had slipped down round her ankles. Her legs ached, her body protested, but on she went.

When at last they reached the bank of a stretch of water, she walked straight into it, up to the level of her knees, her sabots sticking on the muddy bottom. She tried to bend down and pick them up, for she had walked straight out of them. White Fox reclaimed them and dumped her and them into the canoe. She lay in the bottom of it, so inert that he did not even bother to tie her. He pushed the canoe out into the river and began to paddle. This time they went into the setting sun, but Mireille paid no attention to its beauties. She slept.

Darkness fell, and the moon came up, obscured by gathering clouds. The night was still and warm

Mireille, waking from time to time, was conscious only vaguely of the change from day to night, but of little else. She didn't even wonder what kind of man

White Fox was, that he needed no rest, like other men.

It was finally the quiet which woke her. There was no more gurgling or rushing of water against the frail side of the craft. She put her hand outside the blanket in which she seemed to be wrapped, and discovered only space. Her eyes were wide open but could distinguish nothing in the dark. White Fox must have carried her to this place.

Slowly she realised that she was lying on the ground on a bed of leaves. They formed her blanket, too. As she stirred, she was aware that her captor slept quite close to her. So he was human, after all!

He had not tied her. Could she—should she—try to escape? Escape to where? As he had said, she could never retrace the way she had come. If she tried, she might fall into the hands of other, fiercer Indians. What did White Fox mean to do with her when he had her back in his village? Torture her? Make her a slave? That was what the Iroquois did with their prisoners. Mireille knew a terrible fear, and at the same time a sense of utter loss and despair. She bit back a sob and lay in complete misery as the darkness began to lighten into grey.

White Fox was lying on his side, and she could distinguish the shape of his body, the angle of his head, even the outline of the knife he carried in its sheath. If she could reach that knife . . . Silently, she crawled closer to him. The leaves rustled under her and over her and she held her breath. He did not stir.

With infinite caution, she came closer, and her hand snaked out and grasped the sheath of the knife. It was half out when his fingers closed on her wrist. They struggled, and she held the knife for a brief moment, but she could not use it, such was the pressure he exerted on her arm. Then he held her fast.

'White Fox did not tie you up, and you try to kill him!' he snarled at her. He snatched the thong binding her hair so quickly that she cried out as her hair caught in it. He paid no attention to her gasp of pain, but fastened her arms behind her back and then threw her from him.

Mireille lay where he had discarded her. White Fox sheathed his knife.

'The golden-haired one would be wise never to try that again, or White Fox will not deal so gently with her.'

He sat in the leaves, regarding her and scowling. 'It was well enough done. Doubtless Red Fox would praise his woman—were he here.'

That was too much for the girl. She began to sob, tears streaming from her eyes. 'You devil!' she cried, 'Pierre is not here—nor ever will be. He is dead, dead, dead!' With every repetition of the word she beat her heels against the leaves, and they flew up into the air and as quickly fell back. 'I didn't mean to use the knife on you, but on myself.'

White Fox was calm. 'Your man is not dead.'

'Not dead?' Mireille screamed. 'I saw him die before my very eyes.'

'The Golden One is mistaken. He is not dead, only wounded. He lives.

Hope flared up in her. 'How do you know? I saw what I saw.' No, she couldn't believe it!

'White Fox has seen many men die. Such a wound as he received bleeds a great deal, but it is not fatal. He will get well and follow the golden one's trail. She has no need to steal knives.'

Mireille only half believed him. 'You mean he'll come after me'

'White Fox has spoken. Sleep while you may.' He settled himself among the leaves again, and within seconds was breathing deeply.

She lay uncomfortably,until at last the tears dried on her face and she slept again. This time, there was a ray of hope in her dreams. White Fox had said Pierrie was alive and would come after her. She woke, asking herself how long it would take him. White Fox was nowhere in sight. Her arms were still bound.

As she was struggling to raise herself from the bed of leaves, he appeared, a large fish in his hands.

'White Fox will free your bonds if you will promise to try no tricks,' he offered.

'I promise,' Mireille agreed readily, her eyes on the fish, her stomach rumbling with hunger.

White Fox released her, and directed her to gather sticks for the fire which he had already lit. The fish was quickly cooked, and as soon as they had eaten it, washed down with water from the river, he doused the fire and raked the ashes carefully out of sight.

Once again, they travelled by canoe. All day, White Fox paddled tirelessly, and Mireille, now allowed to sit in the shallow bottom of the craft, trailed her hands in the water from time to time to cool herself as the sun became hotter and hotter.

At one point, White Fox approached the shore and cut an overhanging branch from a large-leaved tree. Paddle stilled across the canoe, he plaited several leaves together and directed the girl to place them on her head against the fierce rays of the sun. She did so thankfully, finding their shade very welcome.

All day he scarcely spoke a word to her, and she mulled over her conflicting thoughts. Pierre was always in her mind—and Charles, for Charles, thwarted, would not be easy to deal with. It was all very well for White Fox to be so sure of Pierre's pursuit. Charles might somehow prevent any action on his part. Had he not made him languish in gaol for want of a wife?

It upset her to think of it, and she gave her attention to the wildness of the scenery. On either side of the river were only rocks and trees, a forest of greens and browns, a veritable wilderness. She had wanted to see this vast country, to know about it. Now she shivered at what she saw. How could White Fox go so confidently, with only sun and stars to guide him? He paddled on, taking her further and further into the unknown. Mireille wished with all her heart that she had never left France, never set out to this strange new world.

When at length they halted, the sun was beginning to set, filling the sky with a myriad of colours: reds and pinks, orange and purple. The girl marvelled at the exotic beauty, and shivered too with loneliness and a prickling sense of dread. It was a more rugged shore than this morning's and overhung with drooping branches and mighty trees. To her, it seemed dark and oppressive.

But White Fox seemed quite at home. He ordered her to gather sticks and branches, and to keep close by while he hunted. He disappeared into the thickest brush.

She wanted to call him back. What if he abandoned her here? She shook the thought away and set to work. In this country it was all the same—the men commanded and the women toiled. Perhaps that wasn't quite fair, she admitted to herself, as White Fox returned with a rabbit and proceeded to light the fire.

While the rabbit was cooking, he showed her where she might gather berries, and mushrooms and roots to accompany the meat. He rested while she did it. The mosquitoes descended on her in droves, and she hit out at them until she realised that this only made her drop some of the berries.

The meal was good, even if unsalted, and the fire kept away the insects, much to her relief.

As they ate, White Fox advised her to spread some of the grease from the rabbit on her hands and face to counter the action of the sun, which had reddened them. More than a little dubious about this cure, Mireille adopted it for want of anything better. The rabbit was succulent, the roots much better than she would have expected, the berries sharp and sweet.

'Is this what your people eat?' Mireille asked the Indian.

'Meat or fish at every meal, if the hunting is good.' White Fox sat cross-legged and belched in satisfaction. 'The men of my village are good hunters. Our women and children eat well. No one goes hungry.'

'No one?'

'No one—what we have is shared out for all.'

'All? Orphans—and old people?'

'Orphans are adopted into families and clans. Old people are honoured for their wisdom.'

This was a different White Fox, one who was disposed to talk, and she tried another question, not sure if he would answer. 'And Red Fox's son, Pierre's son—has he been adopted by a family?'

'Naturally—into the family of his woman. Her sister and her man have taken him as their own. They have only daughters.'

'Is he—is he happy with them?'

'Happy?' White Fox looked astonished—if such a phlegmatic countenance could be allowed to express emotion. 'All children are happy. Why should the Golden One ask such a question?'

'Because you said something to Pierre about him missing his father.'

'Ah yes,' the Indian waved that away. 'That was for Red Fox's ears. The white man likes to think his son wishes to see him.'

'It's not true, then?'

'Who knows what thoughts a child has? It may be true. If Red Fox thinks so, it will hasten his steps.'

Cunning devil! Mireille thought to herself, but did not voice her opinion. She did not have time to do so.

White Fox held up his hand. He sniffed the air, and took his axe from its holder. Mireille watched him in alarm as he rose to his feet and held his finger to his lips. 'There is danger!' He melted behind a tree, and she was left alone at the fire.

A minute went by, and then another. She held her breath, straining to hear any alien sound, the hair on her neck prickling.

Two Indians stepped into view—a man and a woman. They halted some distance from the girl, as White Fox came suddenly from behind a tree.

The man spoke, and White Fox answered. They talked for some time while Mireille watched. Her gaze strayed towards the woman.

She was only a girl, dark-haired, dark-eyed, pretty in a flat-faced way, she decided. She wore a deerskin dress, fringed and beaded in an elaborate pattern of reds and blues. Her hair was braided in a single plait, a thick coil of gleaming black which reached to her hips. She sidled closer to Mireille and to the fire while the men talked.

Mireille could see she looked tired, and exclaimed, 'Sit down, here beside me.' She could see no menace in her. She spoke in French, as it was the only language she had. Whether the girl understood it or not, she sat down, cross-legged as White Fox did.

The two men approached the fire. White Fox began to question the Indian maiden. Mireile supposed it was his own language he used.

The girl answered haltingly, her eyes swinging to the man who accompanied her.

To Mireille's eyes, without the spoken word to help her, the girl seemed ill at ease—frightened, even. She could not tell what White Fox made of her story, or what the story was, but he waved her companion to a seat by the fire, and the man produced a pipe and passed it to his host after he had puffed on it.

There was no food left, nor did there seem any inclination on White Fox's part to provide any. They must have eaten already, Mireille concluded, wondering if they meant to stay.

She tried to speak to the girl, whispering, 'Have you come far?' and was met with a blank stare.

The men were still talking and smoking, so Mireille was forced to wait in ignorance of the situation. Sighing, she told herself to be patient. She remembered how long it had taken White Fox to get down to what he wanted with Pierre.

She looked from the girl sitting so dejectedly beside her, to the man who had brought her. Was he her brother, her husband? She guessed there must be some relationship between them. Though both were dark, she could detect no particular resemblance. The girl was slight and pretty, if a bit sullen; the man was squat and short, and his face was heavy and threatening. Mireille felt that if she did not have White Fox's protection, she would fear this man. When he looked at her—as he was doing now—she saw a light in his eyes that she did not like at all. She longed to interrupt and ask what was going on, but she held her tongue. She had no desire to antagonise either of them.

The girl beside her reached out and touched Mireille's hair. She stroked it, and said something in her own language.

To Mireille's surprise, White Fox noticed the gesture. 'She says your hair is like the sunshine, like ripe corn,' he translated for her. 'She wants to know how she may have hair like yours.'

Mireille smiled at the girl. 'She must be born with it.' She mimed holding a baby in her arms, and the girl giggled.

'White Fox, who are they? Why are they here?' she asked

For a moment he looked as though he would not answer, but he relented. 'The maiden is called Little Lynx, the man is Wildcat. They are brother and sister from a neighbouring tribe. The girl was captured in a raid on their village, and the brother has been successful in snatching her back. Wildcat asks my help in eluding pursuit.'

'They're being followed?' Mireille's heart sank. If their pace had been furious before, what was it likely to be now with enemies on their trail?

'Wildcat thinks so. He says he will defend his sister with his last breath.'

Mireille swallowed. She could picture the scene. Painted Indians would descend on them in the dark and kill them, scalping the shining hair from her head. She hung on to it with a shaking hand, and put the question she feared to ask. 'Do you mean to help him?'

'White Fox must. Their enemies are my tribe's enemies.'

Mireille accepted that statement. She had been waiting for it. From the finality of his voice, she knew that he would not be moved from helping. Men were all the same, she reflected. They made the decisions, women had to abide by them, and suffer for them. Men enjoyed a fight. The prospect of battle roused excitement in them. These savages were the same.

She sat in silence, turning thoughts over in her mind. People called them savages, these Indians, but were they so different from other men? Her ideas about them were changing. She had thought of them as scarcely above the level of animals, yet here was a brother who had rescued his sister, and a man who would help them, not to gain anything for himself but because he felt duty bound against a common enemy.

Mireille looked at Little Lynx. Her brother had come after her, as White Fox was sure Pierre would do for herself. If Pierre did come for her, she would be happy—a good deal happier than the Indian girl looked! There was sadness in her eyes that Mirille could see quite clearly in the light of the fire. Why should that be? She wondered about it as the men went on with their conversation. Perhaps it was just the Indian way. She feared for her brother's life—and perhaps her own. That must be it.

The men smoked the pipe again in turn, then Wildcat said something to his sister, and Little Lynx rose to her feet and went towards the river.

'She goes to fetch water,' said White Fox. 'Go with her.' It was a command. 'We shall kill the fire.'

Mireille did not protest. It was said in exactly the same tone that Pierre used. It meant that the girls would douse the fire. She followed Little Lynx to the water's edge.

The Indian girl had a leather bag, which she filled, Mireille had no container, but took off her sabots and filled them. They made three trips there and back.

When the fire was out and the ashes had been covered with soil and branches, White Fox announced the obvious. 'We move on. We carry the canoe. There is white water ahead, but Wildcat knows the trail around it and will lead us. He will go first. You and Little Lynx will take turns at the canoe's head. I shall take the rear.' He allotted first turn to Mireille.

She knew what was expected of her and heaved up the craft on an aching shoulder. Little Lynx walked in front of her, behind her brother.

It was eerie, walking through the woods. Mireille's sabots, still damp, made a noise in the stillness—such a noise that White Fox ordered her to take them off and walk in her stocking feet. Little Lynx carried them.

Every moment Mireille expected a hail of arrows, or a wild yell of attack, but none came, and they walked on almost at a run, fear lending wings to all their feet. She wanted to ask if the four of them would use the canoe when they had finished the portage, but she had not the breath to do so. It seemed to her, however, that there would not be room for all.

When she felt as if she would drop under the strain, White Fox signalled to Little Lynx that she must change places, but he retained his, looking as fresh as when they had started.

Even without her burden, Mireille's steps flagged, and the moon, which had been giving some light, now hid behind a bank of clouds. It was very dark and very still. She tripped over a tree-root, and the sound of her fall was loud in the silence. Wildcat dropped back and helped her to her feet, his hand on her ankles and legs, his voice hissing in her ear.

She didn't like the feel of his hands on her; she didn't like the sound of his whispered remark, nor did she need it translated to know it was an injunction to be quiet, to be careful. She pulled herself away from contact with him, shaken.

They all halted, listening. The only sound Mireille

heard above the beating of her heart and her laboured breathing was the cry of an owl and the shriek of some woodland creature in fright. Then, they went on, pace slowed a little, for the going was rough and uphill.

Mireille walked on mechanically, panting, her feet unprotected now where her stockings had worn away, protesting at every step. When would this forced march end?

It ended so abruptly that she stumbled against Wildcat and would have fallen again, save for his arm about her waist. She wriggled in his grasp, repulsed, dismayed, and he held her fast. His hand stroked her hair.

He released her as White Fox came forward. The two of them conferred in whispers and grunts, and then Wildcat led the way to one side to a sort of hollow, a ditch, almost. White Fox thrust the girls into it and then jumped in himself.

'Wildcat will stay on guard while we sleep. It is time to rest.' He sat upright, but closed his eyes.

Little Lynx lay down. Mireille lay beside her. She was too tired to sleep, but could only envy the other two their complete oblivion. She was too conscious of their danger, of Wildcat on guard above them. She longed for escape from all of them. Ah, if only she could be back in Pierre's house, she'd never complain again about loneliness or strangeness or his over-powering ways! She had been able to talk to him, even if she hadn't always liked him or the things he said. With these people she was really voiceless, dependent on White Fox to translate. What if White Fox were not there? In the perilous situation they were now in, he might not live. What then? She shivered at the thought of how she might fare at Wildcat's hands. As it was, she didn't want him looking at her, touching her. She must keep him at a distance.

She fell into sleep, wild nightmares chasing her, an endless shifting pursuit in which Wildcat changed into Pierre and then to Charles, and she ran from all of them, and woke, screaming, with Wildcat's hand across her mouth.

CHAPTER SEVEN

PIERRE WOKE TO sunshine, to a strange face bending over him, a face he could not put a name to at first. He closed his eyes again, puzzling over it. It wasn't Mireille. Who was it? He opened his eyes again, and the face came into proper focus, concerned, anxious. Ah, he had it.

'Émilie?' he questioned, 'Where's Mireille?'

Émilie burst into tears. They overflowed from her eyes on to his hands. What were his hands doing, folded like a corpse's on the rough linen of a sheet? And what was the woman crying for?

'Mireille?' he repeated again, conscious now of a searing pain in his shoulder. 'Where is Mireille?'

'Gone,' was the answer. 'The boy said the Indian took her, but he was half crazed. He lost his father and his mother, you see.'

Pierre didn't see at all. He could not make head or tail of what she was talking about. Who was the Indian? Why should he take Mireille? For that matter, who was the boy? His head began to clear. In one swift flash he began to remember the scene in the barn. Had White Fox taken Mireille?

'Where's Charles?' he asked. At least *he* might talk some sense.

'Captain de la Croix was carried from here on a litter by six soldiers,' she said, 'after the army surgeon came to attend him. He took the shot from your wound, as well.'

'He's still alive, then? He was only shot in the arm, I think.' Pierre found he was unsure of what had happened to Charles.

'He was shot in the elbow, but they say the arm will be all right—he won't lose it. It is the head wounds which are the worry.' Émilie had dried her tears, and her eyes were sparkling as she gave him the information.

'Head wounds? What head wounds?'

'He was hit many times by a blunt instrument on the head and shoulders—that's what they say. Didn't you see it happen? The boy doesn't seem able to explain it. He says he was asleep and only saw the Indian take the woman.' Émilie licked her lips. 'You must know what happened. Who was the Indian? Why did he bring the boy back? They want to question you, you know.' She sat down by the side of the bed, clearly prepared to hear the whole story from his lips before anyone else should.

'Who wants to question me?'

'Why, the military and Monsieur le Secrétaire. The Captain can't tell them anything yet. He's unconscious, and suffering from a fever.'

'But he'll live?'

'As to that,' Émilie shrugged and straightened the bed-cover, 'no one knows. It rests with *le bon Dieu*. A patrol went out to chase the Indian, but they could find no traces of him. They think he may have had a canoe hidden somewhere.'

'Yes,' agreed Pierre. 'He'll be many leagues away by now. How much of a start has he had? A few hours—a day?' He frowned. How long ago had it all happened?

Émilie's eyes were round, and Pierre could see they were crossed as well. 'It is two days since it occurred. The surgeon said sleep would heal you best of all, and he gave me a powder for you. You have had it all.'

'Two days!' Pierre groaned, and tried to get up. The pain in his shoulder made him grit his teeth. It felt as though a horse had kicked him.

Émilie pushed him back. '*Tiens,* you will undo all the surgeon's good work and start it bleeding again! You must rest until it heals properly.'

'And what of Mireille?' he demanded. 'Each day, she

goes deeper and deeper into Indian territory.'

'*Pauvre* Mireille!' Emilie crossed herself. 'I pray to the Virgin for her. You must do the same.'

'*Bien sûr,*' said Pierre bitterly. 'The Virgin will provide her with wings to fly back to us, will she?'

Émilie crossed herself again and put her hands over her ears. 'Take care, Monsieur, the Virgin is not to be mocked.'

Pierre closed his eyes, a vision of Mireille before them: Mireille exhausted, frightened, not understanding anything. He must go after her. She had shot Charles to save him.

'That's right,' said Émilie. 'Sleep again, for I must send a messenger to tell them you are able to speak now, and you will need your strength for that.' She rose to her feet and left him.

He nearly called her back, and then decided it was better to feign sleep so that he might consider what to say, how to explain what had happened. The boy was considered unreliable: Charles was unconscious. There was only his word to act on. What should that word be? That Mireille had shot her cousin to save him? That was the truth, but would the truth be accepted? Mireille would have to face the gossip and the speculations when she returned—if she returned.

He put that thought aside. Of course she would return. He would see to that! White Fox knew that he would follow. It was just a ruse to force his hand. And that was something he did not want to tell the authorities: that a Mohawk warrior should come to *him* for help against the French. Hell's fire, whatever he said landed him in trouble, and could be contradicted by Captain de la Croix if he came to himself.

Suppose he said White Fox was known to him and had returned the boy out of friendship—how, then, to explain why he had taken Mireille? Could he pretend he remembered nothing? He hadn't seen the blows which seemingly felled Charles, but it could only have been a desperate White Fox who had struck. Wasn't it just the luck of the devil himself that Charles had such a thick skull?

He was no nearer a solution to his problems when the first of his questioners arrived. Pierre had half hoped it might be the Secretary first. At least, he could talk to Albert, try out on him the story he was concocting. Albert would give him a sympathetic ear, at least.

Unfortunately it was Commandant Beauclerc himself who came and settled himself with an escort of two fine soldiers at his bedside. The soldiers stood, the Commandant sat.

'This is a bad business, Monsieur Charbonneau,' the Commandant began in friendly enough fashion. 'I trust your wound is not troubling you too much. Once we have your explanations, our minds will be relieved and we can leave you to your healing.'

Pierre thanked him for his interest and good wishes. 'Unfortunately,' he went on, 'I am not able to give you much help. I find my mind is almost a complete blank as to what happened.'

'Surely you remember something?' The Commandant's expression had changed from solicitude to incredulity. 'If we discuss it a little, some of it will return.'

Pierre swore softly to himself. *Sacré-bleu!* This one was a wily one. It was the same ruse he would have tried on one of his company when he was in the army.

'Certainement,' he agreed. 'I remember the Indian was in the barn. He called me in by putting the boy in the doorway.'

The Commandant nodded. 'You were armed?'

Pierre hesitated for only a fraction of a moment. He nodded. 'I had a musket.'

'Was it loaded?'

'Yes, I had been teaching my wife to handle it.'

'Your wife was with you?'

'Yes, you must know that from the boy. He ran to her.'

'You went into the barn. Why was that?'

'The Mohawk called me in. He didn't want to be seen in the open. He seemed to think he would be blamed for taking the boy in the first place.' Pierre paused. 'He said he wasn't guilty, that he had rescued the boy from the ones who had taken him.'

'You believed him?'

'He swore it was the truth.'

'But still—a Mohawk—do they know truth?' The Commandant did not raise his voice.

Pierre might have shrugged, but remembered his shoulder. 'I had no reason to doubt him. The boy was there.'

'Your wife and the boy followed you into the barn?'

'Yes.'

'You didn't think to prevent them?'

'It happened so quickly. I couldn't stop them.'

'And then did you discover who the Mohawk was?'

Pierre could see no harm in admitting some knowledge. 'White Fox—I traded with his people some years ago.'

'When did Captain de la Croix arrive?'

'Almost right away.'

'He was armed?'

'Yes, he had a musket. He turned it on the Indian. He seemed to think it was White Fox who had attacked the boy's family. I tried to explain that it wasn't.'

'But it might have been?'

'I didn't believe it was.'

'So you shot Captain de la Croix to prevent him carrying out his duty.'

'I did not shoot Captain de la Croix!'

'Ah, the Indian had a musket, did he?'

Pierre was beginning to feel trapped. Why had he said he had a musket when he went into the barn? It struck him suddenly that the Commandant had already a very good idea of what had gone on in the barn. Where had he got that knowledge?

'He must have done—or else he seized mine.' Pierre frowned. 'That's where it begins to get hazy. Captain de la Croix shot me. Your surgeon took the bullet from my shoulder. You must know that.' Yes, it was better to blame White Fox for shooting Charles. They'd never catch up with him. In any case, it must have been his hand that felled Charles.

'Someone shot you. There's no disputing that.' The Commandant's face was stern.

'Well, then,' Pierre sensed reservation in the man but plunged on anyway. 'It's as I said, the Indian shot the Captain. The Captain shot me. The whole thing was unfortunate and could have been avoided.'

'That wasn't the way you said it the first time. The first time you gave a different sequence. You said the Captain shot you first, then the Indian shot the Captain. Which story is right?'

'It was a slip of the tongue the second time. The Captain shot me. The Indian shot the Captain. How else would he have got my gun?'

Pierre was beginning to sweat. How could he have been so clumsy as to give the Commandant that opening? Charles had shot him first, and that was why Mireille had fired.

'Why would the Captain shoot you? No, no, it doesn't make sense. I think I must believe the Captain's story.'

'The Captain's story?' Pierre could not believe his ears. 'Is the Captain able to speak?'

'Does that surprise you?' came the swift retort.

'I was told he was unconscious.'

'So he was, but this morning changed that. It looks as though he will recover.'

Commandant Beauclerc studied his hands, which now formed a steeple. 'Your musket was found in the barn, thrown to one side, we must suppose—by the Indian. Why would he throw it down? A musket is a much-sought-after prize by our dusky brothers. Can you advance any reason why he would abandon it?'

'No, no, I can't—except if it was as the boy says, that White Fox took Mireille, he would need his hands.'

'Of course, so he would. How foolish of me not to

have seen that immediately!' The Commandant's smile was frosty. 'It is only the boy saw the kidnapping.'

'What do you mean?' Pierre had begun to feel the worst was over, but now he was on edge again.

'The boy may have been mistaken, have confused dream and reality. Perhaps your wife took the opportunity to take to the woods.'

'Run away? Why would she do that?' Pierre half rose, but his shoulders forced him back.

'You've only been married a few days, have you not? Perhaps she saw a chance to escape. These hasty marriages sometimes cause violent reactions—quarrelled a lot, did you?'

'No, we did not.'

'She took to the life, did she? Come, Monsieur Charbonneau, you can confide in me. I'm a married man myself. I know things don't always go smoothly.'

Pierre was getting angry. He and Mireille had had some differences: there was that moment when he had thought she meant to turn the musket on him. But run away from him—never? 'Nonsense, where would she go? I suppose you searched the woods, and found no trace of her.'

'As you say, no trace has been found—but the forests are immense.' The Commandant was bland, conciliatory almost. 'You understand we have to consider all the possibilities. Your wife is Captain de la Croix's cousin. He seems to think she was not altogether happy.'

'How would he know?'

'He says she spoke to him about it.'

'When? Where?'

'As to that, I don't know. The Captain is very weak still—too weak to make a proper statement, but I must take heed of what he says.'

'You must take heed of what I say, as well. I have as distinguished a record as the Captain on the battlefields.'

'So I believe, or I would not be here myself.'

'Take my word for it. My wife would not have run

away from me. I had given her no cause.' Pierre's voice was steely, but there was a niggle of doubt in him. Mireille was a gently-born girl. Could his swift initiation of her into a working housewife have turned her against him? No, he wouldn't believe it! It was just Charles trying to undermine his position, to make him look ridiculous, unreliable. The blows to his head had only served to sharpen his cunning.

'Captain de la Croix is very anxious that his cousin should be found. He implores that the army should send a company to trace her. Is that your wish also?'

Pierre studied the Commandant's face. The eyes were cold and challenging, but everything in Pierre rose up at his suggestion.

'It would be the wrong tactic. That Indian will be long since gone into hostile territory! They'd never find him, and a great number of the company would never return. It would be like the shambles of last year's campaign.'

'Don't you want your wife back?'

'Yes, I want her back, but not at the expense of a hundred lives thrown away! They would not succeed. Send Indian scouts. They'd have a chance.'

'You'd trust your wife to them?' The Commandant shook his head. 'It is perhaps as Captain de la Croix has hinted. You have a mistaken confidence in the red man. No, I can't do as you ask. You must let wiser counsels prevail.'

'That means you'll do nothing?' Pierre's tone was bitter, defeated. Every minute, every hour, lost made pursuit more impossible. If he could move . . . But he was not going to mention that to this man.

'In a few days'—the Commandant rose to his feet—'a week at most, when both you and Captain de la Croix are able, we shall try a re-enactment. We must get to the bottom of this business. You will hold yourself ready, Monsieur Charbonneau.'

'Certainement,' agreed Pierre, 'I am not likely to be

able to take myself anywhere else!' He gestured to his wound.

'So the army surgeon informs me.' The Commandant's tone was pleasant.

So pleasant that Pierre told himself he must be on his guard. He had the distinct impression that one of the soldiers might have been left behind on guard if it had not been so apparent that he was too weak to do anything.

The visit of Monsieur le Secrétaire Albert Morel later in the afternoon did nothing to dispel Pierre's sense of danger and of frustration.

'Captain de la Croix was your enemy before.' Albert confirmed his fears. 'Now he is determined to destroy you! Consorting with the enemy is punishable with death. With you out of the way, he will be free to marry Mireille.'

'If he can find her,' Pierre pointed out.

'Suppose he knows where she is?' Albert suggested. He held up his hand to silence Pierre's objections. 'Just suppose that Captain de la Croix caught up with your Indian friend, who had, in spite of your belief, taken the boy, killed his parents, razed the homestead. Suppose he made a deal with him—to bring the boy to you, to stage a fight . . . '

'No!' Pierre interrupted him violently. 'Why then hit Charles on the head . . . risk killing him?'

'It didn't kill him, did it? Doesn't that make you wonder—an Indian whose victim recovers? Indians aren't usually so careless with their blows! This White Fox is a young, strong man?'

'About my age,' Pierre felt as if the breath had been knocked from his body.

Albert Morel went on, emboldened by Pierre's silence, 'The Indian then took Mireille to some agreed hiding-place—some place just out of reach of armed patrols. He could be holding her there now.'

'No,' said Pierre, but there was little conviction in his

denial. 'Mireille would not agree to that. Why, she shot him!'

He cursed his tongue when Albert exclaimed, 'She shot him? You didn't tell that to the Commandant.'

'No, I didn't. And you mustn't tell him either.'

'Why not? It makes your case stronger. Don't be a fool, man.'

'And what does it do to her?'

Albert considered for a moment. 'She could say it was an accident. He might agree with her. They may be laughing at you, having trapped you. She was very insistent about marrying her cousin, wasn't she? Perhaps I did wrong to meddle as I did—it seemed such a chance to even scores—but see what I have landed you in!'

'Don't blame yourself, Albert.' Pierre felt complete despair engulfing him. 'I was eager enough! A pretty face can make fools of even the strongest of us. Yet I'd swear . . . '

'Think about it,' said Albert. 'She is his cousin, tied to him by blood. Did she ever suggest to you that she wanted to return to France?'

'She wasn't with me very long.' Even now, Pierre found he wanted to believe in her, to think well of her. She had lain in his arms and returned his kisses; been moved, he would have sworn, by their lovemaking. 'Ye-es, she said we could both go back to France and claim her lands.'

'Ah-ha!' Albert rubbed his hands together. 'That might just have been to put you off the track. What did you say to that? Did the idea commend itself to you?'

'No, it did not. I told her my life was here, that I had lands of my own—a future . . . '

'How did she take that?'

'She seemed disappointed.' Pierre came out with the words reluctantly.

'She could have gone to him—put the proposition to him.'

'I suppose she could have. They met in the woods. She didn't tell me about that until I questioned her.'

Pierre had met double-dealing before. It had sickened him then; it overpowered him with loathing now. He had been taken in by lying eyes, by an innocent expression. He remembered the hatred in those eyes when she had turned the musket on him. Yet she had shot her cousin. Even now, fool that he was, with her duplicity clear before him, he wanted to deny it, to put his trust in her. He groaned aloud.

'I haven't said these things to upset you, *mon ami,*' Albert apologised, 'but to put you on your guard. My guessing may be wrong. After all, only you know what sort of girl she is, how things were between you.'

Pierre nodded dully. Ah yes, he knew. In his heart of hearts, he knew. And some of it must be laid at his own door. He had chivvied her, forced her to work she was not accustomed to, been impatient with her, challenged her that she did not trust him, thrown the fact of his previous marriage in her face—what had he given her to make her turn to him?

There he was, trying to excuse her again, to make her treachery seem less. A curt goodbye was all he managed for Albert. Then he turned on his good side and could have wept—for himself—for her—for the sheer waste of it all. What did it matter what happened now? Let Charles have his re-enactment. He had been an idiot to trust White Fox, to trust Mireille. Why did he always believe the best of people? Would he never learn?

When Mireille woke, cramped and stiff and still tired, there was only a strip or two of dried meat to eat, and water to wash it down.

White Fox and Wildcat had a short discussion with each other before the canoe was carried to the river's edge. Mireille could not tell what they said, but she judged from their voices that it was not altogether friendly, and this opinion was reinforced when Little Lynx made faces at her and mimed a quarrel. They evidently resolved it, for the girls were bundled into the centre of the boat, and Wildcat took the bow position and White Fox the stern. White Fox had a proper paddle, and Wildcat made do with a branch from a tree, which he hastily fashioned into shape.

Little Lynx began to sing once they were out from the shore, and Wildcat turned round to hush her. It seemed to the watchful Mireille that there was some argument between the two of them as well, but the Indian girl was quiet.

The paddling went on, blades flashing in the sun, fish jumping, dragonflies hovering over the peaceful water. It was very hard to believe they were being pursued. Perhaps the enemy had been thrown off the trail. At any rate, they didn't have canoes; they would have been clearly visible on this open stretch of water.

Mireille found her eyes closing, her back supported by Little Lynx's back, for there was no longer room for her to lie down with these extra passengers. The long day wore on, hotter than yesterday, and sultry as well. Between dozes, she kept glancing at the sky. It seemed to her to be darkening, and she was not sorry when White Fox towards mid-afternoon gave an order to Wildcat.

Wildcat was clearly not disposed to obey it, but grumbling he pulled in. This time it was a rocky shore they landed on, and Wildcat, after the canoe had been hidden in some bushes, led the way to a shallow cave in the rocks. It was scarcely big enough for all of them, but it would certainly offer shelter from the threatening rain.

Again there was an exchange of opinions between the two men. Since Little Lynx waited impassively, Mireille did the same, fanning herself with a large leaf. At length the girls were dispatched to collect wood, but were told not to go far away. Wildcat and White Fox started fishing. By the time they had collected sufficient firewood, some berries and wild potatoes, Little Lynx spoke to her brother.

Whatever she said to him earned his grudging approval, and she led Mireille to a sheltered pool, where she stripped off her dress and went for a swim. Mireille, with a grateful sigh, did the same. She couldn't swim as well as Little Lynx, but she was delighted with the feel of the cool water against her skin and pleased, too, that her mother had allowed her the freedom of bathing in the enclosed stream on their property in those far-off days in France. True, she hadn't bathed naked there, but no one could see here, with only Little Lynx in attendance.

As the Indian girl circled round her, Mireille was astonished to hear her singing a tune that recalled home to her, and she was singing it in English! Mireille knew the words in French. But Little Lynx sang very quietly: *'The first good joy that Mary had, It was the joy of one—To see the blessed Jesus Christ, when he was first her son.'*

Mireille was astonished to hear the name of Jesus Christ from Indian lips in the middle of nowhere. Tears rose to her eyes as Little Lynx came to the chorus: *'Praise Father, Son and Holy Ghost to all eternity.'* She hummed it with her, saying the words in French under her breath.

'English!' she whispered. 'You speak English?' She could not have explained why she whispered. Perhaps it was just that she was overcome. 'I, too, I speak a little.'

The Indian girl laughed aloud, but she too kept her voice very low. 'I learn from a missionary! Oh, how I have longed to speak to you, to say what is in my heart so that you and I will understand each other! Sh-h-h, my brother must not hear us, must not know we speak together.'

Mireille had difficulty in following this spate of words, for the Indian girl seemed to have no trouble at all with the language. She made her repeat it over again until she had the full sense of it. 'Why your brother . . . not know?' she questioned in very halting English, for she had only a slight command of the language from the days of her childhood and a curé who had taught her Latin, and added a little English for good measure.

At first Little Lynx gave no reason, but wanted to know who Mireille was, why she was here, what her relationship with White Fox was. She could not understand that Mireille was White Fox's prisoner, and kept exclaiming, 'Does the mighty Mohawk treat his prisoner so kindly? She is not even tied—she is not treated as his slave!'

Mireille tried to explain that she was not so much a prisoner as a hostage, but was not sure that Little Lynx grasped the distinction. At any rate, she nodded her head wisely and gave some information about herself.

'I was taken prisoner,' she confided. 'And I found favour in the eyes of a brave—as you have with White Fox. He wished to make me his wife, but before he could do so, my brother took me away.'

Little Lynx's expression was so sad that Mireille's heart went out to her. 'Have you told him?' she asked.

By means of gesture and halting questions, Mireille found that Wildcat had been told, but had not wanted to hear of his sister's feelings. In fact he had dismissed them as nonsense. Running Wolf, Little Lynx's suitor, had followed the trail of the fleeing brother and sister. It was him they ran from.

Before the first slow raindrops began to fall and the girls left the pool, Mireille had the bare bones of the story, and all her sympathies lay with Little Lynx. A short week ago she would not have believed it possible that she could feel involved with the problems of a wild savage, indeed that a wild savage could love and suffer for that love. Now she thought of Little Lynx not as a savage but as a girl like herself, whose love life was difficult, impossible. She felt a bond between them. As they shook the water from their bodies and dressed, they made a pact of silence, of secrecy, of friendship, which excluded the men completely.

Then they went back to cook the fish, to watch the rain fall from the heavens, to sleep in the shelter of the cave, to dream of escape and happiness, to hope for a way out.

For the first time, Mireille hugged a feeling of lightness, of optimism to herself. Pierre would come after her. He would find a way to her.

CHAPTER EIGHT

IT WAS STILL raining the following morning. Mireille looked out at it. So did White Fox. He grunted. Little Lynx and Wildcat surveyed it, too. Wildcat shrugged, and began to talk to White Fox.

Mireille could see that whatever he said did not please White Fox. He shook his head, and began to feed the fire. He gestured that the girls must fetch more wood, and she followed Little Lynx out into the pouring rain. She was glad to be out of the cave, glad to be able to talk to the Indian girl again.

'White Fox says there is no one following us, but even if there were, this is a good place to stop and rest. He wants to make a proper paddle so that we may go faster. He wants Wildcat to hunt for game. He says a turkey or some pigeons would keep us in food for some days.' Little Lynx piled branches into Mireille's arms.

'Is he sure that no one follows us?' she asked, seeing the desolate look in the other girl's eyes.

'I don't know. He may be right. Perhaps Running Wolf has returned to his village. He was on foot and we have come by canoe. It would be hard for him to keep up—perhaps impossible.'

'If we stop here for a while, he might catch up,' Mireille suggested, rain trickling down her face. 'But if he does catch up, what will he do? If he takes you back, Wildcat will follow, and so will White Fox.'

'I know,' Little Lynx agreed. 'Wildcat will fight him, and one of them will be killed. I can't let it happen. What am I to do? I'm wretched, unhappy, torn in two.'

'And wet through,' Mireille pointed out, shivering. 'Let's go back. We'll think of something.'

They went back loaded down with wet wood, which had to be dried out before it could begin to burn. The cave became steamy and was made more uncomfortable by a change in the direction of the wind so that they began to cough with the smoke.

Wildcat had gone hunting. White Fox went with his axe to chop a suitable piece of tree, and the girls were left on guard. It meant they could talk some more.

Their talking did them little good, because all they could do was to go over and over the problems Little Lynx faced; the problems they all faced. She knew the territory, and told Mireille there was some rough country ahead. She said she supposed White Fox was going this way to avoid the white man's wrath, that he was not keeping to the easy, direct route.

Mireille had guessed as much. She found it comforting to have a friend to talk to, for she had begun to consider the Indian girl as such.

'My brother does not like to take orders from White Fox,' Little Lynx confided. 'That is why he quarrels with him. He is not an easy man.'

Mireille had already decided that for herself—and she had decided, too, to keep as far away from Wildcat as she could, because of the way he looked at her.

'If only we could make them go more slowly, it would be better for both of us,' she confided in her turn. 'Pierre will not be able to come after me until his wound has healed.'

Mireille was trying to explain the whole situation when White Fox returned and they were forced to keep quiet again. He settled down to whittle at his wood. After a few hours, the rain stopped, and a weak sun parted the clouds. White Fox went down to the water's edge, and the girls could see he was examining some sort of trap he had made. There was an eel in it, and they watched him hold it up in triumph.

That was when a bear walked out of the brush that bordered the shore.

The girls cried out in alarm, and White Fox turned

to face the creature, his hands gripping his catch.

The bear moved forward, hungry.

White Fox stepped back, and would have been all right, except that he slipped on the wet stones.

The bear was upon him, slashing at him with one tremendous claw across his chest, but he had the presence of mind to throw the eel at the bear. It caught him on the mouth, and deflected his attention from White Fox.

The screaming girls, rushing from the cave to the shore, startled the creature further, and he left, eating the eel and crashing back into the bushes whence he had emerged. Mireille was terrified that he would return, as she and Little Lynx half dragged, half carried the Indian to the shelter of the cave.

White Fox made no sound as they bathed the claw-marks. Fortunately they had not gone very deep, but there was a great deal of blood, and it must have been very painful.

Mireille tried to stanch the flow of blood with a strip torn from her petticoat. Little Lynx ran out of the cave and fetched some moss from the base of a tree. The French girl watched in astonishment and some trepidation as she dressed the wound with the moss. Then she bound it up, holding it in place with the petticoat length.

'Stay with him,' she directed Mireille, 'while I fetch herbs and medicines.' That, at any rate, was what she thought she said, though she was puzzled where medicines could be found here.

When Little Lynx stepped into the forest, Mireille was worried as well. What if she should meet the bear? White Fox lay as one dead, whether from shock or loss of blood. He was cold to the touch, and she built up the fire and wrapped his deerskin tunic round him. It was all there was to cover him. She had never felt so helpless in all her life.

Little Lynx was gone a long time, and it was Wildcat who returned first, carrying a turkey and four pigeons. He dropped them all when he saw his sister was missing, and looked so menacing that Mireille led him immediately to White Fox.

It was unfortunate that she and Wildcat had no language in common, for White Fox seemed unable to explain anything, not even the marks on his chest.

Wildcat was in a frenzy of impatience when Little Lynx reappeared. She calmed him down, and he took the birds outside to clean them.

She showed Mireille how to pound the herbs she had brought into powder, while she boiled some water in the only container they had, a large tin pan that her brother usually wore at his belt. Mireille had thought it at first to be a strange sort of ornament, but now she saw it served a practical purpose as well.

Little Lynx mixed some of the powder with the water, and signed to Mireille that she must spoon this into White Fox. She did it with the aid of a rubbery sort of leaf. He made terrible faces while he took it, and this struck Mireille as funny. He was making more fuss over the medicine than he had over the injury!

Little Lynx took the liver, kidneys and heart from the turkey and boiled them into a broth for White Fox. Then it was left to the girls to cook the birds, which they did over spits, turning them constantly.

Wildcat watched this activity for a while, and then stalked away without an explanation. It seemed to Mireille that he had assumed an air of complete authority over the party. He did not have to offer reasons; he was free to do as he chose.

'How long will White Fox be like this?' Mireille whispered to the Indian girl, drawing her to one side.

Little Lynx shrugged. 'A day, two days; perhaps longer, if the wound does not heal. We shall not move from here. Wildcat sees that. He has gone to think, with the help of the Spirits, what is best to do.'

As always with Little Lynx's conversation, Mireille had to puzzle not only over the English words but over the meaning the girl meant to express. When she said 'the Spirits,' the sense of that was not clear to her. Were these Indian Spirits of a heathen religion, or the saints whom all good Frenchwomen called on in times of need? She would have liked to know, but her English was not good enough.

However, when Wildcat returned, he did not immediately announce the results of his deliberations, but ate a great helping of turkey, some mushrooms and wild potatoes.

The girls divided a plump pigeon between them, and encouraged White Fox to take a little meat as well as the soup. More wood was collected for the night, but Wildcat would not allow the girls to swim in the little enclosed pool.

'He says it is too dangerous, that we must stay together,' Little Lynx managed to tell her.

Mireille wanted to know what else he had decided, for brother and sister had had a long conversation after the meal.

'He thinks tomorrow we must go on.' Little Lynx was hesitant. 'He says White Fox will be strong enough.'

'You don't agree?'

'He says White Fox can lie in the bottom of the canoe, and I must paddle.'

'Can you?'

'Yes, but it is not a good piece of water. There are many rocks.'

'But you'll do it?'

'If I must.'

There was no time for more. So Mireille lay down on the floor of the cave, close to Little Lynx and close also to White Fox. Sleep was a long time coming. She could see Wildcat on guard at the cave's mouth, but that gave her no sense of comfort. If White Fox did not recover, what would her fate be?

Captain Charles de la Croix sat up in bed, his arm in a sling, his head bandaged. Despite the gruesomeness of his appearance and a recurring headache, he was feeling satisfied, almost happy. Let Pierre Charbonneau look out for himself; he had the upper hand now!

That morning, the Captain had had a most extraordinary piece of luck. Some French officers out on a hunt for deer had gone rather further than they had intended and had found the slashed-off hem of a woman's brown dress. They had brought it back, not quite sure if it had any relevance, but when a white woman had been captured by Indians, anything might be a clue to her whereabouts.

They had hurriedly taken it to Pierre Charbonneau, and he had admitted that it might be a piece from the very dress Mireille had been wearing. The colour was right.

Some time afterwards, Charles had been shown the material, and had agreed that that was indeed the colour of the dress and the type of material. An independent witness had been found, too—one of the girls from the bride-ship, but not Émilie, the one who was nursing Pierre. In fact the girl who had come forward was married to the man who served in the grocery shop. She was a big, broad-beamed farm girl and made a good witness, so they said. She was very positive it was Mireille's dress: she would know it anywhere. Mireille had worn the dress on every day of the voyage.

Charles had wanted to know how Pierre Charbonneau had taken the news.

'Very calmly,' he was told. 'One might almost suppose it was not his wife who had disappeared, but some neighbour woman, from his coolness.'

'He always was a deep one,' was Charles's rejoinder, but he smiled to himself. He had Pierre where he wanted him! Now was the time to act. The blows to his head had not dimmed his cleverness.

Mireille would never return. He had her inheritance within his grasp. He had made it his business to find out that she had not even signed the marriage certificate with her own name, but only with a large X. Fate had played into his hands admirably. With her out of the way, there was only Pierre to silence, and that he could and would do!

Charles summoned an official to hear his statement, and a clerk to write it all down. In it, he accused Pierre Charbonneau of treason against the Crown in shooting an officer of the King and consorting with the enemy, and added for good measure that he suspected a plot on the part of Monsieur Charbonneau to get rid of his wife and claim her lands. If one charge failed, another was sure to stick. Pierre Charbonneau would be either a dead man, or so long in gaol that he would never chase after Mireille. Yes, she was as good as out of the way, and Pierre with her!

He lay back, well satisfied. All he had to do was to wait. The due processes of law would work for him.

In the morning, White Fox had recovered enough to oppose Wildcat's plans for the day. He refused to move, and pointed out that the canoe was his and that Wildcat was his guest, not the other way round. He spoke in his own language, and in French as well, to make it clear to all.

Wildcat accepted this edict with a poor grace, and stalked down to the river. It was not clear to Mireille whether he communed with any Spirits down there, but he did bring back a very large eel for their lunch, and he had no tussles with the bear.

After a short nap, White Fox enlisted the help of both girls and walked as far as the pool with them. He sat in the sun, on guard against any comers, to prevent the girls being surprised. He was not only out of sight of them, but out of earshot as well.

At first the girls only frolicked in the water, enjoying themselves in the sunshine. But when they lay on the furthest rocks to dry, with their hair spread round them, they were able to talk.

'Wildcat is very angry,' Little Lynx admitted. 'He makes no secret of it. I guess you can see that.'

'Yes.'

'I don't know if White Fox is a match for him.'

'Because he's hurt, you mean? But they are supposed to be friends.'

'Wildcat says you are not treated as a prisoner. He asks White Fox why this is so.'

'And what does White Fox say?' Mireille felt a twinge of alarm. Little Lynx was trying to tell her something.

'He says it is no concern of Wildcat's how he chooses to treat his prisoner.'

'What did your brother say to that?'

Little Lynx appeared suddenly unwilling to tell her. 'He—he does not agree.'

'Tell me what he said.'

'The Golden One would not wish to know.' Little Lynx reverted to the more formal Indian way of speaking.

'He would make things harder for me?' Mireille asked, wanting and not wanting to know at the same time.

'He would use you,' Little Lynx whispered. 'He says that is what women are for.'

Mireille recoiled at that. She understood exactly what Wildcat meant. She had seen his eyes upon her.

'White Fox will never permit it,' Little Lynx went on comfortably. 'Don't worry, just stay close to White Fox.'

'Yes,' said Mireille.. She shivered, and began to dress. Wildcat might be somewhere in the immediate vicinity at this very moment. All her pleasure in bathing disappeared.

Little Lynx seemed to have no such qualms, and lingered on the rocks. White Fox at length called to them, and they went to help him back. He seemed a little stronger for his sunbath.

Again, that evening, the girls fetched more wood, bringing in large armfuls, and Little Lynx sang as she collected her load. As far as she was concerned, Mireille thought, she had no fear of pursuit or of bears coming out of thickets at her. For a few minutes she watched the other girl. She was so graceful, so happy, a slight smile on her lips. Well, it was the life she was born to, and she was used to it. Would there come a day when Mireille had grown accustomed to it also? Already she had adopted some of the Indian ways. She spread the grease from the meat on her arms, legs and face to protect her from the sun and the attentions of the mosquitoes. If anyone from France should see her now, would they recognise the person she had become in this short time? How many days was it? She frowned, trying to recall.

There was a fine moon, and Mireille watched it from the cave. Little Lynx had persuaded her brother that she must stand guard to let him sleep for at least part of the night, and he had reluctantly agreed that he would watch for the first part and Little Lynx for the second, thus allowing White Fox to rest as much as possible. Mireille hardly heard them change places. She had chosen to lie on the other side of White Fox, away from Little Lynx—and from Wildcat.

Usually all of them were astir by sunrise, or very shortly after. Yesterday, there had been a fresh fish caught early for breakfast. But, waking suddenly that third morning, there was no smell of roasting fish, only the knowledge that the sun was higher in the sky, that it was later. Mireille lay quiet. Perhaps she was mistaken. White Fox was asleep. Wildcat was not stirring.

She looked to the cave's entrance for Little Lynx, and could not see her. Would she have gone to catch a fish? To fetch more wood? The fire seemed rather low. Mireille quietly got to her feet and stole to the entrance. No Little Lynx was visible at the shoreline.

It was a lovely morning, and she had no feeling of alarm. The myriad noises of the woods were all about her—birds calling to each other, trees rustling in the breeze, insects whirring. Probably Little Lynx was playing some sort of game with her. If she sat on the rock, here in the sun, the way the girl had been teaching her to do only yesterday, and listened and watched, she would hear or see something. Smiling to herself, she settled down.

There was no movement in all that expanse of wood and water. Lulled by the complete peacefulness of it, Mireille almost dozed off, but she was shaken to complete wakefulness by Wildcat emerging from behind her. Clearly he was looking for his sister.

Mireille shrugged, miming that she did not know where Little Lynx could be. A stinging blow brought her to her feet, and she was made to understand that she should start to look. She would have gone back into the cave to seek White Fox's protection, except that Wildcat blocked her way. He raised his hand again, and Mireille ran towards the woods. Little Lynx must be there.

But she wasn't. There was no trace of her in all the little paths they had used yesterday for wood-gathering or mushroom-picking.

Mireille did not know what to do. She wanted to go back, as she hated being in the woods alone. She hid behind a tree, watching to see what Wildcat was doing. He was still standing by the entrance—and relieving himself on the rocks.

She waited. If necessary, she would wait till Little Lynx or White Fox appeared.

But there was no Little Lynx. It was White Fox who finally called to her from the cave mouth. She ran to him.

'I can't find her!' she told him. 'I don't know where she is.' She made no mention of Wildcat hitting her. She was too worried for that.

It was White Fox who thought of the canoe, and Wildcat who stormed down to the beach where it was cached. He ran back. The canoe was gone.

Mireille helped White Fox down to the water, and both men searched for traces of what had happened. They could see that the boat had been pulled from its hiding-place, but on the rocks there was no trail to follow.

Mireille watched the Indians. Wildcat sniffed the air, as though some clue would be borne to him on the wind. White Fox knelt on the ground. But neither found anything. There was no trail. Little Lynx was gone. So was the canoe.

Wildcat turned angrily to White Fox, and screamed at him in a long tirade which sounded accusing to the girl's ears. He pointed at her.

White Fox translated. 'He says you must know something, that you planned it between you.'

'We planned nothing!' Mireille protested. 'How could we?' She did not know whether she should repeat what Little Lynx had told her of her desire to return to her captor.

White Fox tried to calm Wildcat, but he kept pointing at Mireille.

'He says you have worked magic on his sister, and spirited her away. He demands that you return her. He insists she would never have left of her own accord.' White Fox spoke in French.

'How could I?' she asked. 'Do you believe that?'

'White Fox does not know what to believe. Wildcat insists that we set off in search of his sister. Every minute that we stand here is a minute lost. He grieves for her.'

Mireille looked at Wildcat. Far from appearing to grieve, he was clearly angry. She was sure he would have seized her and throttled her had White Fox not been there. As it was, he shot her a look of such malevolence that she took a step back.

'Come,' said White Fox, 'you know something. I can see it in your eyes.'

'I only know that Little Lynx was sorry that her brother recaptured her. He didn't ask her if she wanted to be rescued. She was going to marry a man in the village where she was taken. She said he followed her.'

White Fox's eyes narrowed. 'How does the Golden One know this? Did Little Lynx speak French?'

Mireille shook her head. 'No, English—the missionaries taught her, and I too speak some English.'

'The English are the Frenchmen's enemies! How can it be that you speak their tongue?'

'I learned some when I was a child. I don't speak it as well as Little Lynx, but we managed to understand each other.'

'And you kept your talk secret—why was that?'

'Because Little Lynx said her brother should not know. She said too that he would harm me. She was right. This morning he hit me when he forced me to look for her. Don't tell him what I have said. He will kill me.'

'He will not kill you,' White Fox assured her. 'Nor will he harm you while White Fox draws breath.'

Mireille was considerably comforted by that statement, but White Fox turned to Wildcat and gave him some explanation. It seemed to her that Wildcat was not pleased with whatever he said, and made another impassioned speech. This time White Fox provided no translation, so she was left to wonder. He questioned Wildcat. The answers were surly.

Mireille stood by the water, looking from one to the other, excluded from their deliberations. She hoped with all her heart that Little Lynx and Running Wolf were together again. To have run away seemed altogether admirable, but to have stolen the canoe without a word of her intentions was another matter. Of course it meant that they couldn't follow—but it also meant that they couldn't go forward either without difficulty. How would the two Indians resolve this between them?

To Mireille's surprise, White Fox sat down on one of the rocks, waving Wildcat away. He fixed his eyes on the water and squatted there, immobile, drawn into his own thoughts.

Wildcat went into the thickest part of the woods, and Mireille was left, undecided as to what she might or might not do.

White Fox refused to speak to her. She did not want to go away from his presence, not even as far as the cave, though she thought longingly of the food cached safely there. She was very hungry. But worse than the hunger gnawing at her belly was her fear of Wildcat. He was her enemy. She knew that with certainty. Little Lynx had warned her of him. Had she known yesterday what she meant to do? Was that why she had spoken against her brother?

Mireille sat down on a rock away from White Fox. If he could commune with his Spirits, so could she. Why didn't he tell her what was going on? She was his prisoner, and powerless. Would he feel bound in honour to search for Little Lynx? She shivered at the thought of retracing their steps without the canoe. If she had known hardship before, she would know more on foot. Where was Pierre? Why had he not caught up with them? Perhaps he had, and Running Wolf had disposed of him. That chilled her to the bone.

White Fox at length stood up and went back to the cave. He looked like an old man, bent over. Mireille followed him disconsolately. He went into the cave and lay down.

'Bring me some food and water,' he called to her.

She rushed to build up the fire and to heat the remains of the soup. He drank it, and demanded meat.

She broke off a turkey-leg, and brought him that. Obviously he was trying to build up his strength. What did that mean?

She helped herself to a wing, and ate it. If Wildcat went off on his own, he might claim all the meat as his. He had hunted for it.

At last, she risked a question to her captor. 'Does White Fox mean to try to follow Little Lynx?'

'White Fox has not decided yet. Perhaps the bear's mark was a sign of the Spirits' displeasure with White Fox. He took his friend's woman, and he has been punished.'

Mireille was surprised. This was the nearest, she guessed, that White Fox would get to admitting that he might have made a mistake in snatching her away. It gave her no inkling, of course, of what his next step might be.

White Fox sighed. 'Where is the Golden One's man? Where is Red Fox?'

That was a question Mireille constantly asked herself. She had no answer to it.

'White Fox feels danger all round. White Fox is troubled.' With this pronouncement, he closed his eyes.

Mireille wished she could do the same. It seemed a singularly strange way to her to face trouble. He gave her no directions, no commands.

All she could do was to keep watch. She went to the entrance of the cave and let her eyes rove over forest and water. If there was danger out there, she, at least, must be on her guard. She took the new paddle White Fox had fashioned as her only weapon.

CHAPTER NINE

CAPTAIN CHARLES de la Croix was fuming. What was more, his head was aching abominably and the surgeon wasn't pleased with the progress of his arm. He tut-tutted over it, looked grave, and announced that he was of the opinion that nerves had been damaged and he could not be answerable for its absolute recovery.

'Who else was responsible?' Charles had replied in a vile temper, only to be told that whoever had fired the musket was the culprit.

The surgeon obliged with a long technical explanation of the effect of musket-fire on human bones and sinew, but the upshot of his words was that the good Captain might never be able to flex his elbow again. 'Mind,' the surgeon added, 'it's early days yet, but my experience, which is considerable, leads me to believe that full movement of the elbow may be seriously impaired.'

That was daunting news enough, but more was to follow from a different source.

As there was no proper hospital in Trois-Rivières, Captain de la Croix had been put to bed by his landlady, Madame Veuve Bourassa, a lady with a comfortable figure in her forties. She was still pretty in a rather overblown way, and the coming of the army in such large numbers to the small settlement had been a considerable benefit to her. She had opened her home—and some said her heart as well—to them. The surgeon, for one, was a constant visitor.

Charles and two other officers were billeted with her, and she made them all very welcome. She was a splendid cook and a great gossip. All the news of Trois-Rivières came to her, and she obligingly passed it on. When she bustled into Charles's room with a cup of hot tisane after the doctor's visit, he knew he was in for a spate of information. His head protested that it could do without the widow's chatter, but before he could silence her, she was out with it.

'What do you think, then? It's all round the town this morning! That Pierre Charbonneau has gone—just like that! Gone! One moment he was lying in his bed as pale as the sheet which covered him, the next he was nowhere to be found. They do say the Commandant is furious. Where can he have gone? I say the Indians have carried him away. Well, *le bon Dieu* knows he's gone among them for years; he bears a charmed life. One time they were going to kill him—kill him and torture him, for that's their way.'

She paused for breath, and Charles was inclined to stop the flow by asking if she didn't mean that the torture came before the killing. But the news was too serious for frivolity. It was devastating!

'Gone? Where can he have gone?' Charles asked, his mind trying to sort it out.

'Some say they were going to arrest him. They would have arrested him before, save for his reputation, but I say a man like that should have been put in gaol at once—turning a musket on an officer of the King!' The widow plumped up Charles's pillows. 'There, that's better, isn't it?' She went on.

'I hear the Commandant called in that Albert Morel, Monsieur le Secrétaire. All his airs and graces were for nothing. The Commandant gave it to him that he must have warned him about the arrest, that he'd helped him. But there, I shouldn't be telling you all this—it was told to me in confidence!'

'It shall never go past my lips,' Charles assured her with the most charming smile that he could manage, when the information was eating away inside him. 'After all, I am directly concerned! Please tell me all you can.'

The widow bridled a little and smoothed the counterpane. 'So long as you won't think I'm an idle old gossip?'

Charles assured her he had no such thoughts. 'What did Monsieur le Secrétaire say?' However Madame Veuve Bourassa came by her information, it was usually very close to the truth.

'Monsieur Morel denied all knowledge of Pierre Charbonneau and where he had gone. He declared himself surprised, because he had counselled him that he must oblige the authorities with the re-enactment. That was a point of law, and he had always been a law-abiding citizen, and so had Monsieur Charbonneau.'

The widow licked her lips and sat down on the chair by the bed, just hovering on the edge, as though she might leave at any minute.

Charles smiled at her, and she continued, 'Monsieur le Commandant didn't let him get away with that! He said Monsieur Charbonneau had ben gaoled for not taking a wife, and that moreover there was a good deal which needed explanation about the wife he had taken. That was one in the eye for Monsieur le Secrétaire, *n'est-ce pas?* For we all know that Monsieur Morel had a hand in that affair.'

'Did Monsieur Morel volunteer any information about the marriage?'

'As to that,' the widow shrugged, 'I don't know. You must understand that voices can go lower as well as higher, and listeners don't always hear everything. Not that listening ears are trying to hear, you understand. If a person just happens to be outside a door, they can't help but hear—as I'm sure the good Captain knows.'

The good Captain did know, but all the same he would have given a good deal to know what had been said about the marriage of Pierre and Mirielle, and Monsieur le Secrétaire's part in bringing them together.

'Was there nothing else?' he probed. 'When exactly did Pierre Charbonneau do his disappearing? Today? Yesterday?'

'How like the Captain to go to the heart of things!'

Madame Bourassa beamed at him. 'No one quite knows. It seems that Monsieur Charbonneau had a constant stream of visitors yesterday—and the day before. They questioned that cross-eyed girl about it. She says half the settlement was in and out of his bedroom. Would you believe it—she can't remember the exact time when she last saw him! She sounds a bit half-witted. Really, they should examine these girls properly before they send them over here as brides! They think the colonists are so desperate for a woman—and the dowry—that they'll take anything!'

'Yes,' said Charles sifting his way through this long discourse. 'But when does she *think* she last saw him?'

'The last time she can positively remember was the day before yesterday. It seems he refused to talk to anyone—just turned his face to the wall. They all tried to make him talk, but he wouldn't; he'd gone very strange.'

Charles did not like the sound of this at all. 'Who came to visit him?'

'She didn't know any of their names. She's new here, and she says she didn't think to ask them. But one or two have come forward—a soldier who served with him, and a farmer nearby. They agree with her story that he wouldn't speak, but they swear he was there in his bed.'

'That's not much worth if he didn't speak. He could have been gone for two days.' Charles wished his head would stop aching. He wished he was on his feet again. What a perfect opportunity missed! If he had been able to go after him . . . He could imagine it . . . Pierre Charbonneau could have been shot resisting arrest, and all his own problems would have been solved. Instead, Pierre Charbonneau had escaped his net—the man had always had friends. No doubt it was his friends who had come to his rescue. What a story they had made up between them—a man who wouldn't speak to them, who lay in his bed, face turned to the wall. Rage engulfed Captain de la Croix.

'Leave me,' he commanded Madame Veuve Bourassa.

She was all sympathy as she rose to her feet. 'Is the Captain not feeling well?' she simpered in that tone women seemed to reserve for the sick or wounded. 'The Captain need not upset himself. A patrol has been sent after that scoundrel Charbonneau. They'll have him back to face his actions, and it will be the worse for him that he ran away.'

'When they have him back,' Charles ground the words through his teeth as he lay back. 'If they have him back . . . *Sacré-bleu!* Charbonneau has the luck of the damned!'

Mireille spent the longest two days of her life in watching White Fox. She tended him, kept up the fire, and even managed to catch a few fish.

Wildcat had done as she feared, and taken half the remains of the turkey and a pigeon as well, which had left only a small store for herself and White Fox. Then he had gone.

White Fox had not seen fit to tell her whether he would return. 'It is as the Spirits will it,' had been his dictum. 'It rests with them.'

'Are we to wait here, then?' she asked, impatient with the idea of waiting on unknown and unacknowledged Spirits.

'White Fox is unable to walk over the mountains; the Golden One knows that,' was his only answer.

She was left to her own devices, fearful that Wildcat would not return, equally fearful that he would. She spent long hours sitting at the mouth of the cave, searching the trees and the river for some signs of life. There was none, nor did any Spirit come to advise her, though in her desperation she even appealed to them.

On the morning of the third day since Little Lynx had disappeared, White Fox walked as far as the water. The claw-marks of the bear had scabbed across his chest, and he threw aside the moss and petticoat bandage and bared them to the sun.

He didn't look well, but Mireille was relieved to see that he had decided to live. She ran after him, wanting his company—any company save her own.

'It is a fine day!' she said as she sat beside White Fox on the rocks.

'Brother Sun is shining,' he agreed. 'White Fox might catch an eel today, or some pigeons. We must prepare.'

'Prepare? Prepare for what, White Fox?'

'For the long walk in the mountains.'

'Why must we walk in the mountains?'

'We have no canoe, and the river path is dangerous.'

'Why dangerous?'

'Our enemies will take that way.'

'What enemies?' Mireille asked, glad at last to be given some answers.

'The enemies of White Fox and the Golden One.'

'Who are these enemies?' The information was not easily come by. 'Is Wildcat one of these enemies you speak of?'

'He is the Golden One's enemy. He lusts after her.'

'He's gone after his sister, hasn't he? Will he return, then? Do we wait for him?'

'Not after today. Today we shall catch many fish, and by the time Brother Sun reappears in his circle, we will be on our way. It is a long climb. We will be slow, but White Fox will hide all traces of our path.'

'How long will it take?'

White Fox spread his arms wide. 'How high is the sky? How deep is the river? The Golden One thinks everything has an answer. I have noticed that about her before. It will take as long as it takes. Before the next moon is full and round, the Golden One will be in my village.'

Mireille shivered at that. Somehow she had thought knowledge would make things easier, but it only made them more definite. Every day she was separated from Pierre, every league they travelled, made him and their marriage seem more unreal. The only reality was here; here where they must prepare for the morrow. She picked up the length of her petticoat which had been used as a bandage, and taking off her sabots, waded into the water to wash it. It would serve to wrap meat tomorrow, when it had dried in the sun.

White Fox rose to his feet and set a trap for an eel. He caught four fish as well, before he again sat down to recoup his strength.

Mireille cooked the fish, and later she baked the eel he had trapped.

They had a stroke of luck towards the evening, for a small turkey walked right out of the bushes and regarded Mireille with curiosity. While she clucked to it, White Fox stole up behind it and despatched it quickly. He was so pleased that he showed Mireille where she might pick edible greens and more wild potatoes, only a little way in among the trees.

While the turkey was cooking on a spit over the fire, they ate their meal of fish and vegetables. Mireille found she was very hungry. It was too bad, she reflected, that Wildcat had taken his pan with him, but she didn't have long to think about it, for instead of the splendour of the sunset she had expected, the sky had clouded over and little forked tongues of lightning began to shoot across it in the gathering dusk.

'Heat lightning,' pronounced White Fox. 'Make haste to gather wood in case the rain follows it.'

The girl did as she was told, sniffing the air as the Indians did. It smelt different. The afternoon had been sultry, but now the air seemed lighter. The wind was rising, too. By the time she had collected sufficient wood, it was pulling at her, pushing her along. As she reached the cave, the first fat drops of rain fell.

She scurried inside, just in time. The heavens opened, and thunder sounded loud in her ears. Inside the cave, the noise was thrown back at her. The wind tore in, nearly extinguishing the fire, and then retreating so that it smoked and caused both of them to cough and splutter. The rain drummed down. The lightning flashed. Mireille put her hands over her ears and hid her face in her skirt. She'd always hated thunderstorms, and this one terrified her. It was so close, so immediate. She tried to think of other things, of her home in France, of Émilie and her kindness on the voyage over the sea, of Pierre caught out there in the storm, perhaps.

Why did her thoughts always go to him? White Fox had said he would follow her. Surely, if that were true, he would have found them by now. No—in awful clarity she saw that she would have to abandon hope of rescue by Pierre. White Fox was her only protection. She depended utterly on him. She realised that she had not attempted to escape because she did rely on him. He knew the way through this wilderness. He was her guarantee of life, and she wanted to live—in spite of the hardships—in spite of the storm. It would pass. She prayed that it would pass, to the Virgin and to the saints, and she wondered if White Fox prayed, too. She did not find that strange, for the Spirits he talked with must be as real to him as the saints were to her. She crossed herself at that thought.

The rain fell all night, but the thunder and the lightning moved away, growing quieter in the distance. Mireille fell asleep, comforted by the soft chuckle of the fire, and warmed by it.

In the morning it was still raining, but only a fine drizzle. To the girl's eyes it seemed set in for the day, but White Fox said it would soon stop and then they could go. While they waited, they breakfasted on turkey, and wrapped all the food as best they might. They put it in bundles, some cotton-covered, some in deerskin cut from White Fox's tunic. They tied them with thonging, and filled a leather bottle with water.

The Indian kept going to the cave mouth and looking at the sky, uneasy, muttering to himself. When the rain stopped, to her surprise he didn't immediately load up and leave, but instead motioned her to follow him to the shore. He took the head of the eel, which he had carefully put to one side yesterday, and with it in his hands signalled to her to pick up the new paddle he had made. Did he mean her to take part in some strange ceremony of farewell, of propitiation?

Mireille went with him, a few paces behind.

When he moved into the bushes the bear had come from to attack him, she did not want to venture in, so she stayed on the rocky beach. She put the paddle down.

Five minutes went by, and ten. He did not reappear. Should she go after him? Call out to him? While she hesitated she heard a noise, and spun round. It was nothing—the snapping of a twig. She faced the water again.

She felt her waist encircled by a powerful arm, and a hard hand covered her mouth. She bit at it, struggling and writhing to be free. A glimpse of her captor showed Wildcat! Oh God, she was lost!

Her fight was frenzied, but she was dragged down, forced down on to the shale. He took his hand from her mouth for a brief instant, and her screams filled the air. '*Aidez-moi, aidez-moi!*' she shouted twice before her own skirt was lifted up and thrust into her mouth. Wildcat was on top of her.

Helpless, she stared into his wild eyes. Triumphant, wicked, they proclaimed his vicious intentions. Rage and fear engulfed her equally.

She managed to raise her knee and strike against his back. Her fingers clawed his face, but he laughed aloud, and struggled with her petticoat.

Even as he laughed, White Fox was upon him, his knife in his hand. Unfortunately it only raked his back, and both Indians were rolling down the shale away from the girl, who lay cowering, unable to believe in her reprieve. She managed to raise herself to her knees and gazed upon the struggle.

The weakened White Fox was proving no match for Wildcat. It would all be over between them very shortly. Already blood was oozing from White Fox's earlier injuries, and one of his legs had assumed a strange shape where it had hit against a rock. The fight was almost lost.

Mireille's eyes fell upon the paddle. Her hand groped at it and seized it, despite the flailing bodies. She sprang to her feet and brought it down on Wildcat's head. The thick end caught him squarely above his ear with a resounding thunk, and his body stiffened and lay still.

Panting, sobbing, she sank to the ground. Had she killed him or only maimed him? She didn't know whether White Fox lived. Both Indians lay quiet as the dead.

She was lying in a puddle of water, and it was the consciousness of its coldness and wetness that made her shiver and get to her feet again—that, and the fact that the red blood was still trickling from White Fox's chest and mingling with the water on the rocks. She stumbled towards him, her feet slow, unwilling, and bent down. He was still breathing. She called to him, but he gave no answer.

She shouted at the empty sky, ran to the empty river.

It was empty no longer. There was a canoe upon its shining surface. Friends or enemies? She closed her eyes. Perhaps she was just imagining it! She opened them again as the sun made a brave attempt to pierce the steamy clouds.

She stood watching, mesmerised, unmoving. She felt no fear, and didn't even try to run away. In any case, where could she have gone? Whatever lay in store must be faced. She waved to them.

There were two Indians paddling. That much she could make out. Another man was in the centre. She noted idly that it seemed a very small canoe. Even before it beached, she knew who the third man was. It was Pierre, Pierre Charbonneau, her husband. Yes, he had come for her! She tried to call out to him, to make him hear her, but her voice for some reason stayed locked in her throat.

When he reached her, it was the same. She couldn't speak, couldn't explain, but stood, wooden, in the circle of his arms.

Like one in a dream, she was aware that he left her sitting on a rock and went to examine White Fox, that he spoke to the two Indians with him and they did what they could for him, bathing his wounds, doing something to his leg that made him cry out like an animal in pain.

Only then did they look to Wildcat. The shrug of their shoulders told Mireille that he was past all help. They laid him on his back, and the tin pan on his belt gleamed in the sun.

Mireille wanted to tell them that it was a valuable item for cooking, but she couldn't get those words out, either. What did it matter? Wildcat wouldn't need it any more. The best she could do was to point to the cave. Smoke was still rising lazily from their fire. One of the Indians went towards it, while Pierre returned to her side.

He took her in his arms. He kissed her. He shook her. He tried to rouse her.

She was aware of it all, somehow it did not reach her, did not touch her. It might all have been happening to someone else. The thing her mind grappled with was the knowledge that she had killed a man. An Indian, one part of her sneered, an Indian who meant to violate her, who nearly succeeded—but still a man. Little Lynx's brother.

She wanted to weep, to cry that she had done it out of necessity, but she was stony-hearted, stony-faced. The tears would not come.

Pierre carried her to the cave, placed her beside the fire, wrapped her in a blanket. That almost melted her. A blanket—where had it come from? They had no blankets here. She frowned, touched it with her hand, stroking its softness, its warmth.

When Pierre brought her a cup—a steaming cup—of something, she drank it docilely. It was tea. Hot, strong tea. Had he found Wildcat's pan, after all?

She saw they found the food and sniffed at it, helped themselves to some of the eel. Well, everyone must eat, but when Pierre tried to get her to try a little, she couldn't get it past that terrible constriction in her throat.

The three of them talked together. She could not understand anything of what they said, but that was no surprise. She had grown accustomed to the ways of men who didn't explain things to women.

She moaned when Pierre went out of the cave, and she followed him to the entrance, blanket still wrapped round her. She felt safer somehow when he was in view. The danger was past, she told herself. Pierre would take her home now. She'd be glad to get there, so glad.

She leaned against the rock wall, savouring the pleasure of that homecoming. Pierre was going to take her home.

Pierre went down to the shore. His Indian guides had wrapped White Fox in one of their blankets, and he was lying on his side, his eyes open.

Pierre squatted down beside him. 'Well, old friend, what have you done to yourself?' He spoke in White Fox's tongue.

White Fox gave him the ghost of a smile. 'As you see, I will live. What has happened to Wildcat?'

'He's dead.'

White Fox looked for the body, but the two Indian guides had taken it away from the rock shelf where it had lain. He nodded. 'The Golden One smote him with the paddle. My brother, you have chosen a formidable woman, a strong woman! She saved White Fox.'

Pierre would have liked to question him further, but he could see he was very weak from loss of blood and the pain of his leg. He needed to be back among his own people as quickly as possible. Pierre made up his mind. He called his Indian companions and explained his plans. They were to take White Fox to his village with all speed. The canoe would not hold them all. He and the woman would stay.

White Fox protested at that. 'The Golden One must

leave this spot. It is not a good place for her!'

Pierre was forced to admit that was true. She seemed to have lost the power of speech, but White Fox's need was even greater than hers.

'Does my brother remember the green valley?' White Fox asked. 'Take your woman there, and White Fox will send a canoe and warriors to find you.'

'It is a day's march from here, and the way is hard,' Pierre protested.

'White Fox knows that, but it is dangerous to remain here. There are enemies.' There was a look of strain on the Indian's face, a white line round his lips. 'The Golden One will tell you all that has happened.' He brushed Pierre's question aside. 'Go, go now! There is food in the cave. Take your woman and go. Only promise that you will wait in the valley.'

'I promise,' Pierre agreed. There was nothing else he could do. White Fox was his blood brother, and he could not callously leave him there to perish. He must be returned to his people and to their care. Sometime in the future, he would return the favour and send Mireille and himself back to Trois-Rivières.

White Fox was lifted into the canoe. The blanket made things easier, but it was painful for him just the same. He managed a speech of farewell before the canoe was paddled away.

'Till we meet again, my brother Fox, may all go well with you. May the sun shine upon you, and your woman favour you with her smile.

'And you, brother,' Pierre responded. 'A swift journey and a safe one.' The paddles dipped into the water, and he waved them away.

He was alone—he and Mireille alone in this desolate spot, and he must tell her as best he could that her adventure had not ended, that they must go on.

He was not sure how she would take the news, if indeed she would even understand what he told her. He had not had the heart to tell White Fox that she was in too much of a state of shock to be able to speak. He had no idea if she would ever be able to explain exactly what had happened here. Perhaps it would be better if she forgot it. Sometimes when men had endured a ferocious battle, especially if it was the first one, all they wanted was to forget that it had ever happened. He must help her.

Yes, White Fox was right. They must move on. Probably it would take more than one day's march. They'd go in easy stages, as easy as he could make them. In his mind's eye he saw some of the terrain they must cover, and his spirits sank. Could a woman endure it?

There was danger in leaving—but if White Fox were right, there was more danger in staying.

Pierre squared his shoulders and went up the rocks to the cave. The sooner it was done, the better.

CHAPTER TEN

MIREILLE LOOKED AT Pierre with uncomprehending eyes. What did he—this stranger who was her husband—mean, that they must leave the cave? Where did he intend to take her? She had watched the canoe leave with frantic emotion. For a moment she thought he was going to leave with it, but he had returned. He had returned, and announced that they were going.

Even with the warmth of the blanket enfolding her, she began to shake. Every nerve in her body trembled, and her teeth chattered so much that the noise frightened her. When he put his arms about her, she had a wild impulse to flee. That was what Wildcat had done—put his arms about her. But she was shaking so much that she had no strength to push him away.

He sat on the rocks in the sunshine, and held her on his knee as her father used to do when she was little. She remembered her father with a slight surge of pleasure. He had been a good man. Perhaps this man was, too.

This one sang to her and rocked her, and gradually, so very slowly, the terrible shivering lessened and then stopped. She did not know the song. It was about a man paddling his canoe across an endless river under a pale moon. She liked the part about the pale moon. It was quiet and far away on the moon. If she were on the moon now, she wouldn't have to think about anything—not even about Little Lynx. Her mind snapped shut on that name, her body straightened. She knew no one called Little Lynx.

She touched Pierre's cheek, ran her finger along his mouth. He could sing. He could speak. Why couldn't she? She didn't open her mouth. She knew she couldn't speak.

'We're going to a lovely, peaceful place,' Pierre told her, 'where everything is green and beautiful, where there are no enemies.'

She looked into his eyes. They were blue. Of course they were blue! Her husband had blue eyes. That was what she had first noticed about him, the blueness of his eyes. What did he mean about going to a beautiful place with no enemies? Did he mean heaven? They weren't going to die, were they? Not now, not when he'd at last come to her! She tried to tell him so, but no words came.

'There, there,' he soothed. 'There's nothing to upset yourself about. I know the way. You'll like it there. But first we must get ready. White Fox said there was some food. Will you show me where it is?'

Why was he treating her like a child? Mireille asked herself, but she went inside and showed him the food. He began to pack it in a leather pouch.

When it was stowed away, he took the blanket from her and packed that in as well. Then he put the whole pack on his back.

'Come,' he took her by the hand. 'You will soon be warm.'

The way was easy enough at first, but soon they began to climb. The path was muddy in places, and Mireille slipped a good deal.

Pierre went first. He would not let her fall behind, but told her she must hold on to him when the going was rough. She was grateful to do so. If she had thought the steep climb was hard, she was to find the descent on the other side even more frightening. It looked so deep and sheer, and she gasped at the sight of it.

He did not lead directly down it, but zig-zagged across the face, following the faintest of trails where branches reached out to lash them, creepers and thorns tried to trap them. Mireille had some fine scratches on her legs. She was only glad she still had her ragged stockings to offer some sort of protection. Eventually they came to the bottom, rock filled and barren. Pierre allowed her to rest.

'We're around the headland,' he told her. 'It shouldn't be quite so bad now.'

There he was wrong. Last night's rain had seen to that. There were puddles of all sizes to negotiate among the rocks. Mireille stubbed her toe against a sharp submerged stone, for Pierre had made her remove her sabots and carry them. She lost her footing, and would have been completely soaked had he not grasped her by the shoulders and pulled her out.

They were walking parallel to the river at a short distance from the shore, and she could see, as she halted to allow her breathing to become even again, that the rocks abounded there as well. She wondered how the canoe had fared. Pierre motioned her on impatiently. He led the way through overhanging rocks, through a tunnel-like inlet where they both had to crawl on hands and knees like animals. She was crying with fatigue now, but he forced her on and on.

Only when the sun began to descend lower in the sky and the perspiration was dripping from every pore in Mireille's body, did they come to a place with large flat rocks.

She would have sunk down on one of these, but Pierre prevented her by harshly taking hold of her.

'No, no, there's a turtle! If you had disturbed him, he might have taken your fingers off, or a piece of your leg.'

Mireille shuddered, still dumb.

'You've done very well,' he told her. 'We'll just find ourselves a ledge, and stop for the night. We should be reasonably safe up there.' He pointed to the cliff face.

Mireille looked up. She couldn't climb that! She shook her head.

'Of course you can do it!' Pierre told her. 'Think what a view there'll be up there. We can see for miles. No one will be able to surprise us, either.'

The matter was decided for Mireille by one of the turtles ambling across the rocks towards them. Her feet moved of their own accord. The climb up to the ledge was not as difficult as she had feared. There were natural steps ascending to it, and the ledge itself, when they reached it, was much wider than she would have expected. It went back further than the wall itself, and a stunted bush growing at the edge provided a certain amount of cover, should they want it.

It was surprisingly comfortable to sit on the blanket and share a meal with Pierre. The view was magnificent. The whole expanse of the river shimmered with the sunset, red and orange and purple, followed by the softest pink as the sun disappeared and dusk crept over forest and rocks.

'Tomorrow you shall tell me the whole story of your travels,' he said. He seemed to accept the fact of her muteness and to have confidence that it was only temporary.

They had cold turkey, eel and wild onions, and some nuts that Pierre produced from his pack. Mireille was so exhausted that her eyelids were drooping as she ate. Pierre wrapped her in the blanket on the very inside of their perch and then lay beside her so that his body blocked the outside. She could not fall off.

With a tired sigh, she relaxed against him, and slept.

It was Madame Bourassa who brought the news to Captain de la Croix. 'They say that Charbonneau was spirited away by two Indians.'

'Who says?' Charles opened his eyes.

'Everyone says it. Two Seneca braves, may God have mercy on his soul! They're renegades, spies of the English—that's what everyone knows.' Clearly she had more to add. She sat down. 'Commandant Beauclerc has put out a warrant for his arrest, on a charge of treason. What do you think of that?'

'That's good news! The best medicine I could have had.' Charles smiled. 'He'll never be able to show his face around here again. Are they going to try to find him?'

'*Mais non,* how could they? He'll be down with the English by this time. What will happen to the girl, I wonder, the little wife? Will she be waiting there for him? Poor little body—none of it was any fault of hers.'

'Poor little Mireille,' Charles repeated. 'I grieve for her.'

'Of course,' Madame agreed piously, 'she was your cousin. You have reason to mourn her.' The good widow wiped a tear from the corner of one eye with her crisp white apron-edge. 'Tell me, Monsieur le Capitaine, are there any other relatives? Any who should be informed?'

Charles almost shook his head, and then he began to wonder about informing Uncle Alain. It would come as a nasty shock to him that all his plans for marrying Mireille to his son had come to nothing, and it would serve to warn him, too, that the estate must be kept in good condition against Charles's own return. He began to like the idea.

'There is her uncle,' he admitted. 'I suppose he would wish to know. Madame Bourassa, can you do me a great favour?'

'*Bien sûr,* you have only to name it!' Madame smiled at him, exposing a row of teeth with two gaps, one on either side of her front teeth.

'Find me someone who can write, and I will dictate all the facts of the matter to send to France. I would do it myself, but my arm prevents me.'

'Look no further,' Madame instructed. 'I can write. Wait just a moment, and I will fetch pen and ink.' She bustled from the room.

Charles began to compose the letter in his mind. How should he start it—'*Cher Oncle Alain*'? Strictly speaking, Alain was not his uncle, but it would show family feeling, and demonstrate clearly that he was claiming kinship—and his rights. Yes, '*Cher Oncle Alain,* I write with terrible tidings . . . ' That would do nicely for a beginning.

Charles waited impatiently for Madame Bourassa's return. He was tapping his fingers on the counterpane by the time she settled herself at the little table, which she had pulled close to his bed.

'Cher Oncle Alain,' he dictated . . . '

Mireille woke with the sun in her eyes and Pierre's arm round her. She looked into his eyes, and found they were watching her.

'How beautiful you look when you first awake,' he whispered to her. 'I'm glad I found you again.'

The mist of self-doubt and guilt in her heart ws pierced by this simple statement. For the first time since Pierre's arrival, she thought of herself and of him. She longed to ask him a hundred questions—how he had found her—how he had guessed where to look—how long it had taken him—if his wound had healed . . . She tried to speak, but no words came out, only ugly sounds.

'Sh-h,' he said softly. 'When we are in the green valley, your voice will return. You won't even think of all that's happened to you—we'll just talk naturally.'

Mireille threw her arms around his neck, and held on to him as though she would never let go.

He kissed her gently on the cheek, then on the mouth, smiling. 'Some might say I was the luckiest of men. A wife who can't scold at me, can't question me!'

Mireille hit his shoulder, smiling.

He clasped her hand. 'Careful, *ma petite*, it's tender still. I'll tell you all about it when we're there. Now it's time to get up and continue our journey. We want to be in the green valley before nightfall.' He leaped nimbly enough to his feet and helped her to hers.

They climbed down from the ledge and breakfasted on the shore. Their stock of provisions was dwindling. Pierre looked at it, then took a stick and began to dig in the softer shale. When he uncovered a clutch of eggs, she was astonished.

'Turtles' eggs,' he told her, and wrapped them carefully and put them in his pack. 'Have you ever had turtles' eggs? No? Well, you'll like them—and perhaps be very glad of them.'

They washed in the river in the shallow water at the edge, and Mireille found she was not dreading the day ahead. However hard the way, Pierre was here with her. He would lead her safely.

And lead her he did. Across rocks, fording streams, through mud and along creeper-bound tiny paths. It was hard going, and as the day wore on, Mireille suffered from the heat. Pierre made her a hat of leaves and let her paddle in the shade for a short rest. She would have liked to have stayed longer, feet dangling from a flat rock, cooled by the water, but he said they must go on.

The afternoon was far advanced when they came to what she thought must be an impassable place. They were at the very edge of the river on a narrow path, and the path ended abruptly. Only water, and a great cliff against which it lapped, faced them. Neither did the cliff exactly face them—it just ran solid and unyielding along the very edge of the water. Mireille would have turned back.

'This is the worst part,' Pierre said.

She looked at him dumbly, not knowing what he meant to do. He couldn't mean to scale it! If he did—one false step, and they would tumble into the water, and she could see that it was deep and fierce. She shuddered.

'If you look closely,' Pierre said, 'you'll see there is a way across it—climbing across it. Once we get to the far side, it gets easier. There's nothing to worry about.'

As far as Mireille was concerned, there was everything to worry about. She knew she could not climb that awful cliff. She mimed swimming to the far side.

Pierre shook his head. 'The current's too strong. We'd never make it.'

She looked at him fearfully. That meant that, if they fell, they would be swirled away down river. No, she couldn't—she wouldn't!

Pierre would not let her refuse, but pushed her along the first few steps of the path. 'I shall be right behind you. I won't let you fall.'

Face pressed close to the rock, she crept along, Pierre's arm across her back. Half-way over was a gap where the path narrowed to almost nothing. Mireille's foot started to cross it. She drew it back. It was too much of a stretch. She froze there, rigid.

'Fear has tightened you.' Pierre's hand massaged her back, then the calves of her legs. 'It's only a little distance. Look! There's an outcrop of rock above your head. Hold on to that with your right hand, and stretch your left leg across. Good girl!' He was calm. 'I know you can do it. It gets easier after this. The path widens.'

It was the confidence in his voice that moved her. Gingerly, she reached up her arm. It was as he said—she could cling to the rock. Her foot explored the way.

'That's right, your left hand now—there's another place to grip.'

Mireille never knew afterwards how she accomplished that feat, but accomplish it she did. Her left foot bridged the gap, then thankfully her right, and the way was wider. She almost ran along it.

But it was not finished yet. They had still to reach the top. A series of deep natural steps led up. Mireille needed Pierre's help to negotiate these, but she felt a good deal safer on them because they were so firm and large. Eventually they stood on the ledge at the top and gazed into the valley. Way below them, it shimmered, green and peaceful, a stream threading its way through it.

Mireille looked at the walls encircling it, which were as steep as the one they had mounted. No trees grew on them till half-way down. What now? They couldn't slide down. She looked at Pierre.

He signalled to her to follow, and led the way along the rim. A short way along, there was a gaping hole, and he slid into this and then helped her in. She found herself in a narrow tunnel of a place which went downwards by rock steps. It was dark and dank, but she went on until they came out on a ridge. The valley was still below them, much closer now. There were bushes growing at this level and Pierre scrabbled in them. She thought he had lost his senses, but he pulled out what looked like a bundle of rope.

As she watched, dumbfounded, he let it out, and it formed a rope-ladder that was attached securely to a rock under the ridge. They climbed down it, Pierre supporting her and guiding her feet. When they got to the foot, he pulled on a rope that hung by the side of the ladder, and the whole contraption folded up quite neatly half-way up the distance. Pierre took great care to hide the rope itself in the concealing bushes, so that no one would guess it was there. It took a little time for him to arrange it to his satisfaction.

'We want no unwelcome intruders,' he said.

Mireille could see that intruders would have a hard time getting in. She wondered who had found this place, and how.

Pierre might have read her mind. 'White Fox found it as a boy. It was winter, and he fell into it. Luckily for him, the snow broke his fall. It was spring before he found a way out.'

Very soon they were down in the greenness of the flat land.

Mireille gasped at the beauty of the place, and its size. At the far end, a great waterfall shot its cascade into what looked like a dark pool, with the sides of the canyon beginning to shade the sun into shadows. From there, a shining stream ran bubbling and leaping through the centre, with bushes and rough grass bordering it.

She rubbed her eyes. Yes, there nestling behind a bend of the stream was a dwelling of some sort. Pierre walked towards it. It was low and fairly long, covered in birch-bark. He held open the entrance.

Mireille went in, her eyes unaccustomed to the darkness. The first thing she noticed was that it was dry and snug. There was even a place in the centre where there had been a fire—a hearth of sorts. It was a rough sort of place, but it was a house—a place with a roof, where they might sleep and eat in peace. She turned to Pierre, clapping her hands. She ran outside, weariness forgotten, and began to collect wood—branches and leaves to start a fire.

Pierre followed her out. 'It's not much, my girl, but we shall be comfortable enough. There's game in plenty. See the duck on the water? And there are fish. We'll manage.'

She smiled at him. She could see all that for herself. She reached for another branch, and stopped—something was hissing.

'A snake.' Pierre's voice was quiet. 'Stay still!'

Mireille froze. She could see the creature, its tongue darting in and out of its mouth, its body creeping towards her.

Before it could strike, Pierre brought down a heavy branch upon its head. 'I've never seen one of those around here before!'

Mireille swayed on her feet, her bundle of wood dropping from her arms. She ran to Pierre.

'Oh, Pierre, how quick you were! How frightened I was!' She was crying and laughing, and quite unaware that she was talking. 'You have to kill something which attacks, just like I killed Wildcat. You have to save yourself.'

'Of course!' Pierre patted her back. 'You've spoken! You're talking again!' He spun her round in a circle, holding her hands in the way children do.

They danced in a ring until, laughing, Mireille exclaimed, 'We'll go home now, won't we, Pierre?'

'Home?' he echoed the word. 'Now?'

'Well, not today,' Mireille replied. 'I don't think I

could do all that climbing and walking today, but soon—we'll go soon.'

Was she wrong, or did Pierre not share her enthusiasm for a speedy return? The expression on his face was suddenly serious.

'We'll have to wait for the canoe to come back,' he pointed out.

'Ye-es, I suppose so,' the girl agreed reluctantly. 'But what if it never comes back—if something happens to it?'

'It will come back.' Pierre was infuriatingly calm.

'But what if it doesn't?' Mireille had drawn away from that tight circle, where they had been holding hands.

'Well, then, we shall stay here. There's all we want here—food and water, and a place to live in peace.'

Mireille was forced to admit that was true. She traced a line with her sabot in the soft earth. 'It's not the same as being back in Trois-Rivières, is it?'

'Tiens,' Pierre shrugged. 'So Trois-Rivières has become home in such a short time! In a few days, you'll be thinking of this valley as home.'

'No, I won't.' She began to gather again the wood she had dropped. 'How can this be home?'

He put his hand on her shoulder. 'I'm here. You're here. Isn't that all we need to make ourselves a home?'

Mireille turned to face him. She looked into his eyes, and what she saw there turned her protests to nothing. Pierre was gazing at her as though he liked her, he wanted her. In spite of herself, her heart began to race, and her fingers fumbled with the wood.

'I—I don't know. Sometimes I think I matter to you.'

Pierre had both his hands on her shoulders now. 'What made you think you didn't matter? Silly girl—I came after you, didn't I?'

His eyes were very blue and very direct. Mireille felt the colour rising in her cheeks. 'You might have done that because the Indians had taken me. You might have felt you had to come after me.'

'In honour bound, you mean?'

Pierre's gaze was so tender now that Mireille's legs felt as though they had no power left in them. But she wanted to have things clear between them. 'It wasn't just because I turned the musket on Charles?'

'And saved my life!' Pierre freed one of her hands from the top of the bundle of sticks and, raising it to his lips, kissed it. 'I'm very grateful for that. It made me feel I had a wife who cared for me.'

Mireille's eyes dropped. 'I was horrified at what I had done when White Fox struck him down. He looked so dead. Is he—is he dead?'

'Not he!' He gave a bitter laugh. 'He's going to recover.'

'It's not possible! White Fox hit him so hard.' She searched Pierre's face as if the truth might be written there.

'The devil looks after his own! He'll live. His head will hurt for some time to come—and his arm. Your shot caught him there, but he's getting over it, so they say.'

'Have you seen him?' Mireille felt strangely relieved.

'Not I—I was wounded myself.'

'Yes, of course.' Mireille's hand flew to his shoulder. 'I thought you were dead—that both of you were dead. I couldn't believe White Fox when he said you would come after me.' She felt his shoulder. 'It is all right now, is it?'

'It's pretty well healed. I wasn't able to paddle myself, so that's why I had to take the two Indians. They aren't a pair I'm usually friendly with. But necessity makes strange bedfellows.'

Mireille withdrew her hand as though it had been stung. 'Why do you say that?'

'What?'

'About necessity and strange bedfellows. Is that how you really think of me, as a . . . ' She faltered. 'As a necessity—a strange bedfellow?'

Pierre gave a shout of laughter. 'What a funny girl

you are! Haven't I just told you I think of you as my wife?'

'Ye-es, but you needn't laugh at me!' Mireille would not meet his eyes. 'You married me only out of necessity.'

He put his hand under her chin and made her look at him. 'Never think that, little wife! I liked the looks of you from the first moment I saw you. I'll tell you something I've never told anyone. Before your brideship came in, I went two or three times to see the girls coming down the gangway from the ships, and I never saw one I wanted to follow into the hall.'

'Truly?' A warm glow began to spread around Mireille's heart.

'Truly.' Pierre drew her towards him.

Once more the wood fell unheeded to the ground, and Mireille was gathered close to him. He kissed the tip of her nose, her chin, her mouth, and she clung to him, arms tight round his neck, body pressed close to him. She did matter to him as he mattered to her. He had come after her because he wanted to. She was married to him, and for the first time she acknowledged it was a real marriage. It would endure.

'I take thee for my husband,' she whispered, when his lips finally released hers.

'You are my wife,' he whispered back.

She tugged at his tunic, pulling him towards the clearer ground in the direction of the stream. 'Come, we'll spread our blanket on the sand and celebrate our marriage.'

Without another word, he fetched the blanket from the bark house and went with her towards the stream. He gave it to her and she spread it out. It was her right. She couldn't tell how she had that knowledge.

She removed her sabots and stood on one corner, he on the other with his moccasins slipped off. They met in the centre and he removed her clothes, one by one, casting them to one side on the sand. She took off his tunic and his leather trousers, and kicked them aside.

Naked, they faced each other in the soft glow of the fading sun, which was disappearing fast down the walls of the canyon.

For Mireille there seemed nothing strange. It was a moment of proud awareness. The tips of her breasts rose to his touch, her body strained to his.

Together they sank on to the blanket and the consummation of their union. Delight coursed through Mireille as he touched her, his hands and mouth lingering on her flesh, hers exploring his body.

When he took her, it was an exhilarating climax, pleasure beyond anything she had ever experienced, and she cried out in exultation. They were one.

They slept, wrapped in each other's arms, as the dusk spread across the valley.

When they awakened under a pale moon, they made love again. They did not go back to the bark house all that night.

The velvet sky was their roof studded with stars. The warm night air caressed them. The sand was soft under them. The blanket protected them.

When the first rays of the sun entered the canyon, they bathed in the clear stream, shook themselves dry and put on their clothes.

Their sojourn in the valley had commenced.

CHAPTER ELEVEN

On their first full day in the valley, Mireille tidied everything in the bark house while Pierre went hunting. He took his musket and said he meant to shoot a deer or some duck, or whatever he could find.

There was not a lot to do in the cabin, because it was so simply made. There was the sleeping-shelf to clear, with old leaves and branches on it. She swept them all out with a stick and replaced them with dried moss and sweet-smelling pine. She found a rolled-up fur rug in reasonable condition, and put that outside to air. It would soften the hard shelf.

There was no furniture at all, but she gathered wood for the central fire. If it rained, they would be glad of dry fuel. She noticed, instead of a chimney, a vent in the roof to take the smoke, and she hoped it worked well. She smiled to herself, reflecting that she had learned something from Pierre's lessons in Trois-Rivières! It seemed a splendid time to wash her dress in the stream, and she pounded it against the rocks, standing in the water up to her knees with her petticoat on. She could wash that tomorrow.

By the time she had accomplished her tasks, the morning was fairly well advanced and it was very hot. She placed the blanket in the shade and lay down.

Pierre returned with a deer, which he had dragged back the Indian way with two long branches tied together in a V at one end. He skinned and butchered it—a process which Mireille did not enjoy watching. Then the skin was stretched on a sort of frame to dry in the sun. The meat was carefully wrapped, and stored out of reach of any marauders, except for a haunch that they roasted slowly over the fire. They gathered nuts, berries and roots, and by the time the meat was ready, they had a very filling meal, finished with the luxury of sweetened tea.

So the days passed—one, two, five—and the living was good. They varied their diet with duck and duck eggs, fish was plentiful and easily caught, there were blueberries and nuts in abundance. When they tired of meat, Pierre had a small quantity of flour in his knapsack, and they made flat bread with water from the stream.

They bathed in the shallow waters or swam in the pool at the far end of the valley. They lazed in the sun. In the evenings, they made love on the blanket in the open air beneath the glory of the night sky. But after that first night, they slept in the cabin, for the canyon was beginning to cool rapidly as the sun left it.

They talked a good deal, going over all that had happened to Mireille on the journey with White Fox. Pierre told her stories of the Indians and their ways, their cleverness in hunting, the farming the women did. She wondered sometimes why they talked so much of Indians, but supposed it was only natural in such a setting. She forgot almost everything except the life they were living now. Getting to know Pierre was fascinating, engrossing. She had never met anyone like him, so handy at the ordinary things of life, so ready to enjoy himself with her.

She sometimes spoke of the life she had led in France with its comforts, but it seemed to her, in the freedom she shared with Pierre, that her old life had had more restrictions than pleasures. She almost forgot that this time in the bark house was temporary and would come to an end. When she thought of it at all, she would bring herself back to reality by announcing some little plan for when they were back in Trois-Rivières. If Pierre became silent then, she did not notice it at first.

It came as a shock to her when, after a week had passed, Pierre began watching a little anxiously for the arrival of what he referred to as the rescue party. He inspected the rope stairway at least once a day, and checked often for any signs of activity on the rocky summits, sweeping his gaze round every few hours.

One late evening as they were lying on the blanket on the soft sand by the stream, well fed, with the sky streaked with blazes of orange and red and purple, Mireille said dreamily, 'Let's always watch the sunset when we go back to Trois-Rivières.'

'If we go back to Trois-Rivières,' Pierre amended, rolling over on to his stomach and propping himself up on one elbow.

'If? What do you mean by if?' Mireille still gazed at the sky.

'Just what I said.'

She sat up. 'I don't understand.'

'I should have told you before. I didn't know how to put it. I still don't.'

'Put what? Tell me, Pierre. Is there some reason why we can't go back?'

'Yes. I'll be arrested, imprisoned, probably executed!'

Mireille drew in her breath in a great gasp. 'But why? Why should that be?'

'Because it's generally supposed that I shot Captain Charles de la Croix in defence of an enemy—a Mohawk.'

'You didn't shoot Charles. I did.'

'Yes, and if we tell that story and anyone believes it, you'd be arrested instead.'

'Charles wouldn't see me arrested!'

'Wouldn't he? You must know a different Charles from the one I do.' Pierre picked up a handful of sand and allowed it to drift through his fingers. 'At any rate, it's gone too far for that. It was my musket. I said I was holding it.'

'But that's not true!' Mireille was appalled. 'I'll tell them how it happened.'

'And they'll drop all charges? You're too optimistic, my dear!'

'The boy will speak up for me.'

'The boy fell asleep, as I remember,' Pierre pointed out. 'Who'd believe a boy against your cousin?'

'Whatever you think of Charles, I'm certain he'd want the truth tc come out.'

Pierre shook his head. 'It's plain you don't know him at all. He wants to see me out of the way.'

'Why?'

'So that he can marry you himself and claim your property.'

Put baldly like that, Mireille wanted to deny it, but she was forced to admit that Charles might see her as the key to wealth. His own expectations were slight.

'What's happened to the boy?' she asked instead.

Pierre shrugged. 'Who knows? There was some talk, I believe, of some childless couple taking him—or perhaps Albert Morel and his wife would—they've always wanted a boy. There may of course be some willing relative.'

Mireille felt as if the breath had been knocked from her body. Pierre was very sure that there was no return possible. 'What then?' she asked him. 'Can we never go back? Where shall we go?'

'There's only one place we can go to—Andaraqué, White Fox's village.'

Mireille heard the words with a sense of doom and utter fright. In her heart she had known that was where they were heading all the time—that was what White Fox had intended from the start—but she had hoped that Pierre would somehow find his way out of that. Every instinct warned her against life with the Mohawks. 'No,' she cried. 'No, there must be something else we can do.'

'What?' Pierre sat up, facing her across the blanket.

'Can't we go to the English—or the Dutch? They have settlements somewhere.'

'First we'd have to get there—and when and if we did, we'd have to convince them we weren't enemy spies. Would we be any better off?' He reached out his hand to her. 'Believe me, if there were any other way, I'd take it.'

'But—but if you go to White Fox's village, you'll have to plan the defences *he* wants. You'll really be helping the enemy then.'

'What's the alternative?' he asked bitterly. 'Do you want to die? Do you think I want to see you tortured and killed?'

Mireille shrank from him. 'Is that what they'd do?' she whispered.

'They're quite capable of it to gain their own ends.'

She shivered, and he put his arm about her. 'I can't bear it,' she said. 'Pierre, I don't want to die!'

'Nor I. Nor do I want to help my country's enemies.' He stared bleakly at her. 'We must just fall in with them, and trust to luck that somehow we can sabotage their plans.'

'Is that possible?'

'It's our only chance. You'll have to trust me, Mireille, and keep silent whatever happens.'

'Do you have a plan?' Faint hope stirred in her.

He shook his head. 'No, but even if I did, I wouldn't tell you—it would be too dangerous for you.'

She digested that in silence, clinging to his hand. 'What about your son?'

'What about him?'

'Will they let you see him—take him away from whoever has him?' Mireille knew a sharp jealousy. It was all right for Pierre to accept so easily life with the Mohawks. He had ties of blood with them.

'I should imagine I shall be free to see him, and perhaps have him with me. Indians are generally willing to share the children of the tribe—they regard them as everyone's future.' Pierre's face was calm, his manner detached. Mireille could not tell what he was thinking, if he was yearning to see the boy.

She sighed. 'When will they come for us?'

'Tomorrow—or next week. Be certain that they will come.'

'Suppose—just suppose—they didn't. What would we do then?'

'Prepare to spend the winter here.'

In a way, that thought was equally daunting. Mireille looked round the canyon and was frightened. It would be cold and lonely. She tried to imagine it covered with snow and ice, and the little bark cabin buried under it. What if something should happen to Pierre—or to her?

'Could we last the winter?'

'The problem would be keeping warm. We have no furs to wrap ourselves in, no snowshoes. We would have to build up provisions. It could be done, I expect, but I don't think we need consider it—not yet . . . '

There was an ominous ring to that 'not yet'. Mireille threw herself into Pierre's arms, pulling him down on the blanket again.

'Hold me, Pierre, hold me, love me. The future terrifies me.'

He wound his arms around her, holding her tightly to him. He kissed her, his lips hard, demanding.

There was an urgency in both of them, a feeling that the span of life might be running out, that they might never mate again. Their clothes were thrown aside, their bodies hasting towards the present, the only time they might share.

The climax came swiftly, savagely. Mireille cried out, not in protest but in longing. Ardour was aroused as never before. How cruel if life were to end just as it had truly begun for her! Spent, she lay beside him as the light faded from the sky and the evening stars appeared one by one in the dark canopy of the sky.

After that night, Mireille too watched the rim of the canyon for any shadows against the horizon.

It was another five days—five days which she lived as though each were her last, savouring their sweetness to the full—before the Mohawks came.

It was afternoon when they appeared, five figures at the edge of the cliff. Mireille saw them first as she was sitting in the shade to escape from the fierce heat of the sun. Pierre was fishing. He looked up when she called out, and stood with his eyes shaded against the glare, searching the skyline.

'Yes,' he said and left the fish to their freedom. 'I shall go and welcome them. You start that last big piece of venison roasting on the fire. They will be hungry.' He went with his long, loping stride towards the far cliff side.

Mireille built up the fire from its ashes, and soon the last of the deer was roasting over it. Pierre might accept the coming of the Mohawks with equanimity, but she could not. It would change everything.

When the Indians arrived, she met them with steaming tea made in the only big container they had. It was made of leaves picked up by Pierre and flaked by herself. A few remaining spoonfuls of honey sweetened it, and it was passed from one to another with every sign of enjoyment.

Pierre introduced them, giving their Indian names, which meant nothing to her. There were two boys of fourteen or sixteen, she judged, and they were White Fox's nephews. To herself she called them Little Fox and Slightly Bigger Fox. They said their uncle was recovering well, but had not been able to make the journey himself. The other three were warriors in their twenties, perhaps. Two were very dark and fierce-looking with green paint on their faces and a single blue feather in their hair, which they wore in a long plait down their backs. They wore only the cut-out bare-bottomed leather trousers of the same pattern as those White Fox had sported. She noticed that they had fewer beads adorning theirs. The other man was evidently the leader, from the way they all deferred to him. He had a slight frame, with a scarred face, and one of his fingers was missing. He spoke some French, and called himself Running Deer. He was dressed in a deerskin suit such as Pierre himself wore, and the tunic was worked in very elaborate patterns of coloured beads and was heavily fringed. It was a beautiful garment.

They all ate the meat when it was ready, and vast quantities of wild potatoes which Mireille had set to bake under the fire. Fortunately she had gathered both berries and nuts that day, and there was enough for all.

When the meal was finished, they all showed their appreciation by enormous belches, and then Running Deer passed the peace-pipe round, offering it first to Pierre. None of them seemed to think it strange that Mireille sat in the circle round the fire with them. She did not understand much of what they said, but every now and then Pierre or Running Deer translated for her benefit.

They spoke of mighty battles which had been fought between the Mohawks and their enemies. Running Deer told her of the peace of the canyon and why it was a special place for them. Young braves came to test their skills as hunters and survivors here. Why, only a few moons ago, Little Fox had won his first spurs as a warrior in this very place. Little Fox beamed at being thus singled out, but Slightly Bigger Fox assumed an expression of boredom and nudged his brother to show less emotion.

Eventually, Running Deer announced the plans for the next day. 'We leave at first light. Blue Feathers One and Two will provide fish to break the long fast of the night. The boys will make sure all fire is out and all water bottles filled, all food packed.' Nothing was left to chance: all duties were detailed, and watches for the night appointed. It was agreed that, since the night was fine, the warriors would sleep outside, leaving the bark cabin to the Frenchman and his woman.

'I'm not sure whether that's meant as a mark of esteem,' Pierre confided when they were alone inside the hut. 'Or just a gentle reminder that we are prisoners.'

His half-jesting remark made Mireille realise anew just what their position was. Though the party seemed friendly enough, she felt uneasy, and it was a long time before she fell asleep.

Leaving at first light, to Mireille's dismay, meant their getting up when it was still dark. But everything had been attended to. There was succulent hot fish for breakfast, hunks of corn bread, and tea.

Departure was conducted with a minimum of fuss, and she found herself ascending the rope-ladder before she would have believed possible.

It was cold on the rim of the canyon, and the sun was just beginning the day's orbit. Its rays had not yet pierced the gloom of the canyon, so there was no last real goodbye, although the girl would have liked to fill her eyes with it.

She had been dreading the descent of the cliff face to the river, but it was made easy for her because the Indians had brought ropes, and she was lowered by them to the shore. She was surprised to see another very tall warrior waiting there by the cached canoes. She was assigned by him to Running Deer's party.

Pierre was directed to a canoe paddled by Blue Feather One and Slightly Larger Fox. Little Fox and Blue Feather Two took up the rear in the last of the little craft.

Mireille sat in the middle, with the large Indian in front of her and Running Deer behind. They proved themselves magnificent paddlers, moving as one man. Large One must have had exceedingly good eyesight, for he steered them round outcrops of rock and floating hazards. She had conquered the feeling of nervousness that these frail craft caused, and only wished Pierre was with her. His phrase of the night before about being prisoners came into her mind; she tried to forget, concentrating instead on the unfolding panorama of forest and river.

The first sight of the rapids took her completely by surprise. She noticed first the angry swirling against the side of the vessel, and the choppy look of the water ahead. Perhaps it was as well that they were swept along so fast that there was little time to think before they fell over the first lip of the swift spiral of descent. That was when she caught an awesome glimpse of what lay ahead.

It made her gasp and hold tight to the gunwales. *'Soyez tranquille,'* she heard Running Deer say, but his words were almost immediately swallowed up in the roar of the water and the exultant shouting of Large One. He wielded his paddle as a fencer might wield his weapon, judging by instinct when to lunge ahead and when to nudge his way to one side.

As the falls cascaded down the next step, the canoes were engulfed in spray. Mireille was too frightened even to wipe the spume from her face. She clung to her place, wishing with all her heart that she were back in the canyon where it was safe. She did not know how the other two craft were faring, and really had no time to think of them. She saw a rock looming ahead through the flashing water, and was sure her last hour had come. Her lips of their own accord whispered a prayer: *'Sainte Marie, Mère de Dieu, priez pour nous, pécheurs.'* She said it again and again, as the next stage took them down into a heavy mist of falling water.

Then they were through into sunshine and a clear shining mirror of a river. Shuddering, wringing her hair and the tail of her dress, Mireille looked back.

The second canoe, Pierre's canoe, was tumbling over the second part of the falls. Hand to her mouth, she watched it. It seemed incredible to her that it would arrive, but it was soaring now through the third set. Pierre was safe.

The third canoe was not quite so fortunate. Its occupants were thrown out as they reached almost the end of the hazard. Large One fished them out of the water and then directed their capsized craft to them. Seemingly none the worse for wear, Little Fox and Blue Feather Two swung themselves into it. Blue Feather Two scowled, but Little Fox waved and grinned.

'He'll be more careful next time,' Running Deer exclaimed, but he smiled at the lad, a smile that lit up his scarred face, giving it a human lop-sided look. Mireille wondered if he was any relation to the lad.

'Is he your son?' she asked.

Running Deer nodded.

'He's a good lad,' she said.

'He'll be all right when he learns some sense,' was the quick rejoinder.

That made Mireille smile. It sounded so like any father, pleased with his son and trying to keep the pride out of his voice. She warmed a little to Running Deer.

The journey continued all day. The river narrowed and then broadened. The scenery softened. There were no more towering cliffs, but sand at the water's edge and flatter land. The water became so shallow at one point that they all had to get out of their canoes and push them through clinging reeds.

But that, too, came to an end, and they appeared to be in a different body of water—a tributary perhaps of the one they had started from. Trees had their roots in the water and overhung it, making it an unpleasant dank place with swarms of mosquitoes.

Mireille suffered a lot from their bites until Running Deer gave her some dark, horrible-smelling salve to spread on her arms, legs and neck. She even anointed her forehead and the parting in her hair. That helped considerably.

At last they reached a clearer space, and beached on a sandy shore for the evening meal and the sleep of the night. They caught shellfish and boiled them over the fire. Mireille found them delicious, and accepted a piece of corn bread from Little Fox to go with her share.

There was little talking around the fire that night, and they rolled themselves in their blankets under the stars, with the Indians taking turns once again at guard duty. They changed every few hours, and each one, as he came off, built up the fire a little to keep it smouldering through the dark.

Mireille, wrapped with Pierre in their blanket, slept only fitfully, aware of the noises and activity of the night. How much longer would it take to reach Andaraqué? What awaited them there? Pierre might say that things would right themselves in time, perhaps, that Albert Morel back in Trois-Rivières would be doing all he could to ease the situation, but she was tired of the way men went on. Waiting patiently had never suited her—it never would. In her opinion, things got worse for waiting, not better. She saw only trouble and suffering before them.

Morning came, and fresh fish, and another day on the water. This time she was assigned to Blue Feather One and Slightly Larger Fox. Pierre took her place in Running Deer's canoe. That meant she had no one to talk to. In a very short time they appeared to be in the mouth of a river, and Running Deer drew his canoe up beside the one Mireille was in.

'Cover up your hair.' He gave her a piece of leather and some thonging to complete the task, and waited while she did it.

'Your skin's still too fair,' he observed, and handed the anti-mosquito potion to her. 'Daub it on your face. It doesn't matter if you don't cover it all.'

Mireille hesitated. She did not want to use the evil-smelling concoction. 'Why must I?'

'Because Running Deer doesn't want anyone to recognise that you are a white woman,' Pierre answered her question. 'Just do as he says.'

Mireille began to streak her face. 'Are we likely to meet anyone who'd care?'

Pierre shrugged. 'We are coming into Lake Champlain, and there are likely to be others here.' He inspected her critically. So did Running Deer. They conferred in the Indian tongue.

'You'll do,' announced Pierre. 'No one is likely to give you a second glance now.'

Mireille hardly felt flattered by that observation, but she let it pass as paddling was resumed. She thought it was strange that she should be hidden among them, when today all the Indians seemed more relaxed. They even sang as they pushed their way through the water, although she did not think much of the song. The words were incomprehensible, and the tune was dirge-like. Were they trying to draw attention to themselves?

The lake was wide and smooth, and towards mid-morning they passed a small Indian village. Several canoes came out to greet them. One or two of the men in them looked curiously at Mireille, but their eyes did not rest long on her. Whatever story Running Deer told them about her seemed to be accepted.

She supposed it was a good thing that her eyes were brown—not of the sloe-eyed Indian brown, but dark enough to earn no comment. No one addressed her directly, and she said nothing. What was there to say? Rescue would not come from this quarter.

Curiously she gazed at what could be seen of their village. It was just a huddle of huts near the shore. Children were running on it, even standing in the water up to their knees, and women washing. Strange that one never thought of savages as struggling to be clean, but Mireille told herself it must be the same the world over, water was there to be used.

She was uncertain whether the party was invited to land, but Running Deer waved to them, and even stood up in his canoe to make them some sort of speech. It sounded, even in a foreign tongue, as someone making his excuses not to stay. The paddlers took up their steady rhythm again, and the sun climbed higher in the sky.

Mireille's leather hat was making her head hotter and hotter, but when her hand went to remove it, Blue Feather One touched it with his paddle, clearly indicating that the hat was to stay in place. She could not see why, because no one was in sight on the whole wide expanse of the water.

Her head drooped, and, lulled by the steady suck-suck of the paddles and the burbling of the water against the sides of the canoe, she must have slept. She woke, in complete surprise, to see a very large canoe approaching their smaller ones. She was even more astonished, as it came closer, to see that it held soldiers in uniform. They were white men—but they did not wear the blue of the French. Their tunics were red.

Mireille's eyes were large. This was the enemy—the hated British!

The canoe drew up beside them, and the Indian paddlers exchanged greetings. Under cover of the patter of politeness, she was able to observe the British soldiers seated so close beside her. She was even able to overhear a little of what they were whispering to each other.

The two nearest were only youngsters, one of them as fair-haired as herself. He had an open, smiling, face. Out of the side of his mouth he spoke to his companion, a darker skinny lad. 'Take a peek at that, Jo—for an Indian, she's small, but all there. And she's wearing a dress!'

Mireille realised it was herself they were talking about, as both pairs of eyes studied her. She gave them a haughty glance, wishing the bodice of her gown wasn't so tight.

'Would you look at that?' the fair boy began to laugh. 'Do you think she's a princess, Jo?'

Mireille had no chance to hear what Jo thought. Blue Feather One saw to that. He adroitly angled his canoe so that Little Fox, not Mireille, faced the lads.

In a few minutes they were on their way again, but Running Deer once again drew his canoe up alongside. 'What did you think to do, Golden One? Appeal to the English? They are your enemies.'

'I was just looking at them!' she protested. 'I thought that, because they were enemies, they would be different, somehow,' she offered by way of explanation, since one was expected. 'They just look like other men.'

Running Deer must have translated this remark for the benefit of the others, for they all broke into laughter—even Large One, who was the most serious of them all.

'If we meet any more,' Running Deer instructed. 'Keep your eyes down as an Indian maiden would do.'

'Yes.' Mireille was meek. 'But what are they doing here?'

'It is no concern of yours,' Running Deer was quick to tell her. 'But they are here on a hunting expedition with our neighbours. They will not trouble us.'

They met no more soldiers, or any more Indians, as the day wore on. Towards late afternoon, the paddlers began to speed up a little, to race each other.

'They're coming home,' Pierre called to her from Running Deer's canoe. 'They're seeing who's going to get there first.'

Blue Feather Two's canoe shot forward, and Running Deer gave quick chase. They shot around and ahead, leading the way into a little bay—a fine protected place, Mireille had time to note before their canoe too beached, and it was journey's end.

She rose to her feet, and Little Fox helped her out on to the sandy shore.

CHAPTER TWELVE

MIREILLE WOULD NEVER forget the first sight of Andaraqué. She had half expected the whole village to be drawn up to greet them, but there was only White Fox, and he was on crutches. He embraced both Pierre and herself and assured them they were valued guests. He stressed the words, 'valued guests'.

He led the way from the beach, the others following behind him in a procession. Mireille, walking behind White Fox and Pierre, was accompanied by Running Deer. She saw smoke rising into the air first as they approached, and then the totems that marked the boundary of the village. She wanted to stay and study these grotesque painted poles which told the history of the tribe, but she was hurried on.

Suddenly she began to feel she was being watched, and the hair at the nape of her neck prickled with the knowledge. She tore off her protective leather hat. Let them see her hair! It tumbled about her shoulders.

The longhouses of the tribe came in sight, and Mireille gaped at their great size. Dogs were tied under one of the biggest, and they were barking.

Before she could remark on it, they were surrounded by children—little dark-eyed Indian children, most of them almost entirely naked but completely unselfconscious. They looked at her with curiosity, one little girl with two fingers in her mouth. It was their quietness which struck her. French children would have been talking and pushing, nudging each other. But these only looked, bright eyes sparkling. Which one of these, Mireille asked herself, was Pierre's son? She could not tell, and none came forward to touch him.

The women of the tribe were behind the children, and they milled about the French girl. Some were old and wrinkled, some young and pretty, but all stared at her, and the boldest put out her hand to touch the blond mane of her hair.

A plump, smiling little woman appeared on the edge of the group, and they parted to let her through.

'I am White Feather,' she announced in French. 'I will take you to your house.' She took Mireille by the hand and a girl of about seven tagged on behind them as they walked together.

'Small Squirrel, my daughter,' White Feather pointed to the child. 'She will teach you our language.'

Mireille smiled at the girl. Perhaps it would be just as well to be taught by a child. It might make learning easier.

White Feather and Small Squirrel conducted her to a medium-sized longhouse that stood quite tall, completely covered in bark, as the small hut in the canyon had been. They entered it. Under the arched roof was a single immense room of a sort she had never before seen. Down its centre were a series of fires. On either side, running the whole length of the lodge, were raised platforms, divided into sections. White Feather led the way to one of these towards the far end.

Some of the centre fires were burning, and making so much smoke that it hung like a cloud around them. Mireille coughed and found her eyes watering. An unpleasant smell struck her nostrils, and Small Squirrel led her past a pile of rubbish. She could see fish-bones in it, and excrement and dirty rags and averted her eyes.

The section in which the little party came to a halt seemed clean and orderly. Screened off from its neighbours on either side by heavy furs suspended from the ceiling, it formed a room by itself, open to the front and the fires, of course—and also to whomever lived across the gap in the corresponding section of the other side.

'It is yours,' White Feather told her. 'Yours and your

man's. You are welcome among us. May you be happy here.'

Mireille thanked her and climbed on to the shelf. She saw there was a pile of furs in one corner and went over to inspect them. She recognised one as beaver, one as rabbit and one as fox, and ran her hand over their smoothness. They were lovely.

'For you to use,' Small Squirrel assured her. Then she took her by the hand and brought her to the nearest centre fire.

White Feather took a pot from the ashes and poured Mireille a drink from it into a birch-bark cup. Mireille tasted it with some misgiving. It was tea, but the strongest tea she had ever tasted. Perhaps, besides the leaves which Pierre used, they added herbs to it. Slowly she drank it down, trying to show the pleasure that seemed to be expected of her. Small Squirrel and White Feather both had some of the brew.

By now, several women were gathered round the other fires, for it was time to prepare the evening meal. Mireille watched them as she sipped. One of them was grinding something in a bowl, and she learned later that it was corn, the Indians' staple food. They used it for bread, or for filling with meat and fish to make it go further.

Small Squirrel and White Feather were having a little argument in their own language. Mireille thought it must be about what they were going to eat, for Small Squirrel disappeared suddenly and came back with a large piece of meat, which she fixed to a spit over the fire. She made a sign to her to watch over it while she and White Feather ground the corn and mixed it to a smooth thick paste which they fried, pancake fashion. When the meat was cooked, it was evident that the other women's preparations were at the same stage, and suddenly all of them gathered up their food and took it outside to where the men were sitting in a circle.

Mireille was directed to a place beside Pierre, and allowed to eat with the men. She supposed it was because she was a guest—for tonight, at any rate. The other women had to wait until all the men had been served. Only then could they and the children eat. The corn bread was delicious, and the meat tender and succulent.

'It's moose,' Pierre told her. 'They're returning our hospitality of the other night. The speeches will be long, I'm afraid. Once you learn the language, you'll find them more interesting.'

The speeches were long and, of course, incomprehensible to her. She stifled a few yawns, wondering why it was that since she had met this Pierre Charbonneau, she had always to learn new skills. How could she ever master the language? It was so guttural, and they spoke at such length.

After a long time, Pierre nudged her. 'They're talking about you.'

'What are they saying?' she whispered back, finding all eyes suddenly on her.

It was White Fox who was the orator, and he switched into French for the girl's benefit.

'This is a small woman, but a woman of spirit. She shot a French soldier to protect her man, and then she killed an Indian to save White Fox. She slew him with a paddle.'

That raised nods and stamps of approval from the audience, and blushes to Mireille's cheeks.

'I only did what any of your women would have done in the same circumstances,' she protested.

Translated, that earned her clapping and laughing from the women, and a whispered, 'Well said!' from Pierre.

Then it was his turn for audience inspection. He was lauded in Mohawk and in French, and White Fox announced that Pierre was to direct the fortifications of Andaraqué. Other tribes might ask the British or the Dutch for help, but they had asked their blood brother, because their ties with him were strong. He would have their best interests at heart. They were all asked for their help, and all pledged it.

Mireille saw for herself that it was impossible for Pierre to refuse. He was committed to it. Building a wall round a village, she tried to convince herself, was not the same thing as fighting against the French. It was not taking up arms—and yet that was what she had done against her own cousin. It was hard to know what was right and what was wrong. After all, the French might never march against the Mohawks again. They had tried it once, so people said, last winter, and been cruelly defeated by the weather and the forest as much as by the Indians. Another argument occurred to her. Perhaps when White Fox said that other tribes had the British to help them, what he meant was that he wanted no obligations to them. They would make demands for their help. Here, in the wilds, she could begin to understand that the Indians might well feel threatened by all white men.

It was a dialogue with herself which went on over the next few days. Pierre seemed to have stifled all his qualms, and threw himself into the task of the construction with a great deal of enthusiasm and energy. His days were spent at it. Mireille sometimes watched the progress of the work, seeing it beginning to take shape as trees were felled in the nearby forest and erected round the village to a standard height. All the men took part, taking time from hunting and fishing. The women worked, too, moving tree-trunks, making thongs from creepers.

Small Squirrel accompanied Mireille wherever she went, pointing to objects and naming them in her own tongue, getting Mireille to repeat them over and over. Gradually she began to make some headway with the language.

In fact, the language proved easier to come to terms with than the living arrangements. Mireille hated living on that little shelf, sleeping there, surrounded by eight other families, some facing her, some on either side. She felt there was always someone watching. Even at night, when dark fell and the lodge slept except for the ever-burning fires, she could not become accustomed to listening ears everywhere.

She felt unwilling to make love with Pierre, though she was aware from the grunts and groans that came through the fur partitions that others felt no constraints. She turned from him, crying silently when he slept. Those days and nights she had spent with him in the valley were far away. They might have happened to someone else.

'It's not right what we're doing,' she told him one afternoon when she had gone to view the work, and they had managed to find a little privacy a short distance from the others.

'It's all we can do,' he answered, very short with her. 'Be patient.'

She bit her tongue. It was no use berating him, but she wanted to lash out at him, to hurt him. 'Do you know which one is your son?'

'Yes.'

The answer startled her. 'Which one?'

'It's no concern of yours.'

That stung her to anger. 'I want to know. I have a right to know!'

'What right?'

'I am your wife.'

'But not the mother of my son.'

Mireille drew back, hurt. 'Why—why don't you want me to know? It's not natural. Don't you mean to acknowledge him?'

'Acknowledge him—what's that supposed to mean? The boy is happy enough as he is. He thinks he has a family. I see his mother and his father are good to him. They love him, care for him.

Mireille could not bring herself to accept that. 'He has a right to know. White Fox said so, that first time when he was in the barn.'

'White Fox is well named. He has the cunning nature

of the fox. He said that for my benefit, not for the boy's. He thought it might move me.'

'And did it?'

'Yes, of course. I'm human, whatever you may think. I take pleasure in my son—in his sturdy body, in his smiling face. He is part of me.'

'But not of me—not even to know him.'

'Do you want to know him?'

'Yes!' The cry was wrung from Mireille.

'Why? What good will it serve?'

'Because he's yours.'

'*Bien.* So you shall, then. But promise you won't interfere.'

Mireille looked into Pierre's eyes. Sometimes in spite of their blueness, she would swear he was an Indian—he thought like them, acted like them.

She sighed, 'I won't interfere.'

Pierre gave her a sudden smile. 'You know him already—Silver Badger—the little lad who sometimes tags after Small Squirrel.'

'Are you sure? He doesn't look like you. He doesn't have blue eyes.'

'I can't help that.'

'No, I suppose not. No one has mentioned his name to me—perhaps they thought I would know it.'

'Peut-être.' Pierre shrugged. 'Whatever you do, don't go out of your way to speak to him. When White Feather thinks the time is right, she may let Small Squirrel bring him to play with you. Give no sign that you know who he is.'

'Why?'

'Because that's the way she wants it. Hasn't she been generous enough already? She shares her daughter with you.'

Mireille admitted that that was true, and that she was very grateful for the girl's company and help. Would she ever understand these people she lived with?

'And another thing,' Pierre went on. 'All the women in the longhouse we live in are related.'

'That's strange, isn't it?'

'Not strange at all. Woman are considered important in a tribe. Inheritance comes through them, not through the men. Women own property. When a girl marries, she brings her husband to live in her house.'

Mireille was astounded. The whole thing turned French customs and ideas on their head. 'Does that mean,' she asked slowly, 'that you lived in this house before—with your Indian wife?'

'With Little Beaver—yes. White Feather is her sister.'

'Then they all compare me with her?' Mireille was not sure why that should upset her, but it did.

'That was a long time ago. They're willing to judge you on your own merits.' Pierre put his hands on her shoulders. 'They may ask themselves why you draw back from me in the nights.'

Mireille coloured to the roots of her hair. 'There are so many ears, so many eyes.'

'That's all?'

'What else could there be? It makes me feel so uncomfortable.'

'I know.' He put his finger to her mouth and rubbed it gently. 'You must learn to forget the others.'

'That's very hard.'

'Yes, I seem to have brought many difficult things to you.'

Mireille put her hand over his. 'Each time I begin to get used to something, everything changes!'

'You're doing very well. Many a girl would have given up before this.'

That was praise indeed, and she felt better for it. 'I'll try to do what you want,' she promised.

He was unable to answer her, for he was called back to the wall and a slight altercation between two of the workers.

Mireille's hand was taken by Small Squirrel. 'Come with me,' she said very importantly. 'Brown Bear, the wife of White Fox, wishes to see you.'

Mireille went with the child, who brought her to the

largest longhouse of all, and to the very top end of it. Brown Bear was waiting for her. She was alone in the big building, sitting on a chair with intricate carvings of animals down its front.

She welcomed Mireille, calling her Golden One, as White Fox did.

When Brown Bear clapped her hands, a woman darted from the shadows and served the inevitable herb tea that accompanied any social interchange. Mireille accepted it, surprised that Brown Bear did not serve it herself.

'That woman is her slave,' Small Squirrel whispered.

Mireille, sipping her tea, was invited on to the shelf, and sat cross-legged on its floor. Why was the woman a slave? she wondered. She was an Indian much like Brown Bear in looks—tall and thin.

Brown Bear had no French, but the slave did, and she addressed Mireille. 'My mistress says she has a gift for you. She begs you to accept it with her gratitude for saving her husband's life.'

'I need no gift,' Mireille protested, and, the words translated, Brown Bear smiled and held her finger to her lips.

'Just the same,' the slave continued, 'Brown Bear's heart is overflowing. She has made you a dress to wear with her compliments.'

Another clapping of Brown Bear's hands brought another woman forward clasping in her hands a deer-skin frock, about knee length and decorated in a marvellous pattern of red, blue and purple beads. It was fringed at shoulder and hem, and was presented to Mireille.

Her hands touched its softness, lingering over it, stroking it. She smiled her pleasure and stammered thanks, quite overcome.

Brown Bear made a long speech. The slave repeated it in French. 'My mistress says it would give her great pleasure if you would try it on.'

Mireille rose to her feet and slipped out of her old

brown dress. She had long since given up wearing a petticoat—it had become so threadbare and torn. She put on the new deerskin, liking its smoothness next to her skin. It fitted beautifully. She pirouetted round for all of them to see. A pair of matching moccasins was produced, and these, too, fitted.

Brown Bear looked as pleased as Mireille, and the two of them partook of another cup of tea to cement their friendship.

When they parted, Mireille would have picked up the old brown dress, but Small Squirrel tugged at her and said she must leave it for the slave. Since the woman's apparel was even more tattered than the old frock, Mireille was quite willing. She handed it to her and was thanked. She gave her her sabots as well, and surprised a tear in the woman's eyes as she handled them.

'Are you a Frenchwoman?' she asked.

The slave shook her head. 'The missionaries taught me French and to love God.'

Her words touched Mireille's heart. She turned back to Brown Bear and asked if the slave might help her to learn the Mohawk language more quickly.

Brown Bear hesitated, and then agreed that the slave might spend an hour or two of every day with her.

Mireille thanked her and asked the woman's name.

'Slaves have no name,' she was told. 'Just as they have no desires or wills except for their master's or mistress's command.'

The slave translated this message with no expression in her voice at all.

Mireille made no comment. Brown Bear had been good enough to offer the woman's services, and the girl went away a little sad, but satisfied. She might be able to make the woman's life somewhat easier.

Mireille went back to her own longhouse, and found that the gift of the deerskin garment had given her a certain status. Small Squirrel took her to the storehouse under the building, and gave her first choice of meat and vegetables for the evening meal. She found her another cooking-pot and two bark cups, and later on when she and Pierre had finished their meal, Small Squirrel and Silver Badger came to play.

Silver Badger was at first very shy, and Mireille ignored him and examined the little girl's corncob doll.

'My father made it for me,' Small Squirrel said. 'My father is the one you call Large One. That's not his proper name, but he likes it.' She giggled. 'Silver Badger will never be as big as him.'

Silver Badger, hearing his name mentioned, came closer and put his hand on the fringe of Mireille's dress. 'It's pretty.' He patted it.

Mireille smiled at him and the child smiled back, a very merry smile, just like Pierre's. It quite took her by surprise. Pierre rolled a leather ball to the boy, and he scrabbled round to catch it.

Silver Badger did not stay long that first time, but wandered back to his own section of shelf and to White Feather. Not a word was said by either Mireille or Pierre. In fact, Pierre took Small Squirrel on his lap and told her a story.

It was a balmy evening, and later on Mireille and Pierre walked by the shore. A big red harvest moon shone down on them, and they sat on a log, watching its reflection in the quiet waters of the lake.

Mireille leaned her head on Pierre's shoulder. 'Nearly everyone's left the house tonight,' she murmured. 'Where have they all gone?'

'On a night like this, they'll sleep out.'

'Where?'

'I expect they're all around us—in the woods, on the shore. It's so warm and pleasant, and a harvest moon brings all the young people out. It's a night when the blood sings.'

'Is it?'

'Of course it is!' Pierre's smile was amused. 'It's a night to be alive. Most of the harvest is in by now, the end of August. The fish have been running well, the wall is going up. It's a time to be grateful to mother nature, to the Spirits.'

'Everything's going well for the Indians,' Mireille sighed.

'Well, most things—not everything for everybody, of course. Blue Feathers One and Two are at odds with each other—and many of the young bucks are feeling the same.'

'Why?' Mireille looked up into his face, not quite sure if he was joking. He had fallen into her habit of calling the two young braves who had accompanied them in the canoe by the names she had given them.

'It's simple, really. It's a girl. Honeybear is her name. The Blue Feathers have always been rivals. Now they both want Honeybear.'

'And how does she feel?' Mireille wound her fingers through Pierre's.

'She hasn't really given any sign. She seems to like attentions from both of them. It's said that her father favours Blue Feather One. His family won't have any trouble meeting the bride-price.'

'What's the bride-price? Does a man pay for a bride?'

'According to Indian custom, the man provides the dowry, not the woman. It's usually a few horses and some strips of wampum—those are the long, intricately-patterned strips of beadwork they use as money. They're pieces of leather, and the beads are made from shells. It's said that Blue Feather Two's family, although they aren't as wealthy as One's, have a wampum belt in which they've used the skin of a great enemy of the Mohawks. That gives it great value.'

'You mean they've cured a person's skin—how would they do that?' Mireille was only half believing.

'They sometimes skin their victims alive.'

'Ugh!' she gasped. Every time she began to think of these Indians as ordinary folk like herself, she was brought up short by some barbaric custom. 'That's horrible.'

'It's their way,' Pierre told her. 'Some think that gives

Blue Feather Two a decided advantage. Blue Feather One might think so, too. He's doing everything he can to make himself more attractive.'

That caught Mireille's interest. 'What sorts of things?'

'He's trying to show what a great warrior he is. That's a bit difficult at the moment, because the braves are all staying close to home to build the defences, and not attacking their neighbours' cattle. He has to content himself with dressing for the part. He does a lot of scowling, and he carries a wooden tomahawk with a great knob on its end everywhere he goes. The latest thing is his hair! He doesn't wear it in a pigtail any longer, but has cut it in a fearsome roach. You know, standing up right along the centre. It takes a lot of grease to keep it like that!'

Mireille dissolved into giggles. She couldn't help it. She thought the roach style was repulsive, but certainly frightening. Blue Feather One began to sound to her like a very conceited fellow.

Pierre laughed with her.

They couldn't stop. They rolled with laughter, hanging on to each other. They laughed so hard that they fell off the tree-trunk on to the sand, still clinging. Mireille's arms were around Pierre's neck, his around her waist, his lips were on hers.

Suddenly all the constraints Mireille had felt through living in this hostile new world of the Mohawk village slipped away. She returned his kisses, pressed herself to him. Her lovely new deerskin dress was discarded, and the feel of his skin against hers, his body muscled and hard, was the only thing that mattered. She ached for him. In the crimson glow of the moon she mounted him, driving his manhood deep within her, trembling with arousal as his hands fastened on her breasts.

It was she who reached climax first, and she cried out in pleasure, raising her head and shoulders like some pagan goddess crying to the mother moon. She felt desperation, satisfaction, fear and love all rolled into one, and when it was over, she lay in his arms, wanting nothing else in life. This was enough; what she had been created for.

She regretted nothing, asked for nothing. What if she and this man could never return to Trois-Rivières or to France, what if he was considered an enemy by his people, to his people? He was her man, her husband. She wanted no other.

Charles read the letter again. *Diable!* His letter to Uncle Alain must have crossed with this one, and he didn't like the tidings this one brought. He read it again. Uncle Alain must somehow have got wind of where Mireille had fled and had had her made a ward of the King. How had that been possible, Charles wondered, and what exactly did it mean for him? The King might have her marriage to Pierre Charbonneau set aside—and might bestow her hand elsewhere. The whole thing would be made easier if Pierre Charbonneau were dead—easier for Uncle Alain, but not easier for himself.

This was going to take some thinking about, some fresh planning, and above all the speedy return of Mireille from the Indians. Strangely, he was convinced she was still alive, but how could she be rescued? If only he were restored to health! He cursed the savage who had laid him low.

Somehow, anyhow, this latest development must be turned to his advantage. The difficulty was—how?

Charles closed his eyes and put his mind to the problem, despite the pounding ache that never seemed to go away. He meant to have Mireille, and her money and property. It should have been his by right.

It would be his. Yes, even if Pierre brought her back, his speedy demise could be arranged somewhere along the way . . . The glimmerings of an idea began to form in his mind. Yes, it might work . . . He started to plan very carefully.

CHAPTER THIRTEEN

THE HARVEST FEAST began with the beating of the drums. At first Mireille was frightened. Their pounding was fierce against her ears, but everywhere there were smiling faces. It was, as the slave had said, a happy occasion, for they were celebrating the bounty of the Spirits. The cellars of the longhouses were stuffed full of food—great quantities of maize, beans, potatoes, squash, and onions, together with dried meat and smoked fish. Enough food for the long winter—enough food to withstand a seige.

The fortifications, too, in the weeks of September had taken shape. The village was enclosed by a quadrangular, triple wall and the wood palisades that comprised it were higher than a man. There were four strong bastions at the corners, all nearly completed now. Pierre seemed to regard it with some pride, and Mireille wondered how he could, when it was raised against his own people. She supposed it was because it was the invention of his mind, and there must be some pleasure in that. Certainly the men of the tribe boasted about it, telling each other and their womenfolk that Andaraqué was safe against any attack by the French or by anyone else. When the French came—if the French came—they would be defeated. That thought made Mireille very uneasy.

Pierre would not talk about the future, about what might happen. 'Wait until it does,' he advised.

Mireille found no comfort in that: it seemed to her that the days ahead would be filled with troubles. Still, for tonight, she determined to be cheerful, to smile. There was, after all, a good deal to be thankful for.

They were still alive, and well fed, adequately housed.

In fact, she had never felt healthier. The outdoor life suited her. Her skin had turned a lovely golden brown, which with her blond hair was very striking. Her deerskin dress set it off to perfection. She had worked in the fields with the other women gathering in the crop, and with the help of the slave, now spoke very passable Mohawk.

In many ways the life of the Indian women was freer than that of a Frenchwoman. They wore only the minimum of clothes, no long skirts, no stays, no tight-fitting collars or waists. Moccasins were comfortable, almost like walking barefoot. In the longhouses, it was a matriarchal society. White Feather was the leading woman in Mireille's longhouse, and since she gave the girl her full approval and friendship, she was accepted by all. Small Squirrel and Silver Badger were as often at Mireille's heels as at their mother's, and she found she loved them equally. They were so open and lively that it was easy to become fond of them.

To Mireille's considerable surprise, the women of the tribe had a real voice in the affairs of the village, and their voices were listened to respectfully in the clan meetings that at first she had found interminable. Since mastering the language, however, she found the proceedings much more interesting. She supposed there would be much talk tonight.

There she was right. Everyone had something to say about the harvest. White Fox thanked the Great Spirit of the Waters for the abundance of the catch of white fish and shellfish. 'It is a sign of favour towards our people,' he assured his audience.

Large One spoke more simply. 'The deer walked out of the thickets towards us, the bear gave themselves up to our arrows.' That met with a roar of approval at his humbleness, when all knew he was a mighty hunter.

White Feather praised the fruitfulness of the earth, which helped the women to grow the corn and produce the babies who would one day be the warriors and maidens of the tribe.

Brown Bear was rapturous about the size of a pumpkin. 'As round as a woman's belly in the ninth month, as smooth as a maiden's skin, as ripe as a warrior's desire . . . ' She went on as though she had tended it herself from the time it was a tiny seed, when everyone knew it was the work of slaves and not of Brown Bear.

As the talking went on, so did the circulation of food: clams, oysters, mussels, shad, bear meat, roasted deer, corn porridge (which Mireille disliked), corn bread, honey, and a drink which was something like wine. She could not decide whether this was made from honey or from corn, or even a combination of the two. At any rate it was unexpectedly pleasant, and was passed freely among them. Even the children had some. She noticed one of the young braves pouring something into a jug of this beverage from which several of them were helping themselves. Berries and nuts and apples completed the repast, and then the men smoked their tobacco pipes.

The feast was interspersed with dancing and ceremonies. In one of these, some of the adolescent boys were given names.

'New names as braves,' Pierre explained. 'Childhood names are forgotten now. These are their names as men. Look, there's Running Deer's younger son. He's to be called "Man Who Sees".'

Mireille wanted to know why.

'Something to do with his initiation into manhood. He must have distinguished himself somehow by seeing what no one else had eyes for.'

'What sort of initiation?' Mireille asked, under cover of the beating of the drums and the sustained clapping of hands which greeted each new name.

'Every boy has to prove himself at hunting, fishing and handling a canoe, and, more than that, he has to be brave and resourceful and manage to come to terms with the Spirits of the earth and the heavens by fasting and praying.'

Mireille was surprised by the serious way Pierre spoke. He seemed to believe in the Indian ritual, even to approve it. Of course, she reminded herself, he has lived among them a lot longer than I have. He knows their customs, the way they think.

The youngsters with the new names grouped together near the large outdoor fire on a bare piece of earth. 'The stomping ground,' Pierre whispered. 'The dance explains some of the trials they had to undergo.'

Mireille watched carefully. To her eyes, there seemed a good deal of pounding of feet and shaking of knives and clubs, but she supposed that defending themselves and frightening and attacking the enemy must be a necessary part of a warrior's training. At any rate, there seemed to be nothing as fearsome about these boys as there had been in her first glimpse of White Fox.

The dance of the newly-fledged braves was followed by one of the maidens. They were girls of thirteen or fourteen, Mireille judged, and it was plain to see that theirs was a mime of girls changing to women. It began with downcast eyes and childish games and progressed to slow steps and glances from sparkling eyes in the direction of the warriors.

Honeybear was one of their number. She was indeed very pretty in a white deerskin dress with very elaborate beading and a pattern worked on the skirt in porcupine quills. Her hair was braided on top of her head in a style Mireille herself often wore. She did not know whether to be flattered or insulted by this imitation. It certainly suited Honeybear, and Mireille could not help noticing the look of plain invitation the young maiden directed at both Blue Feathers One and Two. It made her feel quite ancient.

Every member of the tribe had a turn at being included in a dance on the stomping ground. Even the slaves swirled to the rhythm of the drums, miming enormous burdens, loads too great to carry. This was greeted with laughter and applause, and no sort of rancour on either side. After it, Mireille saw Brown Bear serve her slave with a great slice of bear and a full cup of the wine.

She had no time to reflect on the complexity of their strange customs, for her hand was taken by White Feather, and she was raised to her feet and led to the stomping ground with many of the other women. As she fitted her feet as best she could to the drum-beat and the steps of the others, she was carried along by the theme. Clearly it was calling upon whatever Spirit they worshipped for fertility. In fact it reminded her of a French village dance that the girls did at harvest time.

Mireille understood very well the implications of the female chant which ended the dance, if all the words were not plain to her. She, too, cradled an imaginary baby in her arms and felt Pierre's eyes upon her suddenly. Did she want his child? Not here, her inner voice cried out, and yet there was something deeply primitive and throbbing in the glance they exchanged, in the emotions which the gyrations of the dance had raised in her. She sank beside him again, her head on his shoulder, and saw that many of the Indian wives were sitting beside their men in the same pose.

The moon tonight was paler than the harvest moon of late August, but it was round and full and golden. They would sleep out tonight, all of them. Mireille knew that. The slave had explained to her that it was the custom after the harvest feast. She had said, too, that a child conceived at this time would have good fortune. Mireille had brushed that aside and asked about the maidens.

'The maidens sleep together tonight. No man must touch them under this moon.'

Recalling those words of the slave, Mireille found herself glancing at Blue Feathers One and Two. They were glaring at each other. Was this a night, she wondered, for the two braves to settle things among themselves, to come to blows? She shivered and looked away. It was no concern of hers.

There was now an air of finality about the ceremonies. True, the old men and women were still having their fling. They had been applauded, but a few elders were still moving to the persistent drummers, more to show they could, than to recall past glories. They were mostly old men. The old women were gathering the children together, seeing they slept quietly by the fire.

Couples had begun to slip away into the woods. Pierre took Mireille by the hand, and they made their way by a forest path to a hidden place where fallen leaves had made a natural bower. The drums were softer now, distant and seductive, and it was very peaceful as they sank into the bower, the stars bright in the sky.

Mireille breathed deeply of the quiet night, Pierre's arm about her. She could not share the silence. Her heart was beating to the compelling thunder of the drums, the thunder of her own blood. She was a woman tonight, a woman who wanted what every woman wanted and needed, a man to hold her and make demands upon her compliant body.

Pierre understood the mood of the night, the graceful curve of her arms raised to him, the invitation of her lips. The banked leaves were as enveloping as any feather-bed, the air warm and balmy. They made pagan love on that pagan shore beneath the pale moon. It was almost as ritualistic as the wild dance of an hour ago. Mireille felt compelled in a strange way to invite Pierre to pour himself into her, to suck him dry, to be the essence of woman.

When, spent and satiated, she would have slept, he held her from him for a moment. 'It is a fortunate child fathered by the earth's bounty,' he whispered in her ear.

She smiled, well content if it should be so, and settled against him, eyes closed.

'Nay, we must talk,' he added, 'while we have the chance.' He spoke in French and very softly. 'It is time to think of what must be done now.'

'What do you mean?' She did not want to talk about the future, but she recognised the steely quality of his voice, and sighed, and listened.

'We can't stay here much longer. My work is nearly done. When the French come, it would be better to be somewhere else.'

'Where?' Mireille sat up. She could hear no sound save the faint rustling of a breeze through denuded branches. She was uneasy.

'We could go to the English in New York—that's what they call it now. It was New Amsterdam when the Dutch had it.'

She had no interest in the English—or the Dutch. She just wanted to sleep in Pierre's arms. 'Why should we go to the English?'

'Because we must.'

'Why can't we go back to Trois-Rivières?'

'Because I would be arrested. You know that! I fancy you don't want that to happen, any more than I do?'

'No, of course not—but the English—I don't like the idea. They're enemies.'

'We're not at war with them at the moment,' Pierre said. 'There's a treaty between us of peace. From New York, we could get a passage to London and then to France. I have still some friends at court. They could approach the King, ask for a pardon. You have lands in France. It might take money in the right quarters.'

Mention of her lands chilled Mireille. Pierre had said he wanted none of them, but now he was claiming them. She tried to push the thought away. She wanted him a free man, didn't she? He had a right to what was hers. It was unworthy of her to hold that against him.

He went on with his plans. Plans he had made without consulting her—plans he expected her to fall in with.

'We'll go by canoe. I brought one here. White Fox will surely give us an escort, and furs to trade, fine furs for the work I've done for the village.'

It was cut and dried as far as he was concerned, all thought out.

Why could she not bring herself to say Yes? It was obviously expected of her. 'How far is New York?' she asked. 'Will they accept us there?'

'I don't know.' There was amusement in his voice. 'I have no way of telling the future. We must throw ourselves on their mercy.'

'And if they don't show mercy?'

'What's the worst they can do to us?' Pierre countered. 'Arrest us as spies? Very unlikely. We'll have furs to bargain with. You, my Golden One, will tell your story of abduction by the Mohawks, and the escape from their clutches. Why, when you turn your eyes upon them and enumerate your adventures, they'll be willing to help you to the last man! After all, you speak their language.'

Mireille was not convinced. It seemed to her that a good deal of the success of this plan depended on her concocting a tale of lies and half-truths. She wondered that Pierre could suggest such a thing.

'I'll put it to White Fox,' Pierre went on blithely, assured of her compliance. 'It's our best plan, our only plan. Sometimes retreat is the only course of strategy to be followed. You must see that.'

To Mireille, it seemed more like running away, and she longed to say so.

Pierre lay back against the leaves, the matter settled to his satisfaction. His breathing was even. Sleep had overtaken him. But Mireille shivered and pressed herself close to his body for warmth, for comfort. She drifted into dreams of prison bars and stormy sea-crossings.

Shortly she woke with a start, cold, in the first faint light of dawn. Was that a cry she had heard, a woman's cry of protest—or had she just imagined it? Had it come from her own lips, her own nightmares causing it? The hairs rose on the back of her neck. There was only silence. It had seemed so real, so frightening. Was it perhaps an omen, a warning? She tried to sleep again, pulled on her dress and cowered beside Pierre, the memory of that strangled cry strong in her ears.

She listened to the noises of the forest, willing them to tell her if there was anyone there, anyone lurking in the half-light. There was nothing but the lonely screech of an owl, the barking of a fox in the distance, and near at hand the scurrying of some night creature, hunting or being hunted.

In the morning when the ordinary activities of the day had begun again, albeit later than usual, the women bending over the cooking-pots or grinding corn, the children playing around them, the men stretching and taciturn, scratching themselves, all eloquence of the evening before disappeared with the festivities, Mireille became conscious of an item of news being passed from one to the other. She did not know who started it or where it came from, but she picked up the whisper, 'One of the braves had been found dead down by the little stream—they're bringing in his body.'

Suddenly the women came out of the longhouses, the children quiet before them, to meet the men carrying the dead warrior in procession. Mireille had not expected to know him, but with a shock of horror she saw it was Blue Feather Two. He had been stabbed. Was it his cry she had heard? She shook her head. It had been a woman's cry.

There was another woman's cry now, as Blue Feather Two's mother recognised her son. His father stood as one turned to stone, and then asked quietly in the hush that followed, 'Who has done this evil thing?' His eyes swung round the circle of men. 'This was no enemy attack. One of you is guilty.'

There was utter silence.

Mireille, used to the Indians' stoic ways, half expected impassive expressions on every face. True enough, faces were impassive, but all swung in one direction—towards Blue Feather One.

He licked his lips, his face paled, his roached head

shook. 'It was an accident,' he stammered. 'It was the drink.'

'How can that be?' they asked, surrounding him in a tight circle, menacing, expectant.

The murdered man's mother broke from the circle and raked his face with the nails of her right hand. She was restrained by her husband, and by White Fox's voice. 'Let him speak. Let him say how it happened.'

The men carried Blue Feather One forward to the stomping ground, and, in circle formation, they all squatted on the ground, waiting.

The whole sorry story came out. Blue Feather One stood before them and told it, looking a very young man. Some brave had had a bottle of brandy, with which he had spiked the wine. Both Blue Feathers had had too much, and, inflamed by it and by their jealousy, had fought to the death.

At this revelation about jealousy—which could not have come as much of a surprise—Blue Feather Two's mother shot a look of hatred towards Honeybear, who was standing near. The girl threw her arms about her own mother and hid her face. There was silence for a few minutes then, as all deliberated, keeping their eyes fixed on the ground.

Mireille did not know what to expect. The penalty for murder must be the death of the murderer, she supposed. That was French law. So she was astonished when the murdered man's father spoke out.

'The price—you all know the price. My son's blood calls for justice.'

There was a mutter of approval.

It was White Fox who looked round the circle and announced what appeared to be a unanimous verdict. 'Ten wampum belts must be paid to the murdered man's family.'

Mireille drew in her breath. 'Ten wampum belts.' Had she heard aright? Was a man's life measured solely in terms of money? Seemingly it was so. There were nods of assent all round.

Blue Feather One's family looked as sick as he did, but they made no protest.

'Is that all?' Mireille whispered to Pierre in rapid French.

'It's probably all they possess,' he replied.

'That's not what I meant. Is there no other punishment?' She was shocked, stunned by what she considered to be the lightness of the sentence. She had believed the Mohawks to be the fiercest of tribes.

'It is their custom. It is enough,' was all Pierre had to add. 'Wait and see what a punishment it is. It doesn't stop with the sentence.'

Mireille turned away from him, wondering yet again that he could accept so completely the Indian ways. He thought as they did, acted as they did. Go to New York—yes, that was what an Indian would do. Her faith in Pierre wavered. She was unsure of him, unsure of herself in relation to him. She knew in her heart that her cousin Charles would never allow her to be imprisoned. But still, he wouldn't hesitate to have Pierre gaoled.

The temptation to disagree with Pierre's plans went round and round in her head throughout the next few days. She seemed to be standing outside herself, observing Pierre, observing the Mohawks. There was a longing in her for her own kind, for her own people.

Strangely, Silver Badger—who had avoided Pierre up to this time—began to follow him about, and Mireille was rent with sudden jealousy to see father and son so completely together, so in tune and comfortable with each other.

'It is good to see, is it not?' White Feather asked her. 'A father and son should be close.'

Mireille only nodded, wondering anew at the Indians' alien ways. White Feather seemed quite prepared to share Silver Badger's affections. Well, she could not!

She did not know whether Pierre had spoken to White Fox about his plans for New York. A wall seemed to have grown between them—a wall she could not surmount, a wall inside herself.

Tribal events overtook her before she could come to terms with her own feelings. The funeral of Blue Feather Two was an event attended by all. His body was put to rest in the tribal burial-ground some distance from the village. The murder price was paid over that very day, and publicly. Part of it was in actual wampum belts, part in cattle, three horses and a cow.

This changed the status of both families. One became rich, the other poor. Mireille began to see how the punishment might have a basis in reason.

Blue Feather One wore an angry, sheepish expression. Honeybear would have nothing to do with him.

'It doesn't necessarily mean she doesn't like him any more,' the slave explained, 'or that she preferred the other, but he won't be able to pay the bride-price now.'

However practical Honeybear's viewpoint, Mireille found it cynical in the extreme.

It was a message which wouldn't be lost on Blue Feather One, the slave was sure. 'He'll attend to it in the quickest way he can—the only way.'

'How?' Mireille demanded.

'He'll raid an enemy village and take some horses for himself.'

Whether Mireille believed this statement or not, the next morning proved the truth of the slave's prophecy. Blue Feather One and one of his brothers rode in in triumph leading several ponies.

'There, didn't I tell you?' the slave asked. She shook her finger in front of the French girl's face. 'But there's more trouble. They've killed in the doing of it.' There was a great deal of relish in her expression.

'Isn't that what happens in a raid?' Mireille was puzzled that this seemed a consideration.

'Yes,' the slave grunted. 'What's an enemy for, except to be killed or brought back as a prisoner—as I was myself? But it's worse than that,' she added darkly.

'Worse—how? You mean they'll attack in return?'

'Trouble,' the slave muttered. 'There'll be trouble. It's

the one they've killed who'll make the trouble.'

Mireille was getting impatient with all these hints, and she shook the slave by the shoulders. 'What do you mean?'

'They've killed a white man—an English soldier.'

'They can't have,' Mireille protested.

'Little you know,' was the sharp retort. 'It'll be trouble for you, too. The English soldiers were staying in that village for some hunting. They won't take this lying down. And I'll tell you something else, too. White Fox won't be helping you and your man to get away to New York. Not if it means that angry English soldiers will soon be here.' She stepped out of Mireille's reach nimbly.

The girl's heart sank. It was one thing for her to make up her mind against New York; it was another to have it made up for her. She would gossip no more with this woman! She went to Pierre with the story.

'Yes, she's right,' he told her. 'Trust the slaves to know first! It'd be too dangerous for us to try for New York now.'

'Why?'

'Think of it,' he advised. 'There's only a small party of soldiers in that hunting expedition, but they and the men of the robbed village will want revenge. The defences around Andaraqué will hold them off, but if we ventured out, they'd be waiting for us. No, no, we stay put—at least for a while.'

Mireille was forced to see the sense of that, but she railed at it just the same. 'It's always just wait, wait, wait with you—always wait and see! I'm tired of waiting,' she blazed at him.

'Tired or not,' Pierre blazed back. 'You'll have to content yourself with waiting! There's no other way. Don't take out your temper on me! It's just the way things are.'

'Things can be changed!' Mireille's anger rose in her. 'Things could be changed, if only you went about changing them instead of falling in with everybody else's plans.'

'Don't be ridiculous,' he laughed at her. 'You don't know anything about planning or fighting. We'll wait. The time will come for action. Just be ready for it.' He stalked away from her, calling over his shoulder, 'Stop behaving like a spoilt child!'

That was the last straw, to be dismissed with a laugh! Mireille watched him go, her feelings churning within her. Why was he always so sure of himself, so sure that he was right and that she knew nothing? Surely, if they had the courage and the spirit to go now, they'd get away safely enough? She thought to call him back and suggest it, but in his present mood he would only laugh at her again. She'd show him. Yes, she'd show him that it was perfectly possible to get away! If she could once prove her point, he'd listen—and then, maybe, he'd act.

She knew where the canoes were kept. If she could get provisions to his canoe, and perhaps some of the furs they slept on as well, Pierre would surely be convinced that escape to New York was still possible. It was bound to take time for the attacking party to plan their pursuit, and even if they did come, they would go back pretty promptly when they saw the walls, the solid walls Pierre had built.

Mireille began to plan her strategy very carefully, smiling to herself. It would not be so difficult. There were still women working in the fields behind the village. She could say she was taking them something to eat, and then slip down to the beach with the food.

Yes, the simplest plan was best. There was no time like the present. She hurried towards the longhouse.

CHAPTER FOURTEEN

MIREILLE FOUND NO difficulty at all in carrying out her plan. No one questioned her about the store of food she took from the cellar. She even found a leather bag large enough for the dried meat and smoked fish, the corn bread and the apples and nuts which she selected.

There was one moment when Small Squirrel and Silver Badger asked to come along with her on her errand, but she soon shooed them away with promises of playing with them later.

Really, it was all very simple. Men made such a fuss about things! They got ready for the journey or for a war with such ceremony, such preparation. All it needed was clear thinking, planning, and swift action.

She deposited her bag of provisions close to the shore, hidden in a convenient bush. She looked around carefully towards the trees, and could detect no movement at all. For an instant she thought she caught a glimpse of white, but decided it was only a feather fluttering to the ground. The woods were very still in the afternoon sunshine.

Boldly she went back through the trees to the longhouse and to her own section of shelf. Which furs to select, she wondered, and then decided quickly to take them all. There was a lovely beaver blanket which should fetch a good price. The fox-skins were superb. The bearskin was a bit heavy—she might have to make a separate trip with that. She bundled the rest together, deciding to take the bearskin first.

Again she made the trip to the beach without any trouble, though it seemed to her that there was a different sort of atmosphere in the woods, now. For the first time, she felt nervous. Of course, it couldn't be anything except that she had begun to worry just a little about Pierre's reaction. What if he refused anyway, and she had to take all this back? She would feel a fool. Perhaps it might just be more sensible to seek him out and show him what she had already accomplished.

She went in search of him again, and discovered that the women and children had started to return to the village proper—to the village buildings enclosed by the new walls. There seemed no panic in their purposeful approach. They were not running or looking alarmed. Yet they had the children firmly by the hand and there was no dallying.

'What is it?' she asked the slave. 'Why is everyone coming within the walls?'

The slave gave her an abstracted look, clicking her tongue. 'Have you seen Small Squirrel? White Feather asks.'

'I saw her with Silver Badger in the longhouse not long since,' Mireille replied. 'Why—why does she want to know?'

'Because a British soldier has been seen coming this way.'

Mireille's breath caught in her throat. 'Does that mean there's to be an attack? Are the Indians from the other tribe with him?'

'Probably, but they have the cunning to remain hidden. He does not.' The slave glided away. 'I'll tell White Feather. She won't need to worry and search outside.'

Mireille thought no more about the children, but went to the corner bastion where she had last seen Pierre. White Fox was with him, and several of the other men. This was no time to tell him about her preparations for the journey. It would be better, she judged, noticing the grave faces, to do as Pierre was always advising, and wait. No one was likely to miss the food, and the bearskin might just pass unnoticed until such time as she could explain its absence.

She lingered, trying to get closer to hear what the men were saying, but they were in a tight little group and, try as she might, she could not get near enough.

She was joined by Brown Bear and her slave. 'The English soldier will talk first,' said Brown Bear. 'That is their way.'

'Is it?' asked Mireille, interested, and curious too, if that was the way the French army would proceed when and if they arrived.

'The Englishman will make demands,' Brown Bear confided. 'I have come to hear what he has to say.' She settled herself on a patch of grass, content to wait.

Mireille found no such comfort for herself. She stood close to the wall, looking out through the chinks, which permitted a restricted view. She began to wish she had not taken matters into her own hands. What if one of the hostile tribe had come upon her in the woods? She shivered at the danger she had courted. She waited, half dreading it, the arrival of the English soldier. She supposed it would be an officer. Would he speak through an interpreter from the other tribe?

By the time the parleying party approached, most of the inhabitants of Andaraqué had gathered in the area, safe behind the walls.

There was no more than a grunt of anticipation from the assembled crowd when the first glimpse of the red army uniform presented itself to their eyes. The British officer strode confidently into view, followed by six of his men, muskets at the ready. A straggle of Indians followed, keeping prudently to the cover of a clump of trees.

'I have come so that a wrong may be righted.' The English officer raised his voice as he alone came to the perimeter of the wall.

Running Deer, who was standing beside White Fox, translated this quickly into the Mohawk language.

The British officer watched impassively while this was going on and White Fox was issuing instruction for a reply.

'The officer is welcome inside to talk.' Running Deer's English was heavily accented, but clear in meaning.

'We can talk here,' was the uncompromising answer, 'where all may hear. The people of Andaraqué have always been allies of the British army. I know they wish to remain so. I have a simple request to make.' He paused.

A halting rendition followed from Running Deer. Impatiently, White Fox signalled to Mireille to come to him.

'Two pairs of ears will be better than one,' he declared. 'Listen carefully.' He snapped his fingers as he spoke to her, then turned to Running Deer. 'Tell him to make his request.'

Running Deer's words were not quite so abrupt, as he dwelt on the long friendship of Andaraqué with the white men.

The request came swiftly and in the form of a command. 'I am Major Ashton, and on behalf of the British people and our great sovereign over the water, I demand that the Mohawk warrior who killed one of my men last night be surrendered to me for punishment and retribution.'

A stir that was almost a sigh went through the ranks of the squatting Indians.

'It was a command, was it?' White Fox turned to Mireille for confirmation. She could only nod.

'Tell him we deal with wrongdoers in our own way,' White Fox instructed. 'There can be no question of handing over one of our braves.'

When this answer was conveyed to the Major, his anger was clear. His voice was cold. 'What does White Fox propose to do? We will wait and see what justice he dispenses.'

This met with a blank refusal from White Fox, and a stirring speech which lauded self-government, and non-interference from allies.

To Mireille's ears it sounded better in the Mohawk tongue than the English. It didn't satisfy Major Ashton.

'Tell him the tribe who accompany him have always been our natural enemies. We have often raided them before—and may again. Ask why our white brothers make friends of them.' White Fox tried a different approach.

This time Major Ashton became as flowery in his reply as any Indian. 'The white man wishes peace with all his red brothers. Let us all smoke the pipe of peace after justice has been done. White Fox knows—as I know— as the great British King across the sea-knows—that a man's followers sometimes shame him by their actions, put him in an impossible situation. Let White Fox show his wisdom and his great qualities as leader by giving up this evil wrongdoer. He cannot wish to protect him.'

Mireille had to supply a few words for Running Deer, and she saw White Fox's face darken as the meaning became clear.

There were grunts of disapproval and anger from the listening tribe. None of them even so much as glanced at Blue Feather One and his brother sitting a little apart from the others.

'Our justice is ours and ours alone!' Running Deer translated the reply in a strong voice.

'Tell us about your justice,' countered Major Ashton. 'Will this miscreant be put to death?'

Blue Feather One's father shook his fist at the speaker. The rest of the tribe shook their heads.

'That is our decision,' White Fox was firm.

'Then think well of your decision, brother Fox. We hear the French are marching against the people of the Five Nations. A great fleet is even now being assembled at Québec. Scouts say there are boats and canoes making ready—so many boats that a man might walk on them from one side of the mighty Saint Lawrence River to the other. The army is assembled—not only the army but the French settlers, too, and many, many red scouts. They mean to raze Andaraqué to the ground.

Will White Fox then turn to his English brothers for help?'

'If he did,' White Fox retorted, 'would they help him? They have signed a treaty of peace with the French. The Mohawks do not fear their coming. Let the British officer look about him. What does he see? I will tell him, since his eyes do not. Her sees a well-protected village, and a tribe which means to protect itself, a tribe which knows how to fight for its rights.'

Of course the Major could see for himself how well defended the place was, how hard to overcome. Otherwise, Mireille mused, he would not have wasted his energy on talk.

He retired to confer with his companions, and the whole thing might have petered out then except for a sudden commotion in the rear of the opposing Indians' ranks.

Mireille strained to see what was causing it. At first she could see nothing. Then, with a shock of horror, she realised that there were two children there, prisoners of the enemy. The children were Small Squirrel and Silver Badger. They were deposited in front of the British commander.

A lengthy consultation followed in plain view of the Andaraqué watchers. White Feather stood as one in a trance, her hand to her face. The other women tried to make her sit down, to speak.

A horrified Mireille asked herself if they could have followed her into the woods. But she had sent them away. Yes, but there had been that instant when she had thought she'd seen a falling feather. Oh God, if she should be responsible! She paled at the very notion. White Feather's daughter, Pierre's son! She saw the expression on Pierre's face and could not even go to him, or reach out her hand to him, so great was her guilt. She knew what was coming next even before Major Ashton came forward again, a child under each arm.

He set them on their feet beside him, in full sight of

all. He neither touched them nor commanded them to be still, but the two stood quietly, Small Squirrel with Silver Badger's hand in hers.

'We found them in the woods, picnicking on a bear-skin rug.'

Running Deer turned to Mireille for an explanation of 'picnicking'. She gave it, her heart cold. She could see the two children, delighted with themselves, reaching into the bag of food, sitting on the bearskin. It was her fault! Although she had pushed them away, they had followed her.

The Major had paused to let his words sink in. He went on, 'It is not our custom to fight with children, but you will understand that I want the man who killed my soldier. He, too, was only a boy, hardly older than these little ones. His mother will want to know how he died, and what I did to those who killed him. Come, let's make a sensible bargain.' His tone was soft and pleasant. 'Two lives for one. Take the children, send out the culprit. We ask no more than that.'

There was consternation, raging anger. A babel of voices rose up from the inhabitants of Andaraqué.

Major Ashton listened to the din, then spoke again. 'You will wish to talk it over. Do so. We shall withdraw with the children. If you wish to send a messenger to see the children are being treated well, do so at any time. No hand will be raised against any one of your village till nightfall. We must have an answer by then.' He departed with Small Squirrel and Silver Badger.

Nightfall was not so far away, Mireille told herself over and over, as the interminable talking went on. It seemed everyone had an opinion, men and women alike. And men and women were pretty evenly divided. The men were refusing to give Blue Feather One to the enemy. In their eyes, he had done what any of them might have done. He had been unfortunate in one thing only: he had killed a British soldier. What had the soldier been doing there? They had no quarrel with him. He had got in the way. It was an accident. There was no reason why Blue Feather One should die—and they had no illusions about British justice demanding his death. It was a matter of principle to stand firm, and regrettable about the children, but the women should have looked to their safety.

The women, with the exception of Blue Feather One's mother, wanted the children spared. Blue Feather One had not consulted them about raiding the enemy—and killing again. It was the second death, after all; the first had been a fellow-brave. It was impasse. All the talking in the world would not bridge the serious split which had developed between men and women.

Mireille listened to the arguments and the oratory with a sinking heart, and a feeling of guilt so deep she couldn't speak. The afternoon wore on. The sun slid lower in the sky, its heat lessening. Nightfall would find them still quarrelling, if this went on.

Gradually some of the women began to leave the conference. Mireille wondered where they were going, and why they chose to go. She stayed where she was, willing Pierre to speak up, to ask for his son's life. It was as he was doing so that the slave sidled up to her 'Come with me! White Feather asks it.'

So urgent was the command that Mireille obeyed at once. She would go to White Feather and tell her the whole story. It would be a relief to confess, whatever happened afterwards.

White Feather was not alone. Two others sat with her—Honeybear and Blue Feather One's mother.

'Will you help us?' White Feather asked, before Mireille had a chance to say anything at all.

She nodded dumbly and took White Feather's hand in hers.

'It may be dangerous!' White Feather clasped her hand.

Mireille looked into White Feather's eyes, the words of her guilt trembling on her lips. She didn't even utter them. She felt that White Feather knew, and tears fell down her cheeks.

White Feather wiped them away. 'We have a plan. The white officer said that a messenger might go to the children. Will you go?'

'Of course.'

'We may not be able to trust the word of such a man,' White Feather went on. 'It is a lot to ask. They might take you prisoner as well.'

A chill of fear went through Mireille's body. 'I will take the chance,' she said. 'What do you want me to do?'

'Speak to the children—and then speak to the officer. You are the only adult woman who speaks English.'

Mireille nodded. She was afraid, but she did not falter. It was right that she should go. 'What am I to say to him?'

'That we will deliver Blue Feather One to him.' White Feather's voice was stern and hard.

Mireille's breath caught in her throat. 'Will we? Can we? What will happen to us if we do?'

'That might be the most dangerous part of all,' White Feather told her. 'The men will be very angry. Do you still agree to go?'

Mireille licked dry lips. 'Yes, I'll do it. Tell me what I must do.'

'Good!' White Feather released her hand. 'Our plan is this. Honeybear will entice Blue Feather One to her side.' She put her finger to Mireille's lips. 'Never mind her reasons. She has them.' Mireille remembered that scream in the night, and looked at the girl's face. It gave nothing away.

'You have only to agree a place where the exchange can be made—out of sight and knowledge of the men,' White Feather went on. 'We thought, since they are all gathered at the front facing the forest, that it might be best to meet the officer at the furthest wall—if he is willing to group some of his men there with the children. There is a gap in the fence, and we will see that it is made bigger. Go now. Hurry! Do not tell White Fox what we are doing. I will attend to that while you go.'

The women got to their feet, and Mireille had no trouble at all in letting herself out of the small gate in the wall very close to where the men were gathered. They simply paid no attention to her, so engrossed were they in their own arguments.

Not until she was half-way over the no-man's land that separated the village from the opposing forces did sheer terror threaten to overcome her, and her confidence almost fled with her faltering feet.

It was Major Ashton himself who came to greet her. He led her to the children, and the pair of them embraced her.

'When will we go home?' asked Silver Badger plaintively. 'My mother will be missing me.'

'He's only a foolish boy!' Small Squirrel was holding fast to Mireille's hand. 'What he means is that he is missing his mother. Have you come to take us home?'

Before Mireille had a chance to answer, Major Ashton broke in, 'There aren't many fair-haired Indians. Where did you come from?'

'Never mind,' Mireille said very quietly. 'I've come to tell you that the women are willing to hand over the warrior who killed your soldier. Listen carefully, because they'll be suspicious if I talk to you too long.'

Fortunately he raised no objections. He listened and he agreed, only making sure that he understood. Then he strolled away so that it might not look as though she had anything of interest for him. By now, Mireille knew, a great number of eyes would be upon them. She hugged the children to her, and they were snatched away by one of the soldiers when they clung to her.

She wanted to protest, to take them with her, but she was led in the opposite direction towards the wall. There was one bad moment when, her back to the enemy, she hurried from the soldiers, half expecting every step to be her last.

Pierre met her at the gate. 'What possessed you to take such a chance?' He shook her.

'I had to.' She couldn't meet his gaze. 'White Feather

asked me. She wanted to go herself, but she was afraid she'd break down before the children and upset them all the more, but she wanted to know they were all right. I've come to no harm, as you can see,' she babbled, relief to be back overpowering her.

She might have said anything, told him the whole tale, but White Fox came to her. 'What did the Englishman say to you?' he demanded. 'What did you talk about?'

'He asked me where I came from. He said there weren't many blond Indians. He wanted to know what you were going to do,' she improvised.

'What did you tell him?'

'How could I tell him anything? I don't know what you mean to do. I went to comfort the children, and to relieve White Feather's fears.'

Mireille was very grateful that she needed to say no more, for White Feather came to her and began asking questions about the children. She told her what they had said, that Silver Badger was missing his mother.

White Feather turned tear-filled eyes on White Fox, but he did not allow her to plead her case. He stalked away, saying, 'I expect the Golden One to stay with me from now on.'

White Feather embraced her, and Mireille only had time for a whispered, 'Yes', before she followed White Fox.

Pierre accompanied her. 'He's angry, of course, that you went. He knows how the women feel, but he's pulled in two ways. He can't abandon Blue Feather One. You understand, don't you?'

Mireille sat beside White Fox, and had to tell her story again to the waiting crowd. She added a plea for the release of the Small Squirrel and Silver Badger, since she had everyone's attention.

She allowed her eyes to rove over her audience. Blue Feather One did not seem to be anywhere. Did that mean that the men had spirited him away, or he had gone to hide, fearing their judgment—or could it be that Honeybear had been as good as her word and enticed him to her? Mireille waited in a fever of impatience for something to happen as the light gradually faded from the sky.

The assembly of the men and women of Andaraqué had fallen silent, whether considering their verdict or waiting for the next move from their opponents, Mireille wasn't sure. They sat in small groups, the circle broken.

There was a stirring, a sigh which might have been a groan, from most of them when the two captured children were brought to the fence by the British Major. The Mohawks climbed the wall of the defences for a better view, Mireille too.

'Take a good look at these, your children, the future of your race,' he said. 'It may be your last look.'

The villagers were silent. The children spoke not a word, though Silver Badger managed a gesture that was not quite a wave, more a salute to the watchers on the top of the wall.

'Before nightfall, I said,' the Major went on. 'There isn't much more time. Be advised that we shall act as grey turns to dark.' He gave a signal, and the children were lifted bodily from beside him by two strong troopers. They were carried to the shelter of the trees out of sight of the watchers.

Mireille's heart was in her mouth. Now was the most dangerous time of all. Could she rely on the British officer to give up the children for Blue Feather One? If he proved false, three lives might be lost. She prayed with agonising fervour that the plan would work, that there would be no hitches, no betrayal. She wondered that Pierre could sit so quietly beside her, uttering no words about his son. Did he not want to rescue him? Did he grieve? She didn't know. Perhaps he, too, was praying.

The English officer had been regarding the walls of the fortifications. 'When I stand before you again, I shall expect your answer.' He strode back to the trees, and seemed to pass among the assembled men there.

'Now, now is the moment,' Mireille said to herself. 'He'll circle to the rear with Small Squirrel and Silver Badger. I must do something to distract attention from what is happening there.' She looked down at the ground. It seemed a long way away.

She took a deep breath and hurled herself down, crying out her alarm. Shaken, sobbing, she lay upon the earth. They all surrounded her, climbing quickly and neatly from their high perches.

Pierre scooped her up. 'What happened? How could you fall? Are you all right?' He carried her from the vicinity of the fence, and the crowd followed them.

Mireille heard a voice crying out in pain, screaming out. It was herself. 'My shoulder! Oh, my shoulder!'

Brown Bear pushed through the crowd to her. She bent over her, knelt beside her, her hands on the shoulder. The pain increased. As those hands did their work, Mireille could stand it no longer. She lost consciousness and the pain was no more. She came to, with only a dull throbbing where the unbearable pain had been.

'It's back in place,' Brown Bear smiled at her. 'It will be very sore for a few days. You must rest, and sleep a lot.'

'I shall carry you back to the longhouse,' said Pierre. 'What a fright you gave us all!' He lifted her in his arms.

'No!' said Mireille. 'What's that noise? What's happening? I must see what it is.'

So great was the urgency of her need to know what was going on that she would have crawled there herself, but Pierre carried her, and found her a place where the slight space between the logs permitted a peephole.

It seemed to her that all hell had been let loose. The villagers were screaming, the attackers shouting and jeering. She shook her head and glued her eye to the crack.

The British soldiers were carrying Blue Feather One high on their shoulders. Both sides were shrieking imprecations, one side in rage, the other in triumph. Mireille knew a moment of complete relief. The children were safe! She sagged in Pierre's arms, resting against the fence, and began to cry.

The rage of the men of Andaraqué reached her, pricking the bubble of her happiness. It was all about her. They might fall upon their enemies. God! What had she done?

She caught a glimpse of Blue Feather One's face. There was terror there. He was only a boy. She cried for him as well as herself, great sobs which shook her whole body. Could no one put a stop to this ugly business, this threatening riot? She added her screams to the others.

It was White Fox who brought sanity of a sort. Silently he raised his bow to his shoulder, and crouching on the topmost platform, out of sight of most of the would-be attackers, shot an arrow. Straight it flew—and true—into Blue Feather One. The boy crumpled onto those who carried him, blood spurting from the wound. He gave up his life without a sound.

White Fox's voice rang out. 'The Mohawks give justice to their own.'

Running Deer translated the quick words—not that there was any need. The action was clear enough to all.

The crowd was stunned into quiet. Fists were raised on either side of the fence, but no one questioned what had been done.

Blue Feather One's body was lowered to the ground. The soldiers moved back at a command from Major Ashton. The opposing Indians melted into the trees.

Only the British officer and the body were before the wall. He looked down at it, then up at White Fox, now standing on the ledge.

'Justice had been done, brother Fox. The children are back in your village. We return to ours. You will want to inter your warrior. I leave him for you.' He made a bow to them all, then turned swiftly on his heel and walked away, his back exposed to them.

No hand was raised against him, nor any voice on either side. There was finality in the very air they breathed—finality, and the dead waiting to be buried. How small Blue Feather One's body looked, lying on the ground, his hair still standing stiffly upwards in that roach.

As the enemy retreated without a backward look, Blue Feather One's mother and father let themselves out of the gate and stood above his body. The mother's keening cry broke out, filling the night with its haunting sound.

Mireille tried to shut it out of her ears, but was unable to until White Feather and the children reached her.

They put their arms about her, and Pierre hugged them all. He spoke to Mireille in French. 'I knew you were up to something when you went outside to them. How brave you were! I prayed you'd come back safely.' He hugged Silver Badger to him. 'Was it a good picnic?'

Silver Badger shook his head.

Mireille never heard his answer. She crumpled to the ground. She never knew either how tenderly Pierre carried her to the longhouse, the others trailing behind, White Feather supplying a bearskin rug for her to lie upon.

CHAPTER FIFTEEN

PIERRE FELT THE time had come for action, but there were several problems in the way. First, and most important, was Mireille, who was in no state to travel. Her shoulder was stiff and swollen, and she had developed a racking cough and a fever.

Perhaps it was just as well that she lay listless and exhausted in the longhouse, for the men had not forgiven her for the death of Blue Feather One. They laid all the blame for that at her door, although Pierre knew the original plan had not been hers. She had confessed to him her part in the children's capture and her feelings of guilt and responsibility. He had applauded her courage. She had brushed that aside, and told him how frightened she had been.

'There's no bravery if you're not afraid,' he assured her. She only smiled slightly at that, and asked what he would have done if she had not come back from that walk across to the enemy.

'Followed after you, of course,' he'd replied. 'Didn't I come here?'

She had held his hand at that. It seemed hardly the time to tell her that the plan he was now considering involved leaving her for a considerable length of time. He still felt the only sensible course of action was for him to leave Andaraqué and travel to New York. But he could not take Mireille. It would be too dangerous for her. As far as the English were concerned, she was a marked women. Her fame would have gone before her with the return of the soldiers to their base. They would hold it against her that she had been involved in a plot that had robbed them of their captive, and made them lose face before the other Indians.

No, he had to put that plan aside. He must remain, even though almost every day brought news of the progress of the French army against the Iroquois. He knew they had set out in boats this time—no more stupid marching through icy forests. Pierre estimated there must be over twelve hundred men on the move, for it was said that the original divisions had been reinforced with colonists. Certainly the fact of their new strategy suggested that the colonists had a clear voice in the arrangements. He decided that a fleet of three hundred boats of whatever small sort would be necessary to transport men and provisions along the waterways. It would be a sight to see! His heart stirred with the remembrance of past campaigns. It seemed that in this one he was destined to play a passive part. Worse than that, he must retreat. The thought of running away was repugnant to him, though he knew all too well that the man who runs away may live to fight another day.

Another factor in his hesitation was Silver Badger, his son. He had attached himself firmly to Pierre since his rescue, and followed him everywhere, a small silent shadow most of the time, imitating the way he walked, the way he stood. Blood calling to blood, he supposed. He smiled to himself. He had grown fond of the lad. He was a boy to be proud of. He had made no fuss when he'd stood with the English officer before the gates but had held himself proudly, uncomplaining, his hand in Small Squirrel's.

Vraiment, it was a teaser. What was best to do for Silver Badger? Leave him with his family, with the only people he had ever known? Pierre had a vision of that life through the eyes of a boy. The freedom of it—hunting, fishing, becoming a brave, living in the woods, on the rivers and the lakes. It was a life he loved himself. Ah, but it was bound to come to an end for the Indians. White men would see to that, however bravely and tenaciously the red men fought. Already the land was being parcelled up between English and French.

Pierre sighed. Was it a flaw in his character that he could see both sides? That was letting his mind slip away from decisions. In the long run, what was best for Silver Badger—to leave him or take him? Always supposing the choice was his. He had little to offer the lad at present. He might find himself in gaol back in Trois-Rivières!

It was White Fox who forced him into a course of action. He took him aside and offered him his pipe to smoke as they squatted on the ground away from the others. This was not a pipe of peace. That was clear from the start.

'White Fox and Red Fox are blood brothers,' White Fox began, taking a long puff himself as Pierre handed the ornately carved pipe back to him. 'But between brothers, there are sometimes differences.'

Pierre waited impassively for White Fox to come to the heart of what he wanted to say.

'There are many among the men of the tribe who hold the Golden One responsible for the dishonour of the tribe.' White Fox held up his hand for silence. 'That it was dishonour, I do not deny. Blue Feather One was surrendered to the enemy.'

Pierre puffed at the pungent tobacco again. 'My brother White Fox acted with great cunning and compassion. He turned defeat into victory. None may say that his arrow hesitated, that his vengeance was not swift. He gave the English officer no cause for satisfaction, the enemy Indians no chance to torture and revile Blue Feather. It was the work of a far-sighted man.'

White Fox permitted himself the ghost of a smile. 'My brother always had a silver tongue.' He puffed again at the pipe. 'My brother has a woman with special qualities.'

Pierre hid his surprise at this abrupt change of subject. 'Red Fox is prepared to follow her to the ends of the earth.'

'I hold her in high esteem myself,' White Fox passed the pipe again. 'She saved my life.' He patted his leg lightly. 'It healed well. There are those who do not look so kindly on her. They wish her to be punished for her part in Blue Feather's death. When the women heard that these others had spoken to me, they came to me and threatened all sorts of things.'

This was news to Pierre. 'What sorts of things?'

White Fox hedged round the subject. 'You know what women are—they say many things.'

'Yes.' Pierre puffed at the pipe, and waited.

'You will scarcely credit what they told me they would do. I have never known them so set against the men—and it was the men who wanted the Golden One punished.'

'Yes, indeed,' Pierre agreed. 'But what did the women plan to do?'

'They planned a terrible thing! 'White Fox shook his head. 'Such a thing as has never been known before. They said they would withhold themselves from their menfolk.'

Pierre exclaimed in wonderment, since that seemed to be expected to him. He hid a smile, marvelling that Mireille had produced such a united response from the women of the tribe. Of course it was themselves they were standing up for—their importance, and their children's. That was what the men had been unable to see in their own loyalty to Blue Feather One.

'They spoke as one woman,' White Fox confided. 'I had to listen and pay heed. There will be no punishments, no reprimands.'

Pierre handed the pipe to White Fox. 'White Fox has spoken with wisdom, with magnanimity. A chief must make decisions. The men will soon forget. More important things will claim their attention.'

'As my brother says. Red Fox may be interested to hear that the leaders of the French force have fallen ill. The commander has been seized by a spirit in his foot—he cannot move. The one they call the Governor suffers from griping claws inside himself. The next in command has come out in sores from the heavy load he is forced to carry. Truly, the *manitou* of the forest and the water is showing his power over the white men.'

Pierre frowned and translated the ailments into more prosaic terms. Commander Tracy he knew was subject to gout. The Governor, Courcelle, had an attack of the flux, and the other man was troubled with either boils or blisters. It might be all to the good for the French cause, for it would mean the colonists might take charge. Surely, that great fighter, Charles le Moyne, must be there from Ville Marie, and the Sieur de Repentigny from Québec. Pierre kept his face without expression. He had no wish to quarrel with White Fox.

'My brother need not fear the French force,' he said, 'He has the best fortifications in the district.'

'White Fox has no fears,' the Indian assured Pierre. 'The French will run from us in Andaraqué. My brother will be able to see that for himself, for he will remain with us. He would not, I know, be so foolish as to try to leave us and go to his countrymen. What use would our walls be then? He might be tempted to tell the soldiers the best places to attack, the easiest way in. My brother knows the strength of my warriors.'

Pierre drew in his breath sharply. 'What are you saying—that I am a prisoner here?'

'Would I say such a thing?' White Fox growled. 'My brother is an honoured guest. I wish to keep him near me.'

These words did not take Pierre in. The threat was implied: if he did not accept them at face value, he would be a prisoner. In effect, he already was. Someone would be watching his every move. 'My brother is kind to me,' he said softly.

If White Fox heard any note of sarcasm, he chose to ignore it and put his hand on Pierre's knee. 'My brother would do well to guard his woman carefully. There are those who wish her ill.'

Pierre received this warning in silence. If White Fox

gave it, it must be real. 'White Fox may be sure I will listen to his words.' He bowed his head. The audience was over.

Pierre sought out Mireille. She was looking no better, and Small Squirrel was sitting with her.

'She eats nothing,' the little girl complained. 'Brown Bear has sent her slave with a potion of herbs, and my mother has made soup for her. If she does not get better soon, the medicine-man must come to exorcise the Spirits which trouble her.'

'No!' said Mireille, propping herself up on one elbow. 'No medicine-man.'

Pierre was inclined to agree. If there were those who wished her ill, the fewer people who came with remedies the better. He looked out of the longhouse door. It had begun to rain. 'Best just to keep warm and to sleep.' He put his hand on her shoulder, sitting beside her. She did not look well, and it upset him.

She reached out to him. 'Pierre, can't we go-home—home to Trois-Rivières?'

So pleading was her voice that Pierre's heart contracted. 'Soon,' he agreed. 'Soon we shall go home. You must get better first.' He wondered that he could utter the words, that they didn't stick in his throat. When she turned her trusting eyes on him, it was all he could do not to run from the longhouse. He waited a few minutes until White Feather came to see Mireille.

Once outside, Pierre strode morosely to inspect the fortifications. He walked along the entire length of the walls. Yes, he'd done a good job—he tapped the wood with his knuckles—good, strong defences. His conscience smote him. They were erected against his own people. He ran his hand down the sturdy post that supported this length. There was no weak spot, no easy way in. The villagers could hold out for months. Their cellars were bulging with every kind of provision. They could withstand a seige, whatever its length.

The knowledge was bitter to his solder's mind. He could envisage too well the plight of any attackers. They would have no stores of food. They would be exposed to all sorts of weather as well as to injuries from arrows, muskets, boiling water poured from the walls.

For the first time, Pierre noticed that the fine rain had turned heavier, and he was getting soaked. The ground was muddy where he stood. He also noticed that he was not alone, for one of the braves watched him. It had begun! There was no escape. It was as White Fox had said: he would not be permitted to leave. They meant him to see how effectively he had built, how he had betrayed his countrymen. Yet what else could he have done, with Mireille to consider? Mireille and Silver Badger. He harboured no illusions as to how the Mohawks would have forced him to comply with their wishes. He had no thoughts about an attempt to escape, to avoid the consequences of this bloody wall. He hit it savagely with his hand, kicked at it. It stood firm, as he was sure it would. He had built it too well.

Pierre stood in the pelting rain for a long time, trying to exorcise his guilt, to find a way out. He hoped the French Army would never reach here—and hoped they would. The settlers needed peace, needed to be free from the constant threat of the Iroquois to their lives and their homes. The Indians had the right to their homes, too. It was his misfortune to be caught between two opposing forces—his and Mireille's.

There was no sense in standing here, he realised at last, becoming soaked to the skin. Cold and unbearably saddened, he went back to the shelter of the longhouse, the brave at his heels not bothering to conceal himself now. Mireille was no better.

Pierre's black mood lasted all that day and the next as the rain continued to fall, and a listless Mireille kept to her fur robes and her place on the sleeping-shelf. It was only with the sight of the sun on the third morning that he began to shake off his depression.

By mid-morning, despite Mireille's protests, he carried her out into the open air to a large boulder where he propped her up, the bearskin about her shoulders.

At first she slumped, huddling into the fur and coughing, but after a little the sun began to warm her, and Silver Badger came and stayed with them, pulling the bearskin over his head and peeping out, imitating the bear's growl and his stiff walk. Pierre was pleased to see Mireille begin to giggle and her eyes became alive again. Why, they might be any family enjoying the late October sunshine of an Indian summer.

News of the advancing French Army was brought to them by an excited slave. 'Two days ago, the French captured an Iroquois village,' she informed them.

'Are you sure? Was the fighting fierce?' Pierre asked.

She smiled, and laughed a bright laugh of triumph. 'There was no fighting at all! The Frenchman surrounded the place, and so frightening were their numbers, that the brave Iroquois left by the back as they came in at the front. What do you think of that?'

Pierre could not believe his ears. He asked for assurances that it was really so.

'Ask the runaways yourself,' the slave suggested. 'Two of them have come here for shelter. No doubt there'll be more of them. They may have lost their appetite for fighting, but they won't lose their appetite for eating—and the white men have burned the village to ashes, with all the food in it.'

Pierre left Mireille with the slave and the boy, and went off to hear the story for himself. Everywhere in Andaraqué the men were clustered in small groups discussing the unprecedented event, and boasting, too, that of course it could not happen there. He came upon one such circle where one of the runaways was holding forth. 'The French are as the sands of the shore, each one exactly like the next,' he declared to his audience. 'And they come in waves, like the angry waters. Their muskets fire as one.'

'You never heard their muskets,' one of his listeners interrupted. 'Did you not say that not a single shot was fired. Isn't that so?'

'It is so, but if they had fired, it would have been as one man and the noise would have split the heavens.'

The hearers chose to be unimpressed. 'Ah, but it didn't happen. If the French come, we shall know how to defend ourselves.'

'They put a spell on us,' the refugee said. 'When they reach here, you will see the might of their warriors and the magic *manitou* who protects them.'

The listeners brushed this aside. It was men—not Spirits, however powerful—who waged war. Pierre alone was willing to believe in the mesmeric effect of such a large force. He knew the Iroquois to be brave fighters, but he knew too that this European method of attack was not their style. The men of the Five Nations husbanded their men and their resources. They preferred the swift, stealthy, surprise attack. Hit and run was their ordinary procedure.

This first village had been burned to the ground, so hunger could be the biggest enemy of the Indians during the coming winter. Yes, this time the settlers must be in charge of the army. They would know the way to fight their enemy. One part of Pierre rejoiced in the knowledge, but the other was appalled by it. If it happened to Andaraqué as it had happened in the first village, children would die this winter for lack of food. He had seen this kind of warfare before—and what it brought in its wake.

He went to see White Feather. She had children. She might listen to him, when the men certainly would not. They were too busy boasting. White Feather heard him out politely, but it was only a few days later, after the similar abandonment of a second Iroquois village, that she paid any heed to his words. Then she sought him out again.

'It won't happen to us, of course, as it has happened to the others—not with our fine walls. But if it should, by some accident, Red Fox, what should we do?'

'Store food outside the village,' Pierre told her. 'In some secret place where your enemies are unlikely to find it. It will be a long winter. Your children will ask you for food, and you will have none unless you move quickly.'

Would it be seen by the French as another act of treachery on his part, he asked himself, as he became aware that the women were acting on his words. They were not informing their menfolk, he was amused to notice. How much food they managed to smuggle out he didn't know, nor did he enquire about its hiding-place. He said nothing to Mireille; better that neither of them know about it.

Pierre had enough to worry about where Mireille was concerned. She made scarcely any progress, and he began to despair of her recovery. What was the matter with her? Every time he spoke to her she had a new catalogue of symptoms. He began to wonder if the medicine-man might be able to cure her where all else seemed to be failing. He would ask White Feather what she thought.

Mireille was feeling wretched. She could not keep any food down, and her whole body ached. She wanted only one thing—to go home. Why would Pierre not name a day when they could start back? She knew she'd be better then.

In the last week, it seemed to her, everyone had been avoiding her, been keeping something from her. What was the matter with the women? She had done what they had asked of her, even a bit more, and they allowed her to lie here unattended. Even Pierre didn't stay with her. He was always down looking at his walls, talking to the other men. White Feather sent Small Squirrel and Silver Badger to her with bowls of soup and choice bits of meat, but she gave her precious little of her own company. Even the slave stayed away. They were busy, the children said. Busy with what? Mireille asked, and received no answer. She felt aggrieved.

It was an attitude of mind she had firmly adopted by the time White Feather one morning did come to her.

Even then, Mireille expected the Indian woman to sit beside her and coax her out of her black mood. But White Feather showed little sympathy, and made only the most perfunctory enquiries about her health. Instead, she said, 'Golden One, it is time you rose from your bed.'

Mireille, who had sat up prepared for the comfort of a long chat, allowed herself to slip down under the furs, even though the day was warm. 'I am ill,' she declared. 'Can't you see that?'

'Nonsense,' her caller informed her. 'You've recovered from your fall. What you feel now is only natural—what every woman feels in the first few weeks after she discovers she is with child. You'll feel better for being on your feet.'

Mireille gasped, 'How—how did you know?'

'Do you think you are the first woman ever to have a child?' White Feather's voice managed to combine comfort and scorn all at once. 'Come, dress yourself and get up! This has gone on long enough. It is plain that the baby didn't suffer when you fell.'

Mireille wanted to explain that she had been worried, that she wasn't ready for motherhood, that she was afraid for herself and the baby, that Pierre seemed to have no plans for returning home. The words trembled on her lips.

White Feather took her hand. 'You must be strong! You must fight for your child—as you fought for my children. When the French soldiers come, do you intend to be still lying there?'

Mireille sat up, her eyes huge in her pale face. 'Are they coming, White Feather? Will they soon be here?' She reached for her dress, not sure whether she was glad or sorry to hear this news. She slipped the leather over her shoulders, and allowed it to fall into place as she rose to her feet. A few tottering steps made her turn to the Indian woman for support.

'You are weak.' White Feather put her arm about the girl. 'You haven't been eating properly. You haven't been outside in days—but that's going to change. Here, try this dry corn bread. It will settle you, and give your stomach something to work on.'

Mireille's stomach heaved at the very sight of it, but she forced herself to eat and to go out into the fresh air. After a while, she began to feel a little better. White Feather let her rest on a tree-trunk for a few minutes, then she set her a few small tasks, tempted her to nibble an apple and some nuts, and Mireille found she was hungry. By afternoon, there was a little colour in her cheeks, and more than a little lift in her spirits.

Pierre came to see her, and did not even notice that she was up and about. His talk was all of the approach of the French army and of the non-existent resistance to its progress.

'What shall we do, Pierre?' she asked. 'Will you fight with the men of the village against our own French people?'

'No, I can't do that—nor can I leave. White Fox will not let us go. I wanted to tell you before, but I couldn't while you were so helpless. We must remain.'

Looking at his set, unhappy face, Mireille began to understand a little of the torment he was suffering. She sat down on the tree-stump and reached out her hand to him. 'What must we do?'

He sat beside her. 'I have failed you,' he groaned. 'It's as you said: I waited and waited, hoping for some miracle. The army is only a short distance from here. We are trapped.'

'There must be some way out?' Mireille still held Pierre's hand. She could not bear to see him so hopeless.

'What way?' Pierre withdrew his hand and gestured with it. 'If the fighting is desperate, the campaign long, how will I not seek to defend myself and you? If the village falls as the others have done, the French will walk in and arrest me for wounding your cousin Charles, with an added charge of building the fortifications here against them.'

'No!' Mireille was suddenly strong—strong as White

Feather had declared a woman must be. 'There will be a time when we'll be able to escape by stealth in the night, or when the Indians themselves leave. We'll live in the forest as they do, hide from the army, if needs be. They shan't take you.'

'Would you do that? Never go back home?'

'Yes.' said Mireille. 'You are my husband. I shall stay with you.'

Pierre looked up, his eyes ablaze. '*Vraiment,* I have married a real woman, a woman to be proud of, a woman to share the good and the bad!' He put his arms about her.

'Whatever happens, we stay together,' Mireille repeated.

It was right, Mireille felt, that they had come to value each other, to be so in accord, but it would be hard never to return to Trois-Rivières and their home.

She was surprised to see Pierre smiling. 'It begins to look, *ma chère,* that we must wait again to see what fate has in store, but with you at my side we'll pull through. I'm sure of it.'

Mireille found she could smile, too. She held Pierre close, striving to hide her fears from him. She was no longer a girl, after all. She was a woman. She had responsibilities to her man, to her child. That knowledge must be kept to herself for the present. She mustn't add to Pierre's burdens. Later she would tell him, and he'd be pleased. But now she hugged the future to herself. Hope lay there—and fulfilment.

Even as they were making their plans, they were interrupted by the slave. 'The French are coming!' She ran up to them, calling out the news. 'Come and see for yourself. You can hear the drums.'

The whole of Andaraqué rushed to the walls, the men with their weapons, the women gathering the children to them. Mireille was pulled along by Pierre. When he climbed to the topmost ledge for a better view, she kept her feet firmly on the ground among the women, and found a spyhole. No more climbing walls for her!

The noise of the drums was faint at first, but it resounded through the woods. Mireille felt that it beat to the beat of her heart, crying out the news, 'The army is coming, the army is here. All you who want to fight, now is the time.'

She looked at the other women. Their faces were blank. Did they hear the same message from the drums? They clutched the children closer, and looked at their men.

The men were brandishing axes, sharpening arrows. They were in position on the walls. There was a great deal of noise and yelling. The slaves had a large fire burning, and were heating water on it. Mireille shuddered at the thought of boiling water descending on the attackers. There was nothing she could do except watch and pray.

The terrible cry of the Iroquois rang out as with one voice, *'Cassee kouee!'* It was the first time Mireille had heard it, and it sent fear to her very bones. She saw that some of the braves had muskets and were priming them.

As the drums became louder and the first of the blue uniforms of the army came in sight, the people of Andaraqué became silent, unmoving. It seemed to her that a ripple of fear went through them all, stunning them, turning them to statues.

Mireille could never adequately describe afterwards the total effect of the arrival of the French army at the gates of the village. It was as though the waters of some giant sea had raced through the forest, bringing panic and terror to the beholders. Each line of men appeared as another wave. Each man was exactly the same as the one on either side of him. Each man had a musket at his shoulder. And the army drums cried out a fearful warning in a sudden crescendo of sound. No wonder other villages had surrendered, had fled!

Men jumped down from the walls, slithered down, fell down. Women turned to the back of the village, dragging and pushing their children. Mireille found herself pulled along with them, for a moment Blue Feather One's mother by her side.

'Get food!' the woman screamed. 'They'll burn the whole place and everything in it.' She pushed a leather bag into Mireille's hand and dragged her to the nearest longhouse, down into the cellar. 'Take what you can,' she screamed, and stuffed meat and fish from the cellar stores into another bag.

Mireille would have run from the place, but she saw the sense of taking food. She grabbed at some smoked fish, turning her back for an instant on the Indian woman.

She felt a sudden stab of pain as she was knocked to the ground, meat and vegetables from the next shelf falling with her, scattering themselves about her, and then a shout of triumph, of gloating, as Blue Feather's mother ran from the place, shutting the cellar door firmly on Mireille.

She fell back, panting, scared as never before in her life. She was trapped! All the food in the world, and she was trapped by her own greed, by her hope of survival! In the dark, she sank to the ground, knowing it was useless to try to open the cellar door. She had pushed against it, scraped her hands and arms in the struggle. She was a prisoner.

The army might never bother to look inside. They might set the whole place to the torch, burning her in it. She began to sob and to beat the ground. Even if they did look first, she would be taken prisoner, or worse. She trembled as she thought of the story of Marianne the Dutch girl, and how she had been used.

Where was Pierre? Pierre would come for her, but he didn't know where she was. No one knew that except Blue Feather One's mother, and she wouldn't tell. She had her revenge for her son's death. Mireille cried out at the unfairness of it. Blue Feather One had died a clean death with an arrow. She would die by fire.

She sobbed again, and shivered with the cold of the cellar. Where was Pierre? Why didn't he come? She would wait for Pierre. She screamed his name again and again. He would come. He must come.

CHAPTER SIXTEEN

PIERRE FLED WITH the others, the whole mass of seething, running Indians. At first he could see Mireille, her bright hair shining in the sun. He tried to fight his way to her, but it was useless. He was carried along by the crowd. Then the women increased their pace and she was borne further and further from him. Still, she could go nowhere except with the others. He would find her shortly, even though he could no longer see her.

As they reached the bottom end of the village and began to struggle through that far gate, he searched in vain for her, examining the stragglers first, then running among the trees, asking for her.

All denied seeing her after the first rush away, and as they were still intent on putting as much distance as possible between them and their enemies, they were not disposed to stop and talk.

White Feather was the most helpful. She said she had been near her, but when she turned her head after passing the longhouses, Mireille had no longer been there. She could not imagine where she'd gone. 'Perhaps she stopped to pick up a child or to help an old person?'

'Blue Feather's mother gave her something,' Small Squirrel suddenly volunteered. 'I saw her.' She repeated it stubbornly, but could not say what Mireille had been given, or think why Blue Feather One's mother would have given her anything.

Pierre searched for the woman, panting with exhaustion to try to find her. When eventually he did catch up with her, she stormed at his questions, telling him he was mistaken. Mireille was no friend of hers! She would have given her nothing! She escaped from his clutches, laughing. He was worried by the sound of her laughter and felt sure she had somehow done Mireille some harm. He must return to the village. He had the strongest feeling that she would be there.

He hesitated for a while at the back gate, then saw the slave struggling with a soldier inside, and that decided him. She should not be allowed to suffer. He could save her, at least. She was entitled to kindness at the hands of the French. She was not an Iroquois, but their prisoner.

He entered the gate confidently, calling out in his sharpest military voice for the woman to be let go. The soldier looked at him, then released her. He knew authority when he heard it. True, this man was dressed in deerskin, but many of the colonists affected that attire, and they had joined the army on this campaign.

'Take me to Charles le Moyne,' Pierre snapped as he saw other soldiers approaching. Fortunately he had seen le Moyne from his vantage-point on the wall earlier on. 'You know the man I mean,' Pierre added. 'The one the Indians call "Akouesson".'

The soldier's face showed that he knew the man, and Pierre blessed his stars that Akouesson would have the authority to search the village if he could convince him of the necessity. He had some slight acquaintance with him, and that should help.

'Pierre Charbonneau, as I live and breathe!' Charles le Moyne greeted him and embraced him. 'They all said you'd be dead and gone, but I've lived with the Iroquois—and survived. Where's your wife?'

'Somewhere in this village, I believe.' Pierre wasted no time in coming to the point. 'Will you help me to find her?'

'Ay, gladly. What do you want me to do?' The legendary fighter signalled to two of his men to come to him. They were dressed as both he and Pierre were, in deerskins. 'Quickly,' he called out to them. '*Vite*! Even now the longhouses are being fired.'

Pierre could see that for himself, and was very

alarmed. Great stores of food had been taken out of two of the cellars, and the rest were going to be put to the torch without entering them, because of the danger of stragglers being inside ready to pounce.

Gathering others about them as they ran, the four hurried to the longhouses and began to search.

The fourth one yielded Mireille. Charles le Moyne himself picked her up from the cellar floor and carried her outside, calling out to Pierre. Her eyes were closed, her face deathly pale. Pierre feared to touch her. Was she lost to him at this late date?

'What's the matter with you, man?' asked Charles le Moyne. 'She's alive! She opened her eyes and looked at me. I don't know why she closed them again.' He gave a great laugh.

The slave then appeared from inside the same longhouse, carrying a fur rug. She spread it on the ground, and Pierre laid Mireille on it, chafing her hands, talking to her, begging her to wake up. The woman elbowed him aside, and bathed the girl's face with water and held her head between her knees.

Consciousness returned to Mireille, and she sat up, and began to cry.

Pierre took her in his arms. 'Thank God you are safe!'

'I followed her in,' Mireille shuddered. 'And she pushed me aside and shut the cellar door on me. I thought I would be burned to death!'

'Don't even think of it,' Pierre murmured. 'Put it from your mind. You're safe.' He had no need to ask who had shut her in. He knew; it all fell into place. It had been Blue Feather One's mother. He should have guessed before. White Fox had warned him to be careful.

'I knew you'd come,' Mireille whispered, and he held her closer. He surrendered her to the slave only when Charles le Moyne at length summoned him to one side.

'I speak to you as a friend,' he declared, seating himself on a tree-stump as Pierre stood in front of him.

'I know the ways of the Iroquois—and I know that some white man must have helped them with the design and building of this strong wall.' He gestured lazily at the fortifications. 'A fine piece of work it is! Since no harm was done, and no lives lost, I would keep to yourself any part you may have had in it. The least said about your captivity in Andaraqué the better. You came in pursuit of your wife, and both of you were prisoners.' He winked at Pierre. 'That's so, isn't it?'

Pierre could scarcely believe his ears. 'Yes, but . . . ' he began.

Le Moyne cut him off, 'I expect you were honoured prisoners, but held captive here just the same.'

'Oui, vraiment,' Pierre could agree to that. 'We were trapped here.' It was the truth.

'You might even go back to New France a hero,' le Moyne went on. 'A modest man has his reputation blown up by others! He keeps quiet. They do the talking.' He gave his great laugh again.

Pierre almost smiled. 'Ye-es, but . . . '

'I never heard a man say so many times, "Yes, but . . . " You begin every sentence with it. Yes, but . . . What does it mean this time? That little affair at Trois-Rivières with the army Captain? Even if he hadn't changed his story, could he deal with a hero of the Indian campaign—when he himself stayed safely at home?'

Pierre seized on the other's words. 'Has he changed his story?'

Charles le Moyne laughed again. '*Oui, mon ami!* Now he says it was not you who fired at him, but some Indian hiding outside. He claims he was confused at first—the blows to his head, you understand . . . '

Pierre knew an enormous sense of relief. It was incomprehensible to him that Charles de la Croix should have told a different story and cleared him. What was he planning? Had the blows to his head changed Mireille's cousin? It seemed highly unlikely, but why question it? It was so, and he could only be grateful that it was. His name was cleared. He could return home with Mireille. She would be as relieved as he was when he told her. He went off to do so at once.

He found a different girl sitting by a campfire, surrounded by soldiers and by colonists, all wanting to know how she had survived the ordeal of life with the Mohawks.

Mireille was saying little. The slave was holding forth on her own captivity and slavery, but his wife was just sitting, holding a bundle in her arms. Whatever was it that she held?

Pierre dropped down beside her, trying to see what a ragged blanket hid.

Two dark eyes peered out at him. Silver Badger raised his arms to him, and he clasped the boy in his own.

'White Feather gave him to the slave to give to you. She must have been watching from the outside. She said that now you were with your own people, it was better so. He might starve through the winter with her.' Mireille raised worried eyes to his. 'Will it be all right, Pierre? She didn't know how things stood back in Trois-Rivières. She thought only of the boy.'

'It will be all right,' Pierre assured Mireille. He gave her a swift account of the charges being dropped. He was uncertain how the presence of Silver Badger would be interpreted, but he didn't care. The boy was his, and Mireille was quite willing to have him with her. He gave silent thanks, and did as Charles le Moyne had bid him, by saying as little as possible and offering a home to the slave.

The French army wasted no time in Andaraqué. By the following day the village had been razed, the provisions they had helped themselves to were packed and loaded, and they set off for the colony of New France, secure in the knowledge that the men of the Five Nations had been vanquished without a single shot being fired. The cannon had not even been unloaded from their boats.

Not a life had been lost on either side. If black eyes watched them from the forest, no hand was raised against them. A lesson had been learned.

The three hundred boats of the expedition wended their way home. Pierre, Mireille and Silver Badger were gladly given a place in the fleet. No one spared a thought for the hungry, cold winter ahead for the Iroquois. They were the defeated.

Pierre found that it was as Charles le Moyne had foretold: the less he said, the more his reputation grew. Even the adoption of the boy, his son, was seen as an act of Christian charity, an attempt to cement peace between the two sides, to win the red man to the white man's ways.

Before the return journey was completed, the commander of the expedition summoned Pierre and Mireille to his presence and commended them on their bravery and good fortune. He was especially interested to hear from her own lips how the women among the Mohawks lived, and could scarcely credit that they were regarded as the property-owners and the farmers of the tribe, and had a voice in its affairs. He said he was sure that she would be eternally grateful to be back among her own people and their different ways.

Mireille, who had difficulty in analysing her own feelings, kept silent, and smiled. He seemed to find that sufficient, and dismissed them kindly, saying that of course they would be free to go when they reached Trois-Rivières. They would not be required to go on to Québec with the army.

It was afternoon when they reached the little settlement. Mireille and Pierre were home. Accompanied by the slave and Silver Badger, they set foot on the shore, waving goodbye to the large fleet.

Mireille's feelings were still very mixed. She had supposed there would only be overwhelming joy to be back, but memories of the Indian village rose in her mind as the citizens of Trois-Rivières came forward to meet the small party.

The whole settlement seemed to have turned out. She saw Albert Morel and his wife, Émilie and her husband, and some of the other girls from the boat that had carried them all from France.

At first, everyone she knew hung back. They were used to Pierre appearing in the deerskin garb of the coureur-de-bois, but they eyed herself askance, she felt. It was she who ran to Émilie and threw her arms about her, crying, 'Don't you recognise me? I've come back!'

Émilie hugged her, and began to sob. 'I thought you were dead! I thought I'd never see you again.' She put a hand on Mireille's hair. 'You have all your hair. They haven't scalped you!'

Mireille began to laugh, and so did Émilie as they clung together. 'Yes, I have all my hair! There's so much to tell you.'

But there was no time to begin on her adventures just then. Albert Morel and his wife were embracing her, Silver Badger was tugging at her skirts, and the slave was standing to one side. Mireille drew them to her. Pierre was being hailed by everyone.

Cousin Charles, too, was there, and he came directly to Mireille. She thought he looked smart in his uniform, but there was an empty look about his eyes.

He kissed her, and exclaimed, 'Who's the child? Your husband's bastard?' he whispered to her.

Mireille turned on him angrily. 'He's no bastard!' She lifted Silver Badger in her arms. 'We mean to bring him up as our son.'

'Really? You surprise me!' Charles was still speaking in a low voice.

'And you surprise me!' Mireille retorted. 'I wonder you weren't with the army. I kept expecting to see you. Are you recovered?'

'I shall never recover. You and your Indian friend saw to that. I am ordered back to France and a medical board. My discharge will follow soon afterwards, I imagine. France keeps only the fit in her army.'

Mireille heard the bitterness in his voice and wished she had not been goaded into taunting him. She bit her lip. 'You'll have a pension?' she enquired in a kinder tone.

'A pittance,' Charles nodded. 'That's the way our country rewards its heroes!'

'What will you do?' Mireille was concerned. It was perhaps unfair of Charles to imply he was a hero. It was, after all, his own fault that he had been injured, but she could not forget that she had fired at him. Maybe something could be done for him? He was her cousin.

'Forget about me,' said Charles. 'Casualties are to be swept away—out of sight. You look ravishing, little cousin!' He stood back a little from her. 'The Indian dress suits you. You should continue to wear it.'

Mireille felt his eyes rested on her longer than was seemly, even by a cousin, but she was pleased by the compliment just the same. It was nice to be admired, and she had always liked cousin Charles, she reminded herself. He had always been good to her. Yes, she would speak to Pierre about him, and see if she couldn't break down some of his prejudices against Charles. Perhaps a job could be found for him on her estate in France. She saw with a pang of regret that he held his wounded arm very stiffly. Was that the injury the army wouldn't accept?

She was swept away from him in the press of people wanting to greet her, to touch her, to congratulate her on her escape. Charles disappeared from her view.

When the crowd had begun to disperse, the Morels were very insistent that the little party go to their house for refreshments before they thought of going to their own. Mireille would have demurred, but Pierre accepted so swiftly that she was obliged to fall in with the plan. The journey back had been easy enough, and very safe in such numbers, but she was tired and longing for home.

She took the slave's arm, and with her on one side and Madame Morel on the other, they followed the men. Silver Badger was on Pierre's shoulder.

It was strange, but walking past the neat little houses of the settlement, Mireille felt closer to the Indian woman than to the French one, and she talked to her in the Mohawk tongue, explaining that these were friends and they would eat with them before going to their own place. The slave nodded, and asked how many people lived in each dwelling. She exclaimed when she heard that one family lived separately in each.

Madame Morel wanted to know what had been said between them, and Mireille explained a little of the Indian ways of housing. Madame shuddered at the very thought of sharing accommodation with other families. 'How could you bear it?' she asked.

Mireille replied that she had found it very hard at first, but that now she thought it might be strange to be on her own in a house.

Little Albertine Morel ran to the gate to greet them. She had been at her lessons, and had missed the arrival of the fleet. She threw herself at Pierre, and was enchanted with Silver Badger. She took him by the hand and drew him indoors. She had none of his language and he had only a few words of hers, but it didn't seem to matter. They were soon laughing and playing together. Perhaps she reminded him of Small Squirrel, Mireille reflected, well pleased that he had a playmate.

They sat at a table to eat. A snowy white cloth was spread on it and there was plenty of good French food—slices of pork and chicken, pickles and hard-boiled eggs, potatoes cooked in milk and flavoured with onion and parsley. There was farm cheese, sweet cakes and bonbons. It was so civilised and so French that Mireille almost wept to see it.

Silver Badger, of course, had never seen a fork, and picked his food up with his hands, which made them all laugh until Albertine gravely showed him how she did it. He smiled and imitated her, and made them all laugh again.

The slave would not sit with them, but took her full plate to the back door and ate, sitting on the step. She said she felt more comfortable there. She had developed a natural sort of dignity since gaining her freedom, and had no hesitation in doing as she wished. That she shared the doorstep with the family cat, a large black tom, disturbed her not a whit. For his part, he opened one yellow eye and then went back to sleep, as though visiting Indians and their ways mattered not at all to him.

It was a merry meal, with everyone talking at once, and Monsieur le Secrétaire asking questions and cutting more pork and more chicken. Mireille would not have thought he could be so entertaining and welcoming. It was not until the end of the meal, when the children were playing at the other end of the room near the big fireplace, that Albert Morel became serious.

He looked at Pierre and asked, 'What are you going to do about Captain de la Croix?'

'Why, nothing,' Pierre replied. 'Is there something I should do about him?' He shrugged, 'He's withdrawn his charge, hasn't he?'

'*Mais oui,* but it doesn't end there.'

Mireille looked from one to the other of the men. It was her cousin they were talking about, and she couldn't remain silent. 'He told me he was returning to France—to a medical examination.'

'So he would have us believe.'

'Isn't it the truth, then?'

'As far as it goes.'

'What does that mean?' Mireille was indignant. 'Why do you two always think the worst of Charles?'

'Because we know him!' Pierre silenced Mireille with a glance. 'Listen to what Albert has to say before you spring to Charles's defence.'

She bit her lip, holding on to her temper. She was reminded of the hastiness of her actions in preparing for the trip to New York that had never taken place.

'Come, Albert,' Pierre went on. 'Tell us why you think I must do something about Captain de la Croix.'

For answer, Monsieur went to a desk on the other side of the room, avoiding stepping on the playing children. He came back with a piece of paper, which he thrust into Pierre's hands.

Pierre read it. 'I don't understand! How did this come into your possession?' He passed it to Mireille.

Her eyes skimmed over it, then went back and read it again. It was a document signed by the King of France, giving her hand in marriage to Charles de la Croix. It referred to her as a ward of King Louis.

'What does it mean?' She prayed that Albert Morel would say it meant nothing, that it was some mistake.

'It means your cousin means to marry you—even now.'

'But—but I'm married already, to Pierre!' Mireille could not comprehend the significance of the paper. 'Why does it say I'm a ward of the King?'

'I believe that was done some time ago—probably shortly after you left France—and by your Uncle Alain,' Monsieur informed her.

'Does that mean I'm not married?' Mireille was horrified! Pierre was her husband, and she was expecting his child. Was now the time to tell him?

'There may be some legal doubt about it.' His voice was grave.

Mireille was stunned, and looked at Pierre for reassurance. 'We are married, aren't we? Tell him you're my husband!'

'Of course I am,' Pierre agreed.

To Mireille's ears, his voice somehow lacked the depth of conviction she would have liked to hear there. She felt even more doubtful about him with his next words.

'Is there really a legal doubt?' he asked Albert. 'Come, we must know.'

'As to that, I wouldn't like to express an opinion,'

Albert replied. 'But, after all, you are here in New France, and the King is across the ocean. And, of course, the little brides who sail across that same ocean to the colony are all wards of the King. I think you might skate round that, if it ever came to court!'

He spoke so comfortably about the situation—her situation, Mireille reminded herself—that she was almost lulled into calm. He would not have to face the consequences if she had to tangle with the King's wrath—and one of the King's advocates. Mireille began to shiver. Home was not proving to be the peaceful place she had imagined back in Andaraqué. Monsieur's next question to Pierre struck an even greater chill into her.

'What would you do, *mon ami,* if you were Charles de la Croix and had such a paper? It's only by the greatest good luck that this copy fell into my hands.' He tapped the paper against the table. 'I still have friends at court!'

Mireille could not see where the good luck lay. It would have been far preferable had there been no such paper. She waited for Pierre's answer, searching his face. How could he be so placid, when her whole life had been turned upside down? Didn't he care for her?

His face gave nothing away. When he spoke, it was slowly. 'If I were Charles de la Croix, I think I'd turn my attention to Pierre Charbonneau. He's all that stands in my path to a fortune. Charles won't like going back empty-handed to France with nothing much to live on! Yes, if I were Charles, I might be tempted to take some action against an enemy.'

Mireille looked at him in disgust. What was he accusing Charles of? Self-interest—or something darker, blacker? He was all but saying that Charles would remove him—kill him! No, she couldn't believe it—she wouldn't. It was infamous that they should even consider it! And yet, the paper was there. He planned to marry her—and share her fortune. One followed on the other. She shook her head.

'Can't we ask him what it means?' she appealed to Monsieur.

Both men laughed at that. Even Madame Morel shook her head. 'Albert would as soon ask the Iroquois who has come to scalp him how he means to go about it!' was her tart comment.

'There's only one thing to be done,' announced Pierre. 'I am forewarned. I must make sure to be always on my guard. In fact, if I could somehow trap him into attacking, and had a witness . . . I don't want any more misunderstandings.'

His words hung in the air. Yes, Mireille would want a witness to be present. But how could that be accomplished? If it were true, Charles would want no witness. The very fact that Pierre was not proposing to seek Charles out convinced her in spite of herself that there was real danger for Pierre—and therefore for herself as well. She would not admit it to Pierre, but she did not want her cousin for a husband—not when she had known a real man! The words slipped into her mind, surprising her. It was her misfortune that Pierre felt less of the depths of the feeling she had for him. She sighed, and nearly missed Monsieur's suggestion.

'I shall be your witness.'

'How?' Pierre and Mireille asked together.

'Cousin Charles has not much time. His ship is already at Québec. In a few days it will load furs at Ville Marie and then return, picking him up here. At the most, he has four days to accomplish your demise, marry your sorrowing widow, and say farewell to New France. He will strike as soon as possible—perhaps this very night.'

Mireille felt a thrill of fear. What if it were true that Charles planned to kill Pierre? It could be easily done. One shot from a musket as they walked along the lonesome path to home. He could hide in the trees that bordered the path, or lie in wait in the barn. Even with a warning, how could Pierre avoid an assassin? She trembled so violently that he noticed, and said, 'You shall stay here. I'll go home alone.'

'No,' said Albert. 'It must seem normal, as though you know nothing. He'll watch, of course. Mireille must go with you—and the boy—and I shall go, too.'

'How can that be considered normal—if you are there?' Pierre protested.

Albert directed his gaze to the slave, the cat now on her lap, her back against the door-frame. 'I shall take her place, darken my face, and wear her clothes and a wig. He won't even notice me. A slave is not likely to attract much attention from a desperate man.'

Mireille opened her mouth, but closed it without saying a word. She had told Charles about the slave. He had seen her for himself and scarcely glanced at her.

Pierre nodded. 'It could work, but are you truly willing to take such a risk? Something could go wrong. He might decide to have no witness, and kill the slave first . . . '

'I am prepared,' Albert Morel said. He glanced at his wife, and reached across the table to take her hand in his. 'We are in agreement. She, too, remembers my brother, and how Charles de la Croix dealt with him.'

Mireille looked at the couple, tears rising in the back of her throat. If only Pierre loved her like that . . . Monsieur le Secrétaire was a much braver man than she would have expected.

Pierre looked towards her. 'Are you willing, Mireille?'

'*Oui*. Must—must we bring the boy?'

'*Bien sûr*. We are all in this together.' He sighed. 'He, at least, won't know that we wait for murder.' His face softened as he regarded his son, playing with Albertine. 'Promise that you'll watch him always, and always keep him near you. That's his best protection, for your cousin won't want you to see him at his worst.'

'Oui,' Mireille repeated. 'He'll be at my side.' There was a lump in her throat. Yes, she would keep his son safe—this Indian son—and the one she carried under her heart. 'Is it time to go?' she asked.

'It is time to make ready,' Pierre agreed, and all four of them rose from the table.

Mireille called the slave to her. She would explain the plan, get her to give up her dress, convince her that, for all their sakes, she must hide.

Pierre and Albert moved away.

Mireille began to speak to the woman. It was ironic, was it not, that the dress in question was the old brown one she herself had been wearing when she had set out from Trois-Rivières with White Fox. No doubt Madame Morel would provide the slave with something much better. She had gone to fetch one from her wardrobe, and returned to offer it.

The slave fingered it, and Mireille could see it met with her approval. It was not hard to convince her of the rest.

CHAPTER SEVENTEEN

IT WAS DUSK. A pale moon was rising as Pierre led the way home through the last lonely stretch in the woods.

They had debated the order in which they should walk, and decided that it would seem more usual if Pierre led, Mireille and the boy followed, and then the slave.

Mireille walked steadily on, Silver Badger stumbling a little with tiredness before her. She felt numb rather than afraid. The whole affair seemed unreal. She could not quite believe that cousin Charles would lie in wait for them somewhere, some time. Even yet, she was doubtful. There must be some explanation for the letter from the King, some explanation other than the one the men had seized on. She remembered Charles as a boy, and the feeling of excitement his visits to her home had always brought her. He'd been such a handsome lad, with such devilment in his eyes.

Silver Badger's steps were getting slower and slower, and he was rubbing his eyes. Mireille stooped and picked him up. She'd carry him for just a while.

He was no sooner up in her arms than he stiffened, and cried out, 'Regardez!'

Mireille's mind registered that the boy's warning was in French even as she heard the sound of the knife which took the slave in the shoulder.

Pierre pushed her and the boy into the bushes at the side of the path, and ran back to Albert.

'Go after him,' she heard Albert order, 'I'll be all right.'

Pierre did as he was bid, and disappeared into the trees after the knife-thrower.

Mireille crawled to Albert. The knife was embedded in his shoulder.

'I must go for help,' Mireille whispered. 'You're hurt.'

'No, stay here! Pull me into cover in the bushes. We'll lie flat and wait,' Albert told her.

'I saw an Indian throw the knife,' Silver Badger said unexpectedly in his own tongue to Mireille.

She trembled and repeated this information to Albert as she rolled him towards the shelter of the trees, trying not to hurt him.

'Was there only one?' Albert pulled the boy to him.

'I saw only one.'

'That doesn't mean there aren't any more!' Mireille whispered, squatting beside Albert.

'I have a knife strapped to my leg,' Albert murmured to her, 'Take it! You may need it.' He lifted the bedraggled skirt of the brown dress and Mireille freed the weapon from its hiding-place. She felt just a little better to have some means of defence, and cradled it in her hands.

She would have shown it to Silver Badger, but he was no longer there. She almost cried out, but stifled the sound in panic and alarm. 'Where is he?' she hissed at Albert. 'Why didn't you stop him going?'

Albert made no answer. He lay still and cool to her touch.

*Bon Dieu,*was he dead? Mireille put her head to his chest. He was breathing. She sat back, calling softly, 'Silver Badger! Silver Badger, come back.'

There was no reply. Where had he gone? Had he been snatched from her?

Mireille had never felt so alone. The boy had gone. Albert was unconscious and the blood was seeping from his wound. Pierre was somewhere in the woods chasing an Indian—an Indian? When Charles might be waiting to pounce on him if what they believed was true!

This was worse than when she had been trapped in the cellar at Andaraqué. There, she could have done nothing. Here, she should do something—but what?

Screaming for help, running after Pierre, trying to find the boy? She wasn't fitted for this life. When she'd left France, her head had been full of romantic notions and excitement, but it was not like that after all. In the woods, under the rising moon, it was frightening, terrifying. She thought her heart must stop beating, it was going so fast.

Suddenly, as she knelt, she thought of Pierre and his often-repeated statements about waiting. Perhaps he was right. There were some situations in which all one could do was wait—wait and turn one's hand to ordinary tasks—to what must be done.

She sighed and turned Albert on his face. Her hands found the knife and she pulled, struggling to free it. With a sort of gurgling sound, it came out, and Mireille staunched the spurt of blood with material torn from the brown dress.

Albert groaned and tried to move.

'Stay still!' she hissed at him. 'Help will come soon.'

As if to mock her words, an owl hooted in the distance, a fox barked, the wind rustled the bushes, but Albert breathed quietly beside her.

He surprised her by talking in a very low voice. 'I don't think that it was an Indian. I think it was Captain de la Croix. It's his style—the knife in the back, the attack in the dark. Of course he wouldn't want the slave to see him. I wonder if the knife was meant for Pierre. I almost turned round when the boy cried out. Where's the boy? Has he got him? If he comes for you, use the knife, my little knife. He won't know you have it.'

'Yes,' said Mireille. She shivered. She had used the paddle on that other—that Indian—when she had saved White Fox. She had not thought of that in a long time, but yes, she would use the knife on Charles. If he came for her, that would mean Pierre was done for. She would kill him.

'When I was a lad,' Albert went on, holding her hand, his voice weak, 'my brother and I used to play at Indians. I was older than he, so he always had to die.

He was big for his age and I was always small, but he always took my orders. Strange, wasn't it? He did die first—both of us from the same hand, you might say.'

'Nonsense, you aren't going to die—not from this wound! It's not deep enough for that.'

'I'm bleeding like a stuck pig,' he groaned.

'No, you're not! It's nearly stopped.' Mireille peered at the wound. It had nearly stopped bleeding, but it needed attention. She looked around and saw moss growing at the base of the tree. She freed it with the knife and put it on the wound. The Mohawks did that. White Feather had packed moss into a deep cut when one of the women had hurt her leg. She explained it to Albert as she worked. She added that Little Lynx had done the same to White Fox.

'You're different,' he told her. 'Different from the way you were that first day. You were full of yourself, then, a spoiled rich girl. I wasn't sure you were right for Pierre—but it was such an opportunity to make Charles suffer that I couldn't resist it. I've always liked to bend people to my will.'

'I didn't like you, either!' Mireille tied a length of the old brown dress round the shoulder, binding the moss into position.

'And now?' Albert questioned. 'Do you like me any better?'

Mireille sat back on her heels. 'I see why Pierre trusts you. So do I.'

'You don't waste words, do you?' Albert grunted, but he reached out and touched her knee in a friendly way. 'Pierre was lucky that day. He knew it from the first moment.'

'Did he?' Mireille had given up thinking about the strangeness of the setting. She was intent on Albert's words.

'He looked at you and made up his mind. He hasn't regretted it. He followed you to the ends of the earth—well, to Andaraqué, at least—and brought you back. Now he's fighting for you again. You're a lucky woman—and a brave one,' he added, almost as an afterthought. 'I'm telling you because I'm not sure he ever will—Pierre's found the one woman for him.'

Mireille was moved. She put her hand to her face, covering her eyes. Was it really true what Albert had said? Did Pierre love her as she loved him?

Albert was quiet now. She sat beside him, cross-legged on the ground, the little knife resting in her lap, waiting, waiting . . . It was no use to try to go after Silver Badger. He would know his way in the woods.

Pierre had no doubts as he sprang after the attacker into the woods. It was Charles de la Croix whom he chased. It was Charles de la Croix whom he would fight to the death! This encounter between them had been foreordained since the day he had married Mireille, snatching her from her cousin's arms.

Pierre moved from tree to tree, listening, sliding. His must be the advantage here. He could imitate the Indians in their stalking. He had almost their patience. He halted again. A twig snapped. He slithered in that direction, softly, softly.

It was cold, at the end of October with only a pale moon rising and no stars yet. Again he waited, pressed flat to a tree.

A faint sound alerted him, and he crept towards it. His musket was over his arm, but it wouldn't be his musket he'd use on Charles. It would be his bare hands. A man who would knife a slave in the back deserved to be beaten!

He spared a thought for Albert Morel and for Mireille. They'd be waiting for the outcome, and he must not fail them. Nor must he think of anything except the stealthy business in hand.

The chase went on, hunter and hunted stepping haltingly in the weird dance of death, one pursuing, one seeking to escape and attack again.

Pierre began to realise that he was being led towards the boundary of his own property. The final drama might well be enacted near the barn where it had begun. Was there some trap there, some place prepared to ensnare him—a bear pit, perhaps, a wire before him? This was no time to hurry. It was a time for craftiness and skill. He must test every step.

Even as he thought it, his foot slipped. He drew it back, slithering to safety on his belly as a hole yawned before him. He peered in. If he had fallen there, he'd have no chance at all.

On all fours, he skirted round the pit. This might not be the last obstruction. He was going so slowly he saw the wire as he reached it and managed to avoid that, too. But how many more traps were there before he should come to the worst of them all? He could see it in his mind's eye—the half-open door of the barn and Charles behind it, waiting for him. Would it be with another knife, or with a musket?

There was nothing more to stop Pierre's progress. He came to the thin fringe of trees marking the boundary. The barn loomed before him, its shadow towards him. It was as he had known and feared. Charles was in the barn, or perhaps hidden behind its further side.

Pierre, flattened against a fine old tree, debated with himself the best course of action. This was the place Charles had chosen to kill him. Well, he had no intention of being killed! He must think himself into his enemy's mind. If he were Charles, where would he station himself?

Charles would hope to draw him within the barn. That would be his way, for then he could dismiss him with one blow, fasten the barn door and set the place to the torch. Yes, that would be Charles de la Croix's way. A terrible tragedy, Pierre Charbonneau burned to death in his own barn—and no one the wiser as to who had done it! No musket-shot to alert anyone to his presence, no wound on the body.

Pierre dropped to the ground, and, a shadow in the darkness of the larger shadow cast by the building, made his way by slow crawl around the barn.

There was no sign of Charles. He must be inside, then. Could he draw him out or take him by surprise? There was only the one door. It was closed. Pierre circled to the back of the barn again, an idea forming in his mind. He loaded his musket. Whatever happened, it was not going to be a secret event.

It was an old trick from his army days. He had a length of leather thonging in his pocket, and he drew it out. In this way he'd be able to pull the trigger from a short distance—just enough to give him some small measure of safety. And he had one more advantage: he knew, and Charles could not, just where the wood in the side of the barn was rotten. He set the musket in position.

Now, now was the time to make his attack! He crossed himself and pulled at the leather. The gun exploded into sound.

The sound of the musket-shot echoed in the still night. Mireille heard it and jumped to her feet. Albert Morel, lying helpless and half awake on the ground, heard it too. He groaned, and tried to struggle up.

Mireille dropped to her knees again, restraining him. 'Pray God that's Pierre's gun!' she muttered.

'Listen,' commanded Albert. 'I hear horses. Be quiet, *attendez*.'

Mireille heard the horses' hooves, the jingle of harness and bit. 'It's the army,' she cried. 'The patrol!' She sprang up again and hurled herself on the path, causing the leading horse to swerve violently to avoid her.

She was laughing and crying, both at once, to see Silver Badger in the arms of the second horseman. 'What a clever boy!' She patted the lad's leg.

'Did you hear the shot?' she demanded of the almost unseated rider beside her. 'It came from over there,' she pointed in the direction of the sound. 'They must be near the house. *Vite, vite,* let's go to Pierre! Take care, there is a wounded person over there,' she babbled on. 'He needs attention, too.'

If the leader of the patrol found it strange that a man's voice issued from the figure on the ground, he made no comment but detailed one of his men to stand guard over him. Then he helped Mireille up on to the other soldier's horse. They rode towards the property at a good pace, pulling up sharply when they saw two figures struggling on the earth directly in front of the barn.

Charles had his hands on Pierre's throat. Pierre looked as though he might be trying to break Charles's back. The strange thing was that Charles was dressed as an Indian, in deerskin trousers, his chest bare and smeared with paint. Mireille recognised him only because of his hair, which had, she supposed, been pulled back into a braid, Indian fashion, but had come loose in the struggle. Besides, she was expecting to see him.

The soldiers separated the two, holding firmly to Charles as the attacking Indian. Recognition dawned slowly in the eyes of the leader of the patrol as Charles hurled insults and oaths in French at his captors.

The two men holding Charles were caught off guard, puzzled by the educated French, and loosened their hold for one brief moment. He seized his opportunity and slid from their grasp, running away fast. One of the soldiers raised his musket to his shoulders, and fired.

Charles fell to the ground.

Mireille gasped, stunned by this action.

'The only good Indian is a dead Indian!' the soldier muttered to his mate. '*N'est-ce pas?*' He looked to his leader for approval.

Mireille found herself in Pierre's arms. There was no reason why she should cry for Charles. He had wounded Albert. He would have killed Pierre. But she wept, remembering the boy Charles had been.

'It's better so,' whispered Pierre, holding her close. 'I'm glad I didn't kill him. He might have stood between us. I couldn't have borne that. I love you too much for that.'

His words reached Mireille's heart. Pierre loved her,

truly loved her. Her tears hiccuped to a stop. She threw her arms round his neck. 'You're alive! We're together! That's all that matters. Pierre, we're home.'

Under the pale moon, with the soldiers grouped around Charles's body, Pierre led her into the house, their house. They were home at last.

Silver Badger followed them in.

Pierre raised him to his shoulder and, their arms entwined around the boy, they came into their new life, all three together.

All four, Mireille corrected her thoughts. Now was the time to tell Pierre about the other child, the one she carried, their child.

Softly she began, 'Pierre I have something to tell you . . .'

Tomorrow they would have to make statements, to explain the unexplainable, to unravel the story for authority to hear, but tonight—ah, tonight was theirs.

Silver Badger slithered down, and Pierre held Mireille close to him.

'It's wonderful news,' he murmured. 'The best news in the world!' His arms drew her closer. 'We're home, and that's where I intend to stay.'

Mireille sighed with pleasure. More than all others, those were the words she wanted to hear, had longed to hear.

They were truly home. She raised her lips for Pierre's kiss—and thrilled at it, her bones melting with its intensity, her heart throbbing.

She was Pierre's wife. What more could she ask for? That other world in France was over, dismissed from her mind. She was home.